SUNSHINE
THE INTRUSION
A NOVEL

THOMAS G. ELMER

Printed in the United States of America

ISBN: Softcover   978-1-63871-257-2
       eBook   978-1-63871-258-9

Republished by: PageTurner Press and Media LLC
Publication Date: 06/14/2021

To order copies of this book, contact:

PageTurner Press and Media
Phone: 1-888-447-9651
info@pageturner.us
www.pageturner.us

DEDICATION

To my father George Miles Elmer (75) and my twin Brother Timothy George Elmer (53) for they both now know what lies beyond life.

It was fun, Thanks you two.

Update: My Mother has passed away. February 2020 at 93

Thanks for you help

CONTENTS

ACKNOWLEDGEMENT

I would like to thank the following people,

Wanda Devall who was the first to read my book,

Christopher Berens, Keith Mclaughlin, Martha Hoskins, Lain Riley.

Special thanks to my mother Helen Elmer Who still puts up with me.

Update: My Mother has passed away. February 2020 at 93

To Kristen House for her help in making my story even better.

At the end of time, a moment will come when just one man remains. Then the moment will pass. Man will be gone. There will be nothing to show that we were ever here...but stardust.

Sunshine, 2007

CHAPTER 1

The frigid sunlight broke through the clouds in Canada's British Columbia. The piercing light spread over Menatuline Peak, creating a new morning. It poured out from the clouds and over the white snowy mountaintops into Valley Lake. The birds had already woken and taken to the sky. The fish were jumping from the water catching insects that floated just above the surface of the lake. My cabin, set about sixty yards from the lake, was surrounded by evergreens.

The lake sat between two mountains. To the west laid Nimbus Mountain, and to the east was Menatuline Peak. The cabin sat at the base of the Menatuline Peak Mountain, hidden among the trees.

I stood at the tree line watching the dawn transform into a frozen winter day. The beauty always made a smile spread across my face. *How many others have stood close to here and watched the day begin?* I wondered. Rays of sunshine reached outward from the sun and into the far corners of space on a journey that man may make some day, chasing light beams across the universe.

I stood there on planet Earth feeling all alone, perhaps the only person in sixty miles. The circle had been completed once again for this old rock called Earth. Another year had come and passed for my self-imposed exile. This planet may not mean much to this galaxy, this speck in the cosmos, but that valley is where I had chosen to call home.

The animals owned this very small part of the earth—the bears, cougars, eagles, hawks all fought for their lives. They lived by the rules of nature, the right to live or die. They roamed where they pleased and had the true freedom that humankind gave up long ago. The animals did not try to alter the world around them to make their lives easier. They simply went about the chore of living—something man was never happy in doing.

In the five years I had been there, I tried only to observe life and do my best to prove that this one man could live in harmony with

1

nature. I could hear the calls of the cities of man. They called to me to return to the world that did not work for me. So far, I had managed to put my foot down and say hell no!

As I stood looking out across the lake, a strange sound came to me. It worked its way over Nimbus Mountain, then floated across the lake waters to the tree line—after that, to my ears. It was not the sound of nature, but the sound of man coming this way. The eagles took flight and cried a warning to whoever would listen. More animals through the valley and over the lake passed out the message of the eagles. It was easy for me to interpret the cries: "Man is coming. Man is coming!"

A floatplane came into view from around the Nimbus mountaintop. It flew over the lake and circled back toward Nimbus Mountain to attempt a landing on the lake waters. It slowly descended into the water—little by little the plane got closer to the lake.

The pontoons finally began cutting into the lake as the plane lowered into the water, making a small wake as they descended deeper. As the pontoons lowered farther, the right one appeared to vanish. Then the plane's right wingtip dropped into the water, forcing the plane into a wild right turn, burying the prop into the lake. The plane seemed to stand up on its nose for just a moment. Time came to a stop for me as the plane stood there with its tail pointed toward the sky. The seconds started to tick by, as in slow motion, the plane flipped over on its back in a crash of water. I could see the right pontoon hanging in an awkward angle to the fuselage. The sound from the engine went dead, letting silence once again engulf the area, though it was the silence of disaster. All life was looking and listening to the abrupt quiet and the settling of the lake waters. I watched as the plane started to slip into the lake.

After a few seconds, I came to my senses and moved toward my covered boat. The faint sound of another motor came over the mountaintop. This time, a black helicopter descended over the lake. It hovered not far from where the plane had crashed. The side door to the helicopter opened, and the rapid fire of a mini-gun broke the peace of the valley. The water jumped as each round sliced into it. I guess that dispelled any idea of this being an accident.

I slipped a little way back from the tree line, keeping my eyes on the helicopter. After a few minutes, it lifted up from the lake and headed back the way it had come. As the helicopter passed out of sight, something broke the surface of the water. It appeared to be one of the pontoons from the plane.

I moved slowly to the water's edge, keeping one eye on the pontoon and one on the sky. Quickly, I uncovered my boat and climbed in. The engine started with a turn of a key. I aimed the boat toward the pontoon, opening up the throttle.

I found that if I left the boat uncovered, people would fly by, see it, and land, destroying the quiet with stupid questions. "How's the fishing here?" "How can you live so far away from other people?" Along with an endless stream of annoying questions that always made me want to scream.

I motored closer to the pontoon, still thinking someone else would show up. That's when I saw an arm reach up and over the pontoon. I twisted the throttle more, and the boat accelerated. If someone were still alive, the cold water would kill them soon. As I rounded the pontoon, two people, who had somehow survived, emerged from the plane.

My boat was a special flat-bottom airboat. In the wintertime I could install a prop while removing the outboard motor. I could also add small skids to glide across the ice. Special baffles reduced the noises of both engines and the props, though the prop still made far too much noise for me. However, there was no better way to cross the lake during winter.

I brought the boat up close to the pontoon, just barely bumping it with the bow. I then threw the anchor over the pontoon, away from the two survivors. Pulling on the anchor chain, I caught the pontoon and held it to my boat. I gently brought the starboard side closer to the survivors. Reaching out, I grabbed the smaller of the two by the back of their jacket. The size told me right away that this was a child, despite the survivor's jacket hood concealing his or her countenance. As I tried to pull the child, I could see the other person was not going to release their grip. Reaching out with my right hand, I tore the youth loose amid a weak cry of "No!" from the other person.

After hauling the unconscious child aboard, I grabbed the other one's coat and jerked. They lost their grip, falling away from the pontoon. They immediately started struggling to break loose, but the cold water, combined with the plane crash, had taken most of the fight out of them. I plunged my arm into the frigid water, searching for a belt. My fingers wrapped around one, and I heaved forcefully, bringing them halfway on to the boat. Once again, I thrust my arm into the cold water, wrapping my arm around their leg. With one more tug, I had them both out of the lake.

Before the adult could start fighting me, I began talking to them. "You're safe. You're safe now. There's no need to fight." I was not sure if they understood me or just gave up, but they both lay quietly in the boat. The next step was getting them out of their wet clothes and into some space blankets I had in one of the storage boxes.

I grabbed the unconscious child and unzipped their coat. Pushing back the hood, a boy's face appeared. The other person was still lying on the deck. "You have to get out of your wet clothes now!" I shouted at them. As they started to move, I returned my attention back to the boy. I began working to undress the unconscious boy, I removed his coat, then his shirt.

I glanced over at the other person who was removing their coat. A mass of long black wet hair fell out of the hood. A woman was the only thought that formed in my mind. I went back to work undressing the boy. "Keep your underclothes on," I instructed her.

One of the reasons I moved out here was to get away from the trappings of the outside world. I did not fit into that world. I could not keep a job and had a hard time getting one. So I took my long-time joy of nature and my failing attempts of interacting with people to the great outdoors. I had lived at this lake for five peaceful years. That is, up until now.

I finished removing the boy's clothes and opened a storage box nearest to me. I quickly found the space blankets I kept in there. Opening one blanket, I passed it to the woman, and as I did I took a good long look at her. It was worse than I had thought. I was staring into the face of a young angel of about sixteen. Forcing myself to look away, I opened the other blanket and wrapped the boy in it. I had to get these two back to my cabin and to the heat of the fireplace.

Pulling the anchor free, I threw it over the pontoon again and hooked the anchor rope to the boat. I couldn't leave it floating on the lake. Lacking anything to sink the pontoon with, towing it back to shore was my only option. Who knew if that black helicopter would return?

The two lay on the deck wrapped up tight in the space blankets. I turned the throttle and started my way back to shore with the pontoon in tow. The boy moved, and the space blanket made a loud crinkling noise. Although it was a short ride to shore, it seemed long to me. I kept looking back to see if the helicopter was anywhere in sight.

At shore, I tethered the boat and lifted the boy. "Come on, we have a short way to go," I told the girl.

She got out of the boat and proceeded to follow me up to the trail. Before we had even made it off the small beach, she was falling behind. The plane crash, plus the cold water had taken a lot out of her. Squatting, I had her climb up on my back. Those sixty yards became a mile uphill trail.

I opened the cabin door and walked straight to one of two bunk beds and laid the boy down on one. The girl slipped off my back, and I guided her to another bed.

The cabin was not much, but it had all I needed to live out here. It had three rooms to it. The main room consisted of the kitchen, the dining room (a small wooden table with four chairs), and the guest room with two bunk beds. Shelves ran along the walls of the kitchen and dining area. Two sets, one above the other, in the kitchen held canned food, pots, pans, and eating utensils. Another room was the supply room; containing a multitude of stuff including more canned food, extra tools, clothes, and ammunition. The other room was my bedroom with what few personal items I had from the outside world. Sitting beside the door was a Winchester 30/30. On pegs above the Winchester hung a Smith & Wesson .357/.38 caliber revolver, and a Smith & Wesson 9mm semi-automatic.

I retrieved wool blankets from the supply room then coved both kids. Both of them curled up under them.

After putting two more logs in the fireplace I stepped outside. Picking up my axe, I stared back down the trail; I still had things to do. With the boat, I towed the pontoon to a small inlet not far away, then struck the pontoon several times with the axe. I studied the hole I had put into it, blessed it, then pushed the pontoon away from the boat. It rolled a bit and water began rushing into the opening. I stood there watching it sink in about ten feet of water. The pontoon would still be visible from the air in the shallow water, but I hoped that no one would come looking.

I returned to the boat landing, set aside the kids' clothes, and covered the boat with a canvas drop cloth. Wet clothing in hand, I proceeded back to the cabin.

As I opened the door, a half-naked girl flashed past me, swinging wildly, with a hatchet in hand. She stumbled off the short porch and crashed to the ground. She just lay there for a few moments, then I heard her crying.

Long ago I learned to step to the side of the door before opening it. When I first built the cabin, birds, small animals, and once in a while, larger game would come charging out. For this reason only, she missed me. I picked up the hatchet and embedded it into the outside wall next to the door. As I gently picked her up, her arms reached around my neck, and she held on as I walked back into the cabin.

To think that just this morning I was living in my own private world. Then in only a few minutes, that world was ripped open and torn away. Now I had two children to care for until I could find a safe place for them. I turned one of the four dining chairs around to sit facing the two of them.

They both slept for about three hours while their clothes hung close to the fireplace. I rose from my chair when the boy sat up in the bed. Gathering his clothes, I walked over to him. The boy backed up against the wall as I approached him. Stopping short of the bunk, I could see that he was uncertain of what to make of me.

"Whoa there, son, I'm not going to hurt you. All I'm doing is giving you your dry clothes back," I said softly. I placed his clothes at the foot of the bed. "You need to get into your dry clothes now." I turned back to my chair and sat down. Slowly, the boy reached out and grabbed his clothes.

Not taking his eyes off me, he slipped into his pants and shirt. "What's your name, boy?" I asked him, then continued speaking. "My Name is Wade Hampton." I leaned back into my chair. How long had it been since I used my own name?

"Don't tell him anything!" the girl yelled out. She hugged the blanket tight to her neck. I got up and gathered her clothes, then placed them at the foot of the bed she occupied. "Get into your dry clothes, please." She just stared at me, as if I were the most dangerous person in the world. The piercing glaze from those young eyes took me by surprise. They seemed to drill deeply into my soul, saying, "Go away!"

"Look, I'm going outside and wait for you two. If you feel some need to escape, the back door is right there. That's the supply room; there are backpacks, food, and other stuff for a cross-country journey in there. Feel free to take what you need. I wish you good luck if you go that route. We are some sixty miles from anything you may call a town." I turned toward the door and stepped out.

After a short time, the front door opened and two kids stepped out into my world. I watched their eyes wander over the landscape. The small front porch held one handmade wooden chair with a tree stump that I used to rest my feet on. The branches of the nearby trees hung high over the cabin. These tree branches did three things: One, they helped disperse the smoke from my fireplace. Two, they hid the cabin from planes flying overhead. Three, the limbs helped lessen the buildup of snow, but not by much. There was one negative thing they did, however: They created a real fire hazard for any hot embers that might float out of the chimney. This was not beneficial for the health of the cabin. However, in five years nothing had caught fire.

"Okay, let's start over again. My name is Wade Hampton. I've lived here for five years without any plans on leaving." I quickly added, "Now it's your turn, what are your names?"

"Charles," the boy blurted out in a tired voice.

"Shut up, don't tell him anything," the girl scolded.

I let out a small sigh. "Look, you don't know or trust me. I understand a lot has happened to you this morning. I am a stranger to you; you are scared and confused about what is going to happen here. Well, that makes three of us that are confused."

"Now if you want to make up a name, please go ahead. Anything will be better than calling you young lady, girl, or hey you. Okay?" I turned and started walking down the trail toward the lake. Charles followed right away while the girl with no name stayed on the porch.

"Amanda, my name is Amanda," she offered.

I came to an abrupt halt, then turned, facing her. "My mother's name was Amanda." The memory of my mother rushed to the front of my mind. I forced it back as quickly as I could.

I bowed toward this young girl. "Well, it's very nice to meet you, Amanda. It is my great pleasure to meet you also, Charles. Now, let's see if we can do something about the trust problem that we're having. I am a pretty nice person once you get to know me." Amanda followed me this time as I started toward the lake.

Charles hurried up and got a few steps in front of me. Amanda was happy to remain a few steps behind. I stopped and turned, seeing that the cabin door was still open. I said, "Amanda, could you please go back and close the cabin door? We definitely don't need any animals getting in there." She looked at Charles for a moment, weighing her options. She was deciding whether to leave Charles with me or not. Making up her mind, she dashed back to the cabin. Shutting the door, she turned around and seemed relieved that I had not moved, plus that Charles was still safe. "Thank you, Amanda," I called out.

We all moved down the trail, Charles a few steps ahead of me, while Amanda remained behind me. "Hey Charles, how old are you?" I asked him.

"I'm seven," he answered, "and Amanda is fifteen," he added before his sister could stop him.

"Well, I'm fifty years old," I said, smiling to myself. Every little bit of information could be helpful. I could somehow feel that Amanda was not happy about my questions. What would make a fifteen-year-old this guarded about the smallest bit of information? Perhaps if I had not shut myself out from the world. Maybe if I were fifteen once again I would figure it out. However, that was a long time ago, plus, there had been many bumps in the road too. Whatever it was, I should take it easy on getting them to talk. It had been a big day for all of us.

We came to the tree line, almost where I had stood earlier this morning. Looking out on the water, it was impossible to tell that a plane now sat at the bottom of the lake. I walked them down to the inlet where I had sunk the pontoon, and pointed it out to them in hopes they would see that I had sunk it to keep them safe. As far-fetched as the idea was, I felt the need to show them. Perhaps they would start talking soon. Possibly, they would begin to trust me sooner.

The thought of that black helicopter kept coming back to my mind. I had to get them talking to see what danger they were in. Furthermore, to get a feeling for the danger we were possibly all in.

"Who was flying the plane, Amanda?" I asked. The footsteps behind me came to a stop. A gasp made me turn around. Amanda stood there with her fist in her mouth and look of terror in her eyes. *Brownie points fall to zero. Can a person get a negative number in brownie points?*

Charles, however, answered, "Daddy was flying, and Mom was helping." Tears started to fall. The sobs broke the quiet of the lake. The eagles and hawks seemed to cry out, "Stupid question, Wade. Brownie points: zero."

I remember someone once saying that to move on from tragedy, one must express emotion in one way or another—something I had not done since the passing of my father and brother. My father and brother died in a traffic accident, and two years later I planned my escape from a world gone mad.

My father and brother were traveling to Flagstaff. Somewhere about halfway from Phoenix is a place called Verde Valley. Interstate 17 turns into a steep downgrade for about six miles.

A runaway semi-truck sideswiped my brother's car from behind, forcing it into the guardrail. The front wheels of their car ended up hanging out over the cliff. The sedan behind them could not stop in time, hitting my brother's car. The vehicle slid forward a little more, then gravity took over as the weight of the engine took the car. The vehicle flipped over several times on its way down the rocky cliff.

No explosion happened. No scream was heard, no chance to survive. It was all over in seconds, just seconds to rip them from my life. Now I was truly alone.

I inherited enough money from Dad to allow me to travel. I hiked the United States—first the southern part, then the northern. The Pacific Crest Trail when it was new. The Appalachian Trail years later. I hiked Europe, the Middle East, and Asia. I returned home years afterward to a broken-down farm in Arizona. I sold the land to a home developer. Again, Dad provided me with money to live.

Amanda was not looking at me; Charles was holding tight to his sister. "Amanda, please take Charles and head back to the cabin," I asked her. She stood there as though I had not said a thing. All I could see was a fifteen-year-old girl who had no idea what to do next.

I walked over to both and pulled them to me. "Come on, let's head to the cabin." Keeping my arm around Amanda, the three of us started back. Her feet began to move, and we slowly made our way to the cabin.

I put Amanda back to bed then pulled the blanket over her. She was asleep as her head touched the pillow. Charles sat in his bed for about ten minutes before laying down himself. His eyes closed, then sleep took him also. As tired as I felt, I just could not think about sleep. I walked around the kitchen area and passed a mirror that hung there. I think I scared myself with what I saw.

I took a few minutes to look at the image that stared back at me. A full bushy beard with lots of unkempt whiskers sticking out all over my face, a receding hairline with a brown white mix. The dark bags under my eyes had always been there. At 5'8", I pretty much felt looked down on most of my life, and while not considered short, I was darn close to it. At 140 pounds, I was at the low range for my height. Out here, anything you did was exercise, from chopping wood to hauling water, plus shoveling snow in the wintertime.

I had some PVC pipe shipped in to get running water in the cabin. I dug a five-foot trench from a stream to the cabin. It took me five months to complete the trench because of the cold ground. I laid the pipe so that it went up hill to the stream fifty yards away. I attached a large funnel at the stream end to direct the water into the pipe. The steep incline produced some good pressure. While it looked hideous, it worked wonderfully. With the pipes five feet underground, they had not frozen yet. Now heating the water was still a bit of work. I started getting ready to clean myself up.

Before the water got warm, I started to cut my beard with my hunting knife. Trying to cut the hair on my head was going to be tough, so I decided to leave it alone. I picked up my long unused razor, then pulled it across my soaped face. It was a tug of war between the razorblade and each of the hairs in my beard. After some time, the razor had done its job—the beard was gone. I had not seen this face for a long time myself. It was time for me to rest, but so much had happened this morning that I didn't think I could sleep.

I spent the nighttime hours in restless sleep. When the sun started coming up from behind the mountaintop, I had to go watch. This was part of my morning routine for years. I would go down by the lake to listen for the beginning of another day. However, this time the thought of two kids kept creeping into my mind. I slowly turned and walked back to the cabin. There was only one way to get these kids to their own world.

I had to start planning for a hike out of this wilderness. Until then, I was going to keep up my routine and try to add them into it. I needed to keep myself plus the kids busy until we started the walk out of here. I wasn't sure what I could have them do, but something would come to mind.

The only tree I cut down to make room for the cabin was off to the left side of it. This magnificent tree ended up too close to where I was going to build. After bringing it down, I thanked it for allowing me to see it beforehand. I evened out the stump so I could use it for chopping wood. The axe sat on the stump with a pile of unchopped wood nearby.

I was behind on my woodpile, but if I worked at it, I could catch up easily. Picking up one small log, I laid it on the stump with one end pointing upward. I lifted the axe, then let it fall, embedding it into the log. The two became one until I lifted both the axe and log up, then slammed it down on the stump. The log split into two pieces, and with one half of the log I repeated the steps over again.

Somewhere on the third or fourth log, I felt the silence of the forest set in. I turned, finding the two kids standing there watching me. "Charles, pick up these pieces of wood then go stack them on the other side of the cabin, please. Amanda will you please put another log on the stump for me?"

Both kids complied with my request, doing what I had asked for the next hour. I was getting tired of swinging the axe, so I finally called the chopping of wood over for the day. The next part of my morning routine was to check the water line.

Sometimes something would get tangled in the guard around the water pipe, requiring me to clean it out. I started checking it every morning to be sure I had water for breakfast.

I led Charles and Amanda to the stack of rocks I had placed in the creek. I had a chain connected to the pipe in a way that when pulling on it, the pipe end would lift out of the water. The funnel at the end of the pipe was just a one-gallon water container. I made a hole at the bottom of it big enough to fit the pipe into the container. I then attached a metal screen over the container opening.

The opening was clear this time, so I lowered the pipe back into the water. The container gave into the weight of the pipe and sank into the water, disappearing from sight until tomorrow.

Breakfast was the next thing on the list. Both the kids, I was sure, were hungry because I was starving.

In the time I had been there, I had made friends with some of the wildlife. At this time of year, one old bear would appear in the distance and sniff the air. Once in a while this great beast would stay long enough to let me admire his power and prestige. I was humbled that this creature let me even share this space with him. The first year was interesting: He would appear and roar when I spotted him. If I didn't see him, he would work his way down the hill behind the cabin. He would wait until I got close, then jump out at me. I thought many times he was laughing at this poor human. Only once did he charge me when I was returning from the lake. I had caught four trout for my meals that day. I surrendered all four trout as I moved to the lake. I watched him eat one, then pick up another and walk back into the forest.

I saw him now checking the new smell of the kids. I stopped them and pointed toward the bear. "Do not be afraid, but we are being watched," I said. "He is not a danger this time, but do not trust him ether. Keep your eyes on him as we walk away. Try avoiding his eyes; just watch his feet as we walk. He may look friendly, but to him, you're no more than a meal." Pointing at Charles, I added, "And you're just a snack." A worried look came across their faces.

"Stay close by, you two; don't go wandering around. Other animals out there would love to find you also. Once you get to know how to act around them, they're not so frightening."

The smell of cooking fish filled the inside of the cabin, and even wafted to the outside world through the chimney. I cooked up three of five fish—one for each of us, plus two for mister bear. This was my way of making peace with him, though I doubt others would recommend this way. It seemed to work so far.

I added some natural herbs, then served up the fish for breakfast. I thought it was a great meal for the early morning. The kids, however, did not seem to agree on my choice. When this trip back to their world started, it may be less for meals. The plan at this point was to take it slowly. Then I smiled—*Wait until they see what's for lunch.*

Bear was waiting for me as I exited the cabin with Charles and Amanda close behind. I had them stay by the front door as I took the two fish out far from the cabin. I laid them on the ground and retreated. When Bear believed I was far enough away, he lumbered his way down for his breakfast. This pact he and I had made was strange indeed, but I enjoyed it. To watch this great bear so closely over the years had been an honor. When he finished one fish, he grabbed the other then moved off into the forest, maybe embarrassed by his eating habits—but I doubted it very much.

I'd also made a connection with two wolves around here during the wintertime. They gave Bear a wide berth when he was around. During this time of year, their presence was more often spotted in the early mornings.

I found two young wolves four winters ago. They were tired, hungry, and close to death. I could see the fear in their eyes as I came upon them. After assessing their condition, I hurried back to the cabin. I entered into the food shack thirty yards from the cabin. I grabbed several large hunks of deer meat I had just killed a few days before. I approached the pair only close enough to throw the meat to them. From a safe distance, I watched them slowly move to the meal I had brought. When I saw them start to eat, I left them alone.

Later that day, I returned to the spot they had occupied earlier. All I could see was the flattened snow and some paw prints.

The trail led into the brush as I worked my way uphill. I was surprised to find one of the wolves in a small cave not that far away. Using the binoculars, I scanned the area and peeked as far as I could into the cave opening. The lone wolf stared back at me. It knew I was watching.

I decided to leave the wolf alone so nature could do its thing. As I turned to leave, I noticed the second wolf not ten yards from me. I bowed, asked for forgiveness for intruding on their home. I still leave them something from time to time during the winter months.

To keep the kids occupied, I decided to try teaching them how to build a fire the old way, plus some tracking, fishing, and compass work. I also had to find out what the deal was with the black helicopter. *This should be fun for about five minutes,* I thought smugly.

The third day we started out together, we watched the sun rise up from behind the mountaintop, then listened to the valley come to life. The birds came out of their nest, singing their morning songs. Soon the air warmed enough that the insects began buzzing about. Out over the lake, the fish jumped at the chance to snag a bug or two.

I decided to start the morning with a fishing lesson. Amanda seemed to pick up the fishing naturally. Her casting was almost perfect from the very first try. It only took her three casts to hook her first trout. Charles did fine, but had trouble handling the long pole. However, he did great for a seven-year-old.

We carried our five fish back to the cabin then set them safely into water to help keep them fresh. Chopping wood was the next thing on the list for today. The kids fell into the duties I had assigned them. Amanda set the logs on the stump. I split them, then Charles would stack them. After an hour of wood chopping, it was time for a lesson in outdoor living.

We moved away from the cabin to a fire pit. "We will have a lighter, flint, and matches for the hike out of here. However, it would not hurt for you to learn how to do this." I showed them my socket, bow, drill and fire board. Putting them together and using the bow to turn the drill, I got a little red-hot ember. Putting that into a bird's nest, I made them blow lightly on it until it burst into flames.

"If you get to this point, you have a fire to cook and for warmth," I told them. I put the bird's nest under a small pile of sticks. Soon I had a cooking fire going.

"You will be working on making your own fire in the next few days. But now let's go get breakfast and feed Bear before he gets cranky." We stomped out the fire I had made, then headed for the cabin.

I had to see if these two were up to hiking out. I planned the first hike up the mountain behind the cabin. Maybe show them some tracking and compass work. With Bear and the wolves around, it would be easy to get them used to seeing those prints.

In the afternoon, we climbed the mountain. As we walked along the trail, I started trying to get information from Amanda again. I started the conversation, hoping for better luck this time. "Amanda, I'm sorry, but I need to ask some questions. First, let me tell you about what I know."

She gave me a hard look, like "Oh no, here we go."

"I was standing at the tree line by the lake when the plane came around the mountain," I began. "It looked like a perfect water landing. As I watched, I saw the right wing go into the water. When I started my way to the boat, a helicopter came into view and began shooting. After it left, I started out on my boat, and I saw the pontoon break the surface. I powered the boat to where the pontoon floated on the water." Amanda listened as I talked. "When I saw your hand appear on the pontoon, I added more power to the engine and as I rounded it, I saw you and Charles for the first time. I got you into my boat and then to the cabin."

Stopping on the trail, I looked at her. "Amanda, I need to know what happened. Why did the helicopter shoot at your plane? Why was the helicopter chasing you? Who are the people in the helicopter? And most of all, do you think they will come back? Sorry, but if we're going to walk out of here, the more I know, the more I can be prepared."

Amanda looked up the trail to where Charles was exploring off the pathway. "Charles, don't you wander off, please," she yelled out to him. Charles waved back at her then continued his search for whatever little boys look for out there.

"I don't know much, but those people worked for a man named Jose Hernandez. I think he runs drugs but Mom and Dad never discussed him when Charles and I were around. Dad was very worried about Jose after a camping trip we went on. He and Dad flew off somewhere, and when they returned Dad was scared. He didn't act right for days."

Amanda scanned the trees for Charles. After finding him, she continued, "We left for what Mom and Dad said was just another camping trip, but I saw Dad open a door in the pontoon that broke off the plane. He put a silver-colored box inside, then closed the door. We only were in the air for a short time. After a while, Jose came over the radio and ordered Dad back to Juneau's airport. Sometime after that, Dad tried to set the plane down on the lake—you saw what happened." She stood there watching Charles still exploring.

"Thank you, Amanda, for sharing that with me. I hope I can show you that trusting me with that information is the right thing to do." I put my arm around her shoulders. I was sure I felt her start to pull away, but then relax. "Come on, we have a mountain to climb. If you think this is hard, just wait until we start this hike." I took off up the trail, leaving her standing there. "Okay, Charles, let's get up this mountain," I called out.

In just seconds, Amanda passed me and headed up the trail to Charles. When she passed me, I smiled down at her, and to my amazement, she smiled back.

After two more days of hiking to the mountaintop, the kids looked to be ready for walking out.

On the fifth night, I finally made up my mind that we better get started. "In three days we're off. It's eighty miles out of here to get to Juneau. We need to get started soon—by the time I make it back myself, it will be cold, with the first snow close by. I still have things to get ready for the winter."

I had been building backpacks for all three of us in the quiet hours of the night. Each of us would carry our own bedding, water, compass, and general directions to go in case we were separated. While I planned to do some fishing on our way, the kids would carry their own snacks.

Because of what Amanda had told me, I decided to bring along some firepower. Two handguns, a Smith & Wesson Model 27 revolver, plus a 9mm Smith & Wesson 910 semi-automatic for the close-up protection. I was also bringing a lever action 30/30 mag. Winchester Model 1892 that my father had bought me when I was thirteen. Oh, yes—and also my handy dandy survival knife, which had proven to be more useful than the weapons up to now.

If all went right, I could get these kids back to the world in twelve days at seven miles a day. I would break out the generator, charge up some batteries for lights. Should be a walk in the park; maybe even hire a plane to ride back. So why did I keep thinking about that helicopter?

I woke up thinking that in two more days, the march out of here would start. We would see some wonderful landscape untouched by man. Nature in all is beauty. It was just waiting for us to gaze upon it, to become one with it again.

I dressed, then hiked down to the lake by myself. I know I would miss the moment when the sun reached over the mountaintop again. But I had to get these kids to safety.

As I got to the tree line, three black helicopters circled around Nimbus Mountain. The whoop, whoop of the blades filled my ears. I should have noticed the quiet of the birds on my way here. I must have been too much into my own thoughts.

I stood there watching them as they hovered low over were the plane had sunk. Eight people dropped from two of the helicopters. They bobbed on the surface of the water until together in a group, then disappeared under the water.

The third helicopter started to circle the lakeshore. The cabin was not hidden that well. If they continued this way, they would spot it.

I remained there long enough to make sure that they were going to circle the entire lake. Turning, I started to run back to the cabin. About halfway there I came upon Amanda and Charles headed for the lake.

"We're leaving now!" I hissed. "The helicopter is back, and it brought two more with it. Get your backpacks, coats, and hats."

The kids ran back to the cabin. I could hear the blood banging through my temple veins as I grabbed things. The sound of the helicopter blades became louder than the blood pounding in my ears. *They're coming*, I thought to myself. *Soon they will find the cabin. Come on, Wade, move it! Move it, dummy, move it!*

Finally, I headed toward the supply room. As I opened the door, Charles tried to squeeze by me. "No! Not just yet, Charles!" I said sharply.

The door to the supply room swung open into the main part of the cabin for a reason. I grabbed two metal rods that hung on the inside of the supply room. Both rods had hooks on the end of them. I inserted the hooks into two notches at the threshold of the doorway and pulled up. The plank came loose with little effort, revealing a dark pit below. I pushed the plank out of the way then grabbed the next board, pulling it up.

Both planks ran the full width of the room, so when they were in place, the floor was solid. Each plank had holes for dowels glued to the floor joist below. The handles for pulling the planks from below were now visible.

"Quick, get inside and be quiet, please," I instructed. I got my backpack then dropped it down to the kids. I gathered the two handguns and the Winchester. After grabbing boxes of ammunition, I lowered myself into the pit.

I looked out the open supply room door trying to think of anything we may need. I spotted Charles' coat still on his bed. Climbing out, I rushed over to get his coat, and looking through the front window, I saw four men moving up the path. I lowered a metal bar across the front door. Picking four cans of pears off the shelf, I placed them in the fire. With Charles' coat in hand, I leaped into the pit, falling over all the gear.

Getting to my feet, I reached for one of the planks. Using the handles, I aligned the holes with the dowels then pulled down. Pulling the last plank in place, I heard the front door rattle. The front window shattered as I fell backward deeper into the pit.

Something began banging around the floor of the main room. Just as the bouncing item came to a stop, a small explosion shook the cabin.

Charles and Amanda were both making lots of noise as I moved over to them. "Shh! They may hear you," I warned softly. Pulling then close, I tried to calm them down. "They will find us if you two keep making so much noise." I heard both trying to choke back the fear.

"Get ready, you two; the loud noises have not stopped yet. Just try to be quiet when they happen, okay?"

My heart was racing at not knowing when or if the pears would go off. Charles and Amanda had death grips on my arms. All we could do was wait now.

When the first can decided it was time to explode, we all jumped together. The kids dug their fingers deeper into my arms. The strength of the two kids made me jump again.

From outside of the cabin, I heard a voice. "SHIT!" Then automatic weapons opened up, firing into the cabin. I pulled myself away from the kids to gather our gear together. Putting the packs around the kids, I began searching for the ammunition boxes.

I found the .38 still in its hip holster. The Winchester sat in its deer hide sheath. Standing on my knees, I wrapped the holster belt around my waist. Finding the 9mm in its shoulder holster, I threw it across my back.

The weapon fire had stopped before I had finished my search of the pit. I rounded up the six boxes of ammunition then joined the kids behind the packs. As things seemed to settle down, two cans exploded. The weapons barked out again, and then the last can popped off. We sat at the back of the pit listening to rounds bounce around the cabin. *I am going to have a mess to clean up if I ever make it back.*

One of the reasons I built the cabin there was because of the cave opening I had found. I dug the pit, then filled the walls with rocks for support. The idea was to have a hiding place in case a bear tried to break in.

I figured the bear would check the cabin before coming after me. Running out the back door would just put me back into its domain. But now, the back exit served a different purpose. I could now head into the cave, blocking the escape behind me as I went. I had spent many hours exploring it, so I knew the layout. The exit was not that far away.

I withdrew a small penlight and shined it on my face so the kids could see me. I put my finger to my lips indicating for them to remain silent. Moving to a corner of the pit, I removed the rocks there. In a short time, the entrance into the cave was big enough for me to crawl through. I had the kids pass me the packs, and then they entered the cave. Once all of us were inside, I started putting the rocks back into place. All the time we were moving into the cave, I could hear the men in the cabin talking.

It sounded like one of them was talking into a radio. "Someone was here right before we arrived, Mr. Hernandez. They left some cans in the fireplace that exploded. That's why we opened fire. They must have made it out the back door. I have a couple of men checking out the back, looking for tracks now." After a short pause, he continued. "It has to be them. The plane was empty. Who else could it be?"

"They must have been planning this for some time," the man on the radio said. "We are going to need some trackers out here before they get too far."

"Bob! You tell Freddie to get over here, now!" barked the man with the radio.

"Jesus, Greg, we're all dead if we don't find them—you know that, right?" another voice said.

"Yes, I know it. So let's not lose them now."

The outside light disappeared as the last rock locked in. I turned on my penlight then pushed past the kids. "Okay, stay quiet and follow me. We can make it out of here in about fifteen minutes. Do not panic on me." I reached inside my pack and pulled out two smaller lights and handed them to the kids.

I took the time to load the .38, then the Winchester. I loaded up two magazines for the 9mm, inserting one into the weapon. I then tied the leg strap for the holster, plus connected the shoulder rig to the holster belt. After putting the pack on, we started farther into the cave.

With rifle in hand and the penlight guiding the way, we worked down the tunnel. The kids remained quiet as we stumbled over the uneven ground. Shortly the cave opened enough for me to stand up with only about a half-inch clearance over my head.

All the work I put into building the cabin over the cave just paid off. I kept a slow pace and soon we arrived at the main room. It was not a very big room, but it gave us a place to sit for a short time. I could stretch my legs out while not touching the opposite wall.

Charles sat down beside me looking scared and worried. Amanda pulled out that hard stare of hers from somewhere, though I could see a frightened young girl in her face this time. I sat there listening for footsteps coming after us.

I soon decided that no one was following. However, we still needed to put distance between the men in my cabin and us. I got up and started to move on.

"Come on, you two, we can't stay here," I said as I continued deeper into the cave. Up ahead there were small pools of water that had formed from the melting snow and rain that made its way into the cave. The pools were not deep, but I remember them being very cold.

We had passed a few pools before coming to the deepest one. It stood in front of us blocking our path. It was only a few feet deep and about eight feet long. I removed my boots and socks. "I'll be carrying you two past this pool so you don't get wet. I have other clothes to change into; you, on the other hand, have only what you are wearing," I explained to them.

I first carried the gear across the pond. The water was colder than I remembered. I piggybacked Amanda to the other side, then Charles got his ride. After putting my socks and boots back on, we continued. My trousers had gotten wet, but now was not the time to change them. We still had a few more pools to cross. I could tell that the cave was going uphill now. Soon we would find ourselves at the shaft that led to the exit. Many years ago, I brought a handmade ladder back here. I hoped it was still useful, or this was going to be a short escape.

The ladder stood to the side of the last pool of water looking safe and dry. Walking across the inch-deep water, I examined the twenty-foot ladder for damage. I moved the ladder into place and started to climb. Reaching the top, I dropped my pack to the ground. The exit was only about some ten feet away.

I descended back down then carried Amanda to the ladder. "Stay by my backpack when you get at the top," I told her as she started up.

As she reached the top, I brought Charles across the water. "Now stay with your sister when you get up there, okay?" Charles nodded at me in the beam from the penlight. I watched him make his way to the top. Then I started the climb for the second time today.

Once I got to my pack, I removed a dry pair of pants. With Amanda and Charles standing close to the exit, I changed clothes. Breaking out the plastic bag I had, I placed my wet pants into it. The last thing to do was pull the ladder up. I had to break the ladder apart because it was too long to maneuver in this small space. If they did follow us this way, this was as far as they were going.

Joining the kids at the cave exit, I once more asked them to be quiet. Moving close to the brush that covered the small opening, I got onto my hands and knees. With the Winchester in hand, I crawled through the brush, sticking my head out to look around.

I stood up, took two steps, then looked around again. Trees and ferns were all that was there. Reaching back into the cave, I took hold of my backpack then drug it outside of the opening. Pulling the sheath from the Winchester, I motioned for Charles and Amanda to join me. We all remained quiet while looking for any sign of our pursuers.

None of us saw or heard anything but the birds going about their lives. Amanda spoke in a whisper. "The birds are not sounding a warning, so we must be alright?"

"Good for you, Amanda, for noticing that," I praised, smiling at her. "I'm not sure about being alright, though."

We went up the small trail about ten feet were it crossed the path we had hiked the past few days. Turning left would take us back to the cabin—not the place we wanted to go. "This is the trail we've been hiking. I recognize it!" whispered Amanda.

We made our way to an outlook where we could see the lake. I could see two of the helicopters headed toward the cabin beach. I could imagine them starting to search for us. The only thing left for us to do was to head up the trail toward the Menatuline Peak mountaintop.

CHAPTER 2

G reg paced the floor of the cabin. "Bob! Get John and Freddie in here now." If Jose was going to want somebody's ass, it was not going to be his crew. He'd spent too many years building his company, and he was not going to lose it because of the mistake of Jose's men. *Greg Woods, you stupid idiot, how did you get mixed up with Jose?* he asked himself. Now his wife Caroline and two kids were in danger too.

Three men made up Greg's crew. Bob Singleton was African American, with black hair, brown eyes, 5'8" a little overweight, age fifty-five. Bob was one great helicopter pilot, an even better helicopter mechanic. Bob's wife Marlene was Caroline's best friend.

John Bolger—blond hair, blue eyes, 6'1", age thirty-five. One of the best helicopter pilots in all of Alaska, that Greg knew of. Married to Sandy, a gorgeous woman, funny, filled with energy, blonde and blue-eyed like her husband. If these two ever had children, they would be beautiful kids.

Freddie Aguilera was Mexican American, with black hair, brown eyes, 5'10", unmarried, and the youngest at twenty-six years old.

Hell, it was his fault for getting involved with Jose. All he wanted to do was test the stealth helicopter he had built. Now he was helping track down Tony Carroll. Tony was not supposed to be able to walk out with Jose's financial records. Jose's men were at fault for allowing that blunder—not him.

One of the new and upcoming cartels, Jose had proven to be an enterprising and malicious person. He came into power during the drug wars along the U.S. Border. The Mexican government had connected him to hundreds of deaths while building his empire. Rumor has it that his first murder was his own brother. If the rumors were right, he'd stabbed him to death.

"John and Freddie are here," announced Bob.

Greg looked up into the eyes of John and Freddie. "I do not have to tell you how much more trouble we're in now." The two of them looked nervous, wondering where Greg was going with this. "Tell me once again—who decided to open fire on the plane, and why did you choose to leave the area?"

"I tell you what, Greg!" John spoke before Freddie had a chance to start. "You put four heavily armed people in your helicopter! Then you tell them no, they cannot shoot at the plane! I swear they would have killed us if we had not obeyed them."

"If Jose doesn't like how things turned out, tough shit! Those bastards were in control, not us. They were giving all the orders. I'm sure they'll lie now to save their own butts. Remember, I wasn't asked if I wanted to get involved with these people. That was your doing, boss!"

Greg looked hard at John, then at Freddie. "I know, John," Greg answered harshly. "If I could do it over, I would, but it's too late. We'll all be dead if we don't continue to bring Jose's drugs into the U.S. and Canada."

"You better listen to him, John," came a voice from outside the cabin. Without any trace of an accent, the familiar voice of Jose broke through the conversation. "All of you come out here, now!"

Greg and the others stepped outside to find Jose standing on the edge of the small porch. On the left side of the trail, four men kneeled, hands and feet bound. All four tried to protest, but the gags made that impossible.

Jose walked behind the four then pulled out a steel plated 9mm semi-automatic. "One of you failed me terribly. You were sent to bring Tony and Lynn back to me, not shoot up a plane and leave. Yes, John, one of them did try to convince me that it was your fault. However, be thankful I did not believe him."

One of the men tried to plead for his life. However, the gag made his words hard to understand. Jose aimed the 9mm at his head and pulled the trigger. The man's face disappeared from existence. "Got to love hollow points, don't you?" Jose said with a smile on his face.

Jose looked at his handgun. "Thanks, brother, for the gift."

The body fell forward into its own blood, which flowed out from under the dead man's head. The red ooze soaked the ground, then started to stream down the trail. The bounds around the other three men's feet were cut. A plastic bag was placed around the dead man's head. Two men gripped the dead man's legs then dragged the body toward the lake.

Jose walked over to John. "Remember what happens to people who displease me?" Jose stepped up onto the porch and entered the cabin.

"Someone really lives in this dump?" Jose asked of no one.

John looked angrily at Greg, then at the blood on the ground. "That's us somewhere in the future, Greg. Just a small puddle of blood." John turned and headed toward the lake.

"Bob, Freddie, go with him please; see if you can keep him from getting killed by badmouthing Jose's men."

"Sure thing, Greg," answered Bob.

Greg shook his head as he followed Jose into the cabin. "Was that really necessary, killing that man in front of us? If you get some kind of pleasure out of murdering people, please do not think for a moment others do. One day, Jose—and it will not be me—somebody will get tired of you terrorizing their lives all the time."

Jose sat down, putting his feet up on the dining table. "Fear does a lot of things, Greg. Fear will keep you in line for a long time. Your wife and kids will surely be an asset to me. You keep running around in that stealth ship of yours. Keep bringing my merchandize across the border then they'll be okay."

"Is that why Tony Carroll ran? You tried to frighten him. What was it, Jose?" Greg never let his gaze move from Jose as he sat down on the other side of the table. "You threaten his family, Jose? You take a liking to his daughter. Is that why he took your bank account numbers?"

Greg leaned forward, knowing he was taking a chance, and asked one more question. "So how much longer do you have, Jose? How much time until those investors of yours want your blood or their money?"

Greg saw Jose's eyes harden as he held Greg's stare. Putting his feet back on the floor, Jose leaned forward until the two of them were only inches apart. "When I find them, I'll take their daughter while they watch. Then I'll ship her to South America where, before she's eighteen, she'll be a pro in bed, making men happy. I will even send the boy with her, so he too can make men happy also." Jose let out a short laugh. "I may even keep mommy alive to send her reports on how well her children are performing."

Greg slowly got to his feet then walked toward the door. Before leaving, he turned to Jose. "How many people are here because they want to be? I mean, how many are loyal to you? How many are you paying or forcing to be here? If a higher bidder came along, what would happen then? Whose side do you think I would take if I saw a way out, huh? When everyone finds out you're broke, who will stay around? Like I said before, don't worry about me—I just don't want to be around you if you fall. I won't be the one to take you out, but don't ask me to help you."

As Greg passed the bloodstained ground, he heard something crash inside the cabin. Now he could hear Jose yelling at no one. Greg didn't understand Spanish, so Jose's words meant nothing to him. By the sound of Jose's voice, he had struck a nerve somewhere. *The man has developed a bad temper*, Greg thought to himself.

Greg arrived at the tree line in time to see his pride and joy fly in low over the lake. A one-man helicopter was making its way to the beach he stood on. The body frame looked like a stealth fighter with no flat surface on it. The blades had been the challenge, but in the end, it was a simple design change. They tilted the blades a little more than normal then reshaped them.

John and Bob were standing by a six-man helicopter—a pilot, copilot, plus four passengers. The four helicopters were heavily loaded with different types of surveillance equipment. Finding these people should not be too hard.

"I need you two in the air to start searching the area. If you locate them, radio back to me first. I will send the other Snoopers in with Jose's men to capture them."

John looked at Greg shaking his head while walking to his Snooper.

"Greg, are we ever going to get rid of these people?" asked Bob.

"I don't know, Bob. We can only go along for the ride right now. However, this is starting to look like the right time to free ourselves from Jose. Let's find those people first, okay? Now get into the air, please."

Bob headed off to the boat they found when they landed here. Freddie was there waiting to pilot the boat to the other two Snoopers. "It will be fifteen to twenty minutes before Freddie and I get into the air," announced Bob.

Greg walked over to his stealth copter, and touched his dream that Jose was ripping from him. Of course, it was his own fault for doing business with a drug dealer. He only wanted to prove that his baby could get past the U.S. military's defenses, so he had set up a run off the coast of Alaska.

He had flown the copter to the ship he had paid to be there. The ship had a helicopter pad for Greg to land on. It was here that he first met Jose.

Jose showed him pictures of his family, and then told him to keep them safe—he would be running drugs into Alaska for him.

Why he did not go to the authorities? He still didn't understand. However, he felt it was too late now to seek their help. He just didn't see a way out—until now.

Yes, this was his baby. Raptor was what he had named it. Ready to present to security companies until Jose showed up. It could carry two .50 caliber mini-guns, plus four laser-guided missiles. The body and windows were bulletproof. All made of new lightweight materials, this craft could reach over 260 mph while carrying enough fuel for a 1560-mile range before refueling.

But instead, it now carried drugs where the missiles and the mini-guns had been. Greg removed his hand from the Raptor. His future had escaped him. He was just a drug runner now. To top it all off Bob, John, and Freddie were now in this mess also. However, for the first time, Jose was out in the open, away from his benefactor. Maybe, just maybe, they could break free of Jose way out here.

Jose's pilot had gotten out of the Raptor, so the seat was still warm when Greg sat down. After flipping the correct switch, the radio came to life. Greg adjusted the frequency to communicate with the Snoopers.

Within seconds, John's voice came across the headset. "Snooper One is ready to lift off."

Greg pushed the talk button. "Find them then. We can go home."

"This is getting harder, Greg, but I'm still with you," answered John.

Bob's voice came through the headset. "Snooper Three in the air."

"Okay guys, start search procedures. We know they were at the cabin, so this is home base. Snooper Three heads north from here. Snooper One, you are south. They're on foot, so they could not have gotten far. You are doing a thirty-mile square pattern. Remember, when you spot them, give me a call. I'll be sitting right here."

Within seconds, Bob called out, "Raptor, this is Snooper Three. I found a large metal object in a cove about fifty yards north of the cabin."

"Snooper Three, I will go investigate after the search is over," Greg responded back.

Some fifteen minutes later Snooper Three again broke the silence. "Raptor, I have a hit of three objects moving north, close to four miles away from the cabin."

"Snooper Three, send data to Snooper Two, then wait there for Freddie's arrival."

"Greg, Jose's men want me to put them on the ground now. They are being very direct about it. I can feel the gun against my head."

Shit, thought Greg, then, "Take them two miles ahead of the targets and let them out."

"Roger, Greg," replied Bob.

"John, keep your search pattern just in case this is not them—but who else could it be, right? Maybe they split up hoping to draw ground parties in the wrong direction."

"Roger, Greg," answered John.

Greg looked up to see Jose at the tree line. "Gentlemen, you are on your own. I have to leave for a bit." Greg changed the frequency back to where he had found it, then shut down the radio.

As his foot touched the ground, Jose made it to the Raptor. "We have located three signals—could be one adult and two kids. Bob is dropping off your men two miles ahead of the signals. Freddie and your pilot are bringing more of your men on the other side of the signal. We should have them boxed in soon."

"Good work; perhaps we will all be back to work shortly," stated Jose.

"Bob will stay with the targets until Freddie shows up."

Greg insisted that Freddie ride in the copilot seat of Snooper Two. He was not about to let the Snooper completely out of his control.

Jose was still angry over the last conversation they had. "You stay out here and make sure your men do their jobs."

"Hey, my men have done everything you have asked, Jose. Let me remind you that your people let Tony get away with your records, not mine!"

Jose reached behind his back and pulled out his steel-plated 9mm. "You be careful how you speak to me. I am your owner; do not forget that."

"Pull that trigger and this whole operation stops. You'll have to find another way to get your drugs in. So go ahead, Jose, and good luck. The only reason I'm cooperating is for my family and co-workers."

Greg noticed two of Jose's guards walk out from the trees. One guard was on each side along the path leading to the cabin.

Greg was not thinking of starting an argument in the first place. Jose still held most of the cards in this game, but Tony had the card that trumped any of Jose's. All he had to do was wait. Maybe, somehow Greg could get the account numbers before Jose.

CHAPTER 3

We finally made it over the top of the mountain, then down the other side. We turned north to follow the base of Menatuline Peak before heading west. The plan was simple: Keep walking until I felt we were north of the lake, then head northwest. Make our way around Nimbus Mountain, heading west until we reached Juneau, Alaska. There were a few small villages or homes along the way, but we would only endanger those people by going to any of them. I hoped the cave bit would leave this Jose's people without a way to track us. For now, I worked under the assumption that they were closing in on our location.

The terrain was rough-going until we found an animal trail. We followed it until it turned away from the mountain. My best guess was that we were some three miles from the cabin. We came to a small meadow that would take five minutes to cross. The grass was almost waist deep for me, so Charles was having a hard time getting through.

Each of us stumbled in the grass, plus we found a few puddles of water to step in. With wet feet, we made our way, forging our own trail. Close to halfway across, the birds stopped making noise. The silence was loud after all these years out here. I stopped to look back at the way we had come.

"Amanda, take Charles and keep heading for the trees as fast as you can. I will be right behind you."

Amanda grabbed Charles by the hand, saying, "Come on, we have to go faster."

I could see the trail we had left in the grass. If I could see it, whatever was causing the silence could too. Then I could hear it—the soft whoop, whoop of helicopter blades.

I started running after the kids. I yelled at them to hide in the grass. "Stay there until I say different." I continued making a trail through the grass. If they spotted it, they might think we had already passed here, or maybe some animal had made a new trail. I stopped at the edge of the meadow, dropped my pack, and unsheathed the Winchester. Moving the lever, I put a round in the chamber then knelt on the grass.

A black helicopter came into view low over the treetops. It began to hover, then moved slowly forward. I raised the rifle, bringing the tail rotor into my sights. Looking at the helicopter again, I saw four ropes fall out of it. As the ropes touched the ground, I sighted the rotor once more. I slowly pulled back the trigger, waiting for the hammer to fall. The Winchester rocked back into my shoulder and a loud noise from the round's exploding powder filled my ears. The helicopter made an immediate left bank. I saw a dark object fall out of the helicopter, then seconds later another fell. As the helicopter started to settle, I fired another shot at the cockpit area. The helicopter rocked, dropped down a few feet, slamming into a tree. Now it appeared to be completely out of control.

It crashed to the ground, throwing debris everywhere. I headed back down the trail to find the kids. "Amanda, Charles, follow this trail until you find my backpack, then stay there, you understand me?"

Amanda did not wait to answer. She grabbed Charles and headed up the trail. I had to see if anyone survived—I couldn't have anyone coming up behind us later on. I made my way back to the helicopter, slipping and sliding across the puddles. I came out of the grass to see the demolished helicopter.

The nose was facing me as I approached it. It sat in an upright position, but the landing struts had collapsed on impact. I could see two bodies still strapped into the front seats. I stepped closer, the Winchester ready in my hands. A tree limb pierced the windshield, pinning one person in the copilot seat. Red blood still ran down parts of the bough.

The pilot was slumped in his harness, motionless. I stepped closer to the windshield, where I could see the bloodstain down the front of his shirt. From here, it looked like my shot had found its mark. I had always been lucky shooting all kinds of weapons. I only wish my aim this time was targets or for food.

I could not see the face of the man impaled by the tree. He had on strange-looking goggles covering his face. I walked to his side of the craft. There I found another body crushed under the helicopter. The broken landing struts lay across the back of his legs. He also had a deep gash in the back of his head. He wore a small backpack, to which I cut the straps and threw over by the trail.

Climbing into the helicopter, I made my way to the cockpit area. The pilot appeared to be of Latino descent, as did the copilot. I removed the copilot's strange goggles then pressed them over my eyes. The world changed to bright white dots scattered around outside the helicopter. Thermal-vision goggles came to mind. A power line ran from the goggles to a battery box. As I removed the battery pack, I noticed a nametag on the copilot's shirt: Freddie. *Sorry, Freddie*, I thought to myself. Turning off the goggles, I left Freddie in peace.

Moving to the passenger compartment, I saw that the back wall was covered with electronic equipment. I had no idea what it was all for. In a row of clear plastic doors, I saw another set of goggles like the ones I now had. None of this was useful due to my lack of understanding. I stepped out of the other side of the helicopter.

Out of the corner of my eye, I saw movement. Before I could do anything, I was struck in the mid-section. Dropping the rifle and goggles, I doubled over, then hit the ground. I rolled and came to a kneeling position, wrapping my arms around my stomach area. I looked up into a bloody face of another Latino man wielding a metal part of the helicopter over his head. I rolled onto my back bring my feet up to protect myself, and the metal club connected with the sole of my shoes. I felt the vibration of the blow travel down my legs.

He staggered a step or two, raising the metal club again. He moved to my side so he could try for my head. He swung the club once more. I rolled to my left and heard the club hit the ground near my head. I continued to move while reaching for my .38. When my fingers clasped around it, the man lunged forward for another strike. This time I rolled toward the man, taking his feet out from under him. Shaking his legs from me, I climbed to my feet, pulling the .38 free. I fired two shots at his back before noticing the backpack that he wore. He started to rise up, so I stepped on his back, forcing him back to the ground.

I took another step, so I was in front of my attacker. I placed one foot on each of his hands, putting all my weight on them. His body relaxed and he just lay there, breathing heavily, exhausted and badly wounded from the helicopter crash. I pulled my knife then cut the straps on his pack. I threw it over by the Winchester.

When I examined his back, I could not see any bullet holes. My shots did not exit the pack. Rolling him onto his back, he just stared up at me. I spotted a radio attached to his belt. I pulled it off him and clipped it to my holster belt. His breathing was labored. His faraway eyes did not see me. Walking to his pack, I stuffed the radio and goggles into it. Picking up the Winchester, I examined it for damage. The man's breathing was coming very hard now. He was not long in this world. I stepped closer to him and sat down. Taking his hand, I said, "I cannot save you, but I will not leave you alone."

His face relaxed, then became softer looking.

"I release you into the unknown," I said. Our eyes met again. "I am sorry," I told him.

His body went stiff, and I watched the life leave his eyes. I did not take the time to cover any of the fallen men. I had to find the kids. I know they heard the shots.

I grabbed the packs and headed back through the meadow. If that man had not been gravely injured, I may have lost the fight. I would have to be more careful from this point on. Two kids were counting on me.

They had found us much too fast—the tunnel should have given us a bigger lead. These goggles would have made it easier to find us. All that equipment in the helicopter probably helped locate us more quickly.

I am too old for this, I thought. I hurried to locate Charles and Amanda.

I was not finding being the hunted very much fun. I've found it's always better to be the hunter. Maybe the goggles and radio would help us avoid the hunters. Perhaps we could lose them before long.

My pack came into view, but the kids were nowhere in sight. "Amanda, Charles, where are you?" I called out.

Charles ran out from behind some trees, wrapping his small arms around my waist. Another pair of arms circled around me higher up. "We heard shots and didn't know what to do, so we hid," said Amanda.

"I was really scared when I heard the shots," Charles added.

I dropped the two packs, then put my arms around them. "Good thinking, you two," I told them.

"A deer came out of the brush and scared me. That's what I was shooting at," I lied. They didn't need to know what had happened back there. "Come on, we need to start back up the mountain."

While I was tired and old, we had to be going. We started climbing. On the way up, we came across a small cave, only about six by four feet. I told the kids to crawl in for some much-needed rest.

Finally taking the time to search the two packs from the helicopter crash, I found what looked to be candy bars. "Is anybody hungry?" I asked.

Both kids nodded their heads yes. "Here, try eating these. Keep the wrappers. We will burn them when we can." I poured the pack out on the cave floor. Three pairs of socks, some change of underwear, plus ammunition. A first-aid kit, more food, and water also fell out.

The kids made faces when they bit into the bars, but they ate them anyway. I took a bar for myself and bit into it. It was dry and tasteless. No, it was like how I would imagine what eating cardboard would be like. I dumped out the other pack. I found another set of goggles with a bullet hole in its battery pack. A radio, too, also with a bullet hole. These are where my shots had gone. Then there were more socks, underwear, and ammunition.

While stuffing the contents of the two packs into mine, I noticed a side compartment in both backpacks. I searched the compartments, finding fishing line and about twenty feet of nylon rope. I found room in a side pocket of my pack for those items. Next, I examined the Winchester. I pulled out the cleaning kit and ran some oil inside the barrel. After finished with the Winchester, I picked up the good radio and turned it on.

"Ground Force Three to Raptor; Raptor, are you there?"

"This is Raptor; go ahead Ground Force Three," came from the radio. I recognized Greg's voice as Raptor. The conversation continued as I listened.

"Snooper Two is down. We found four bodies on the ground. Your man Freddie and three of our men are dead at the crash site. We found one more of ours in a tree over the crash. That leaves one unaccounted for."

"Ground three, I will send Snooper Three to assist you. Hold your position until they get there," answered Greg.

"Snooper Three, did you hear that?"

"Got it, Raptor, headed to the crash site. Sorry to hear about Freddie."

"Snooper One, where are you now?"

"Raptor, this is John—sorry, I mean Snooper One. I'm just finishing the first half of the southern search pattern, Raptor. Now flying at ten thousand feet, I still have no human heat signals to report. This could be a great place for hunting deer, if we ever get to that again."

A new name for me to remember, I thought to myself.

Snooper One, I need you to hone in on Ground Force Three's GPS signal. Use their location to start a new search."

"Roger, Raptor, on my way. ETA is five minutes."

"Ground Force teams, let me remind you that we want them alive. Wound them if you have to, but keep them alive. Oh yes, Jose wants the girl unharmed and untouched. He has his own plans for her."

I clicked off the radio then checked that Amanda was still sleeping. I could only imagine what Jose's plans were. I do have a good imagination. I shook my head to clear it of the thoughts that rushed in. I had to get them out of here.

If they could search for heat images from ten thousand feet, what chance did we have in hiding from them? If we only could mask our heat signatures somehow… It looked like a race to the top. I did not see us ascending the mountaintop before the other helicopter arrived.

"Come on you two, wake up. We have to get moving," I said as I shook them awake. "Come on, wake up! The bad guys are at the meadow. We need to go!"

Barely awake Charles and Amanda put their packs on. We headed up again right away. The stops for air were coming more and more as I pushed the kids toward the top. The five minutes for the other helicopter had come and gone. We were still a distance from the mountain crest.

We rounded some large boulders, scaring two deer plus ourselves. The deer bolted up a small animal trail going toward the mountaintop. I knew we should not have used this trail. However, right now, we needed speed, so I led the kids on to it. If our hunters got here, they would use it to get ahead of us. I tore a bush out by the roots then started dragging it behind us. I was not sure this would work, but it seemed to do the trick in the movies I saw as a kid.

Somewhere after an hour and four stops, we made it to the skyline of the mountain. We rested at a place that looked out of sight. I pulled the radio out.

"Ground Force Three, they stopped at the crest of the mountain."

"Roger, Snooper One," came the reply. "How far behind are we?"

"If you keep up the pace, you should catch them in about fifteen minutes."

"I am only getting quick readings on them because of the trees. Ground Force One is about twenty-five minutes away. You will have them surrounded in about thirty minutes."

The trees are blocking our heat signal. How can we use that information? I asked myself.

I had seen old police images that used thermal detection devises before. They always showed the whole body of the person the police were after. The heat signature disappeared when the person ran behind something, then reappeared when they went into the open again.

I took the ground cloth off my backpack. It was big at eight square feet. I used a painter's drop cloth for many things—maybe it would work to hide us. Unrolling the cloth, I pulled it up over my head.

The kids got underneath it and Amanda held up the other end while Charles dragged the bush behind us. We headed north on the ridge top. I hoped this would do the trick as we continued along.

"Ground Force Three, start spreading out now. You are almost on the last-known position. Ground Force One is eight minutes away now."

"Roger, Snooper One, starting to fan out now."

"Snooper One, keep us advised if they move."

I wanted to run but panicking would not help us. I weaved around trees and bushes as we hurried away. The cloth would be easy to spot by eye if someone were close enough, but our new disguise seemed to be fooling the heat detectors. No report of our movement came from the radio. After close to a hundred yards we turned west again. We descended on the lakeside of Menatuline Peak, working our way past the underbrush, until the radio sounded off.

"Snooper One, Ground Force Three. Targets are nowhere to be found. Repeat, targets are not here. Have visual contact with Ground Force One. The signal, no target spotted, please advise."

"Ground Force Three, I am descending to two thousand feet to restart search."

I took two more steps into the brush when the ground disappeared from under me. My foot crashed down, finding packed earth several feet below, knocking me off my center of gravity. I fought for my balance then I felt hands grab my backpack. There in front of me was a long drop to the base of the mountain. I sat down on the ledge behind me then slid backward. I could feel hands helping me move to safety. When my feet made it back to level ground, I fell backward. My backpack kept me from going all the way to the bottom.

Getting up to my feet, I let go of the image I had seen while leaning over the cliff. My hands were shaking. "Thanks Charles," I said.

My heart rate slowed quickly, and I knew we had to get moving. An idea came to me, and I reached into a side compartment in my pack. I pulled out the fishing line and cut some four feet of line, then tied one end to a stick, pushed it far into the ground, and wrapped and tied the other end to a tree. The fishing line was near invisible. I plucked it like a guitar, then listened to it weakly sound off. If the people made the same mistake as I did, they wouldn't live to see the end of it. I could only hope that they would.

I had dropped the Winchester when I fell forward. It landed just a foot away from me, its barrel jutting out over the cliff. Picking it up, I brushed it off and said, "We have to get moving again, but we are going to slow down. Don't need to do that again."

Farther down the mountain, I spotted a small cave. It looked like a good place to regain my wits before going on. The entrance was only about three feet wide and two feet high. Removing my pack, I inspected the inside of the cave. It would be tight, but we could fit with all our gear.

Charles and Amanda crawled into the cave while I pushed in the packs. I moved an old fallen tree to block the cave opening from view. Picking up a branch, I swept the area clean of our footprints.

Inside I placed the tarp over the entrance, using branches to hold it in place. The cave became dark with some light coming in around the edges of the tarp. The kids stretched out and were soon asleep. I sat with my back against the cave wall listening to the outside world. My head snapped up with the sound of someone screaming. The faint thud of something striking the ground made its way to me.

I turned on the radio. "Ground Force One to Raptor, can you read us?"

After a few seconds, Raptor answered. "This is Raptor; go ahead, Ground Force One."

"We just lost another man plus any sign of the trail."

"Snooper One, have you found them yet?"

"No Raptor, no sign of them at all. I am not sure how, but they have found a way to cover their heat signal."

"Snooper One will return to the fuel depot when Snooper Three arrives. He will continue to look for them."

"Roger, Raptor."

"Ground Forces, keep searching for them. They cannot be that far ahead of you."

"Raptor, we need professional trackers out here."

"I got that, Ground Force. We have four on the way. It may be hours before they get here. Now back to work, guys."

"One more man down, plus four more coming in," I muttered to myself.

Lying down on the hard cave floor, I used my pack as a pillow. "Let them stay up. I need to sleep," I said to no one.

"Wake up! Please wake up!" Amanda was almost shouting as she pushed on my arm.

I jolted awake. "What's the problem?" I asked her.

"You're snoring loudly," she answered.

I sat up, rubbed my eyes, then yawned. "Sorry."

"Are you two ready to move on?" I asked.

Charles aimed his pen light at himself. "Do we have to leave?"

"Yes, Charles, the bad guys are not that far behind us," I answered.

Pulling the tarp aside, I let in the sunshine, then carefully crawled out into the world. With the tarp over our heads, we made our way down to the lake. Staying in the trees, we worked our way around the north side of the lake. Now we had to work our way around one more mountain then head west to the Alaskan border.

We hiked until our arms grew tired of holding the tarp. I would have to come up with a better way to shield ourselves with it. I draped the tarp over a large boulder and we climbed under for rest, food, and drink.

I got the radio out and turned it on.

"Ground Force, have you found any sign of them yet?"

"No, Raptor, we are still at a loss on where they went."

"Snooper Three, any luck with you?"

"No, Raptor. I'm thinking they went underground. I'm not getting a reading on anybody but Ground Force One and Three."

"Raptor, we need a break. How about Snooper Three picking some of us up?"

"Sorry, guys, but all Ground Forces are to stay out in the field. Trackers will be here on-site in forty minutes. Snooper One is bringing them in. So rest where you are, Ground Force."

I was just about to turn the radio off when bad news came across it.

"Raptor, we found small footprints here. Looks like a kid's shoeprint. We will search the area for more tracks. Call when the trackers are here."

"Great news about the print, Ground Force. If you find them, give me a call right away."

"Will do, Raptor."

After eating another snack bar, we grabbed the tarp. We had to put more distance between the hunters and us. We planned to head northwest from the lake, up a trail, and start around Nimbus Mountain.

We reached the small stream that ran on the northwest side of the mountain before mid-morning. We turned westward to follow the stream through this valley.

All streams in this area made it to the Nakina River. Follow the Nakina far enough to come to the Taku River. This would lead us to the Pacific Ocean. It sounded easy when I thought about it, but I knew it was still two days past the Nakina River, and we had not even made it there yet.

I remember a line in the movie *PT109* starring Cliff Robertson playing John F. Kennedy. After their torpedo boat was rammed by a Japanese destroyer and sliced in two, most of the crew was still alive.

They used parts of the boat as floats to swim to a nearby island. One of the men said that four miles is a long way. Kennedy answered, "Yes, but it's only three inches on the chart." That's how I felt right then. It's only inches on a map.

A bird flew high above us as we made our way along the creek. Another called out and took to the trees far from us. As we came around a large boulder, a deer bolted pass us. It had been close enough for us to touch it. It ran for some twenty yards then stopped and looked back.

"Shh, maybe she will let us look at her some." Both kids were fascinated at seeing the doe. It only stayed around for a few seconds, but it was a lifetime for me. It turned then ran a little ways more, then looked back. The deer bounded out of sight into the trees.

On we went following the stream until we finally reached a fork where a small stream converged with yet another stream. We could follow this slightly bigger stream on to the Nakina River.

The kids went ahead with the tarp while I tried to keep a watch for helicopters. I turned on the radio to listen.

"Raptor, the dog that this tracker brought has a scent. We are one mountain over from the lake following some creek headed southwest."

"Ground Force One, I have your GPS reading. Snooper One is headed your way," answered Raptor.

Great, I thought as I turned off the radio, *they have dogs*.

I hurried to catch up to the kids. We now needed to lose the dog somehow. Right now, we needed to start looking for a place to spend the night. The sun was already setting behind the mountains. I was looking for small indents in the mountainside that would work. But, if we could find a cave somewhere, that would do us better. As I got under the tarp with the kids, I started scanning for a way up the side of Nimbus Mountain on my left.

CHAPTER 4

John had dropped the four trackers at the cabin beach, then lifted off for the fuel depot. Greg noted that each tracker had a different color beret on his head: red, blue, green and brown. With each tracker also came a Doberman Pinscher with colored collars.

Greg was hoping that Jose would just stay at the cabin, leaving the search to him and his team. However, that was not going to happen. Jose arrived yelling commands and waving his 9mm around. In response, the red tracker un-holstered his handgun. "You better put that weapon in its holster now!" he commanded.

Two of Jose's guards walked out from the trees and aimed their automatic rifles at the red tracker. Greg wished he knew more about small firearms. Whether he knew what type everyone was pointing at each other or not did not matter—one could kill him just as easily as any other.

"I think that you should holster *your* weapon!" Jose countered with a wide grin.

Never taking his eyes off Jose, the red tracker spoke. "Then we're both dead men." He took a step toward Jose.

"You know who I am?'" shouted Jose. "You were sent here to follow my orders!"

The red tracker took yet another step closer. "I don't care who you are," said the red tracker. "I am here because your benefactor asked me to, and you're not him. My orders come from him alone. He did not tell me to jump to your command. I am not planning to start being your lapdog today or tomorrow, understand? I am here to try to retrieve your benefactor's investment—is that clear, mister? Now it is not going to matter where I hit you with this; you'll still be dead."

The three other trackers began to spread out. Two of them—green and brown—took shelter behind Raptor. Blue lowered himself behind the trackers' gear. Each one of them pulled their handguns. Jose now had four handguns trained on him while he stood out in the open.

Jose smiled then laughed while holstering his weapon. "Okay, you win this time." With a wave of his hand, Jose's two guards slipped back into the trees.

"Jose Hernandez: big man in Mexico, small man here in Canada," said the blue tracker, keeping his weapon pointed at Jose.

"Greg, you get those men out to the others fast," Jose said angrily as he turned, heading back up the trail.

Greg was sitting in the Raptor watching. *Just what I need now— more shit*, he thought to himself.

"You in the copter, where do we start looking for these people?" said Red.

"One of the other Snoopers will airlift you to the two teams that are in the field now."

A voice to Greg's left asked, "How many copters do you have here, mister?"

"I had four but one went down on the other side of that mountain," stated Greg as he pointed to the mountain in front of him. "I now have three; two that can deliver you people."

The touch of a gun barrel to Greg's head made him jump. "You one of his men?" asked the green beret.

"No, I have to be here because of Jose," answered Greg.

"Ah, a little blackmail goes a long way. Maybe we could use you on a different mission sometime." All four men laughed at that. "So what do you call them Snoopers for? It just looked like a Hughie helicopter to me with a lot of electronic junk inside of it."

"So why aren't they here yet?" asked the red beret.

Greg commanded into his radio, "Snooper One, Snooper Three, return to the fuel depot. I will meet you there."

"Okay, Raptor, Snooper One already there needed fuel before heading back out there anyway."

"Snooper Three already on the way," answered Bob.

"I hear you, Snooper Three; everything will be ready for your arrival."

Greg felt the gun barrel at his head again. "Could you please stop doing that? I am not one his lackeys nor am I going to be one of yours. We don't have to set you down in the right place yet—or do we?"

"All you had to do was ask," answered the man. The other three colored berets joined in laughing at Greg.

"If something happens to one of my pilots, you may find yourselves walking out of here. Now how do I acknowledge you on the radio?"

The green tracker bumped Greg with the gun barrel yet again. "We'll call you if we need something."

Greg looked at the green tracker. "Oh, so if we find these people before you, we keep it to ourselves, right?" Greg flipped the canopy switch, closing it. He turned the starter switch for the main engine to the Raptor. With the canopy down, Greg was safe from anything he saw that the trackers had with them.

The four trackers moved back away from the Raptor. Their weapons still out were now pointing at Greg.

Picking up the microphone for the speaker system, Greg pressed the key to talk. "This machine is bulletproof, gentlemen. I'm not here to make trouble with anyone, but I will not stand by while you play your silly macho games. You want to go find these people? Good—go find them! Remember that my pilots are going to be delivering you in the right places, hopefully. Now put those weapons away."

The green tracker fired directly at the canopy. Greg lifted the Raptor only feet off the ground, letting it drift toward the green tracker. As the tracker backed away, Greg continued to follow him, keeping just a few feet between them. The green tracker finally broke into a run, making his way to the trees.

Greg heard other shots hit the Raptor. Slowly rotating the Raptor, he stopped when he was facing the red tracker. Moving forward, Greg forced the red tracker to back up into the lake.

Greg keyed the microphone again. "If any of my people are harmed by you, I swear you will not make it out of here."

The Raptor rose to a hundred feet, then headed to the other side of the lake. As Greg traveled to the fuel depot, he knew he had better get John and Bob out of this mess fast.

John had all the pumps running when Bob arrived. As Bob shut down the engine, John dragged the fuel hose to the Snooper. "Come on, Greg, let us kick these guys' butts then get out of here," John said to himself. Bob was exiting the craft as the fuel began to flow.

Greg set the Raptor down a short way from the fuel depot. As he walked into the area, Bob was waiting for him.

"Greg, are we going to do this much longer?" asked Bob.

"No, I don't believe so. I have a plan. You and John are getting out of here very soon. You are not going to die like Freddie did," answered Greg.

"Yeah, well I'm not getting paid enough for this crap."

"I agree, Bob. When we get out of this mess, I promise you a big payday. Course, we may have to haul a lot of tourists around."

"Beats the gig we have now."

Snooper Three finally finished filling. Greg pulled the hose away from the helicopter. "Bob, go pick up two of the trackers; try to get the ones with the red and green berets on, if you can. If not let me know, okay?"

"What do I do with them once I get them?"

Greg smiled at Bob's comment. "Just take them to Ground Force Three then drop them off nicely. Don't do anything else, you understand?"

Bob began to climb into the Snooper then faced Greg. "Whatever you're planning, Greg, be very careful. Too many people lives are at stake."

Bob got into the pilot's seat, then cranked the rotor engine. After a few moments, he lifted Snooper Three off the ground. Bob stayed close to the lake water until he was away from the depot. He gained some altitude then proceeded to the cabin beach.

When Bob was safely away, John moved his Snooper closer to the fueling hoses. The rotor blade had not stopped when John's feet hit the ground. He was mad at how Jose had blackmailed them for work. He was pissed that they were helping to hunt down some kids for Jose. This wasn't how he had pictured his life. Now add these tracker guys, and he was ready to help free the world of Jose Hernandez.

Greg could see that John was in one of his moods again. John had been so easygoing when he had hired him. Shortly before letting himself get involved with Jose, John had started getting angry over things.

"John!" yelled Greg. "I have something special for you to do. First, you're taking Raptor back to Juneau. When you get there follow the instructions I have here."

Greg handed John a folded piece of paper. "Don't read it until you get to the hangar. I don't want any mistakes of you or me saying the wrong thing on the radio. Plus, I'll be answering with the Raptor call sign. That should go without saying that you'll still be Snooper One, get it?"

Greg interrupted John before he could say anything. "Just listen, don't question, please. I got us into this mess. I'll be the one to get us out, okay? Freddie is dead; I do not need another person dying because of this."

"If your voice fades out, Jose won't question it, but if mine does, you know he will start asking questions. That's why I need you to do this for me."

Looking at Greg, John wondered what was on the paper he now held in his hand. "Okay, Greg, but when I read this it better be good news." Still angry, John headed off toward the Raptor.

"Greg!" yelled out John.

Hearing his name, Greg looked back at John.

"Good luck, friend. If we make it out of here, the beer is on me."

John smiled, and then continued to walk toward the Raptor.

Greg heard his friend start the Raptor then watched it lift off for Juneau. "If we live that long, John, the beer is on me for the rest of our lives." Greg finished fueling the Snooper thinking over his plan. He started the Snooper, lifted off, then went to see destiny.

We followed another animal trail up the side of Nimbus Mountain. The sunlight was just beginning to fade; darkness would soon be calling different wildlife out. Moving into open terrain, I saw possible places for caves, but it was Amanda who found the best one.

"Look, there," she said while pointing at a dark spot among some rocks. "That could be a cave, right?"

"Yep, it could be; let's hope we've found a place for the night."

As we approached the rocks, I saw that this wasn't a cave at all. A giant slab of rock fell from above. It formed a space between the slab and the mountain, almost a lean-to made of rock. Laying our tarps on the ground, we wrapped ourselves up for the night. The world outside had to take care of itself tonight. I was just too tired.

"Ground Force One, this is Raptor. Snooper One is headed your way with two trackers. Please give Snooper One your location so he can find you."

"Raptor, location is being sent now," came the reply.

After the GPS reading appeared on the dash display, Greg banked off in a western direction. "Roger, Ground Force One, I have your location on the screen," replied John.

True, John had their location on the screen—but in the Raptor, he headed to Juneau. *As long as the both of us remember that we've only changed helicopters, we should be able to pull this off*, thought Greg.

John was a great friend. Greg had known him for three years now. The man did not let him down once during those years. Sometimes John could be hard to get along with, but so could he. John was loyal to the company. He would do his best for him and Bob.

"Raptor, I'm dropping off red and green with their four-legged monsters now," reported Bob.

"Got it, Snooper Three. Continue search for targets when you can."

"Okay, Raptor."

Greg switched to Snooper One's intercom. "You two strap in and hold on to the dogs. This is going to be about a four-minute ride. I wouldn't want anything to go wrong."

With brown and blue berets settled into the seats and the dogs beside them, Greg banked northwestward in search for Ground Force One. The ground rushed by as Greg headed to drop off his two passengers.

"Ground for…Snooper One is…of your position," John announced as the signal broke up.

Good, John is playing his part, thought Greg. "Snooper One, repeat message; you're breaking up."

"Raptor, I'm…one mile from ground…One," replied John.

"Roger, Snooper One; you're one mile from Ground Force One. Come back to the depot after you drop your passengers off. We will look at your radio. See you when you get here, Snooper One." Greg started to descend to treetop level in Snooper One, hoping that everyone fell for the act.

Greg turned the radio to a different frequency and announced, "All people be advised that Snooper One is having radio problems. He will be returning to the fuel depot for repairs. Snooper Three will keep searching the area for targets."

The sound of Jose's voice came over the headset. "Greg! I want you here at the cabin."

"Jose, you're the last person I want to see right now. I'll be at the depot if you want to make the trip over," answered Greg, hoping Jose wasn't angry enough to actually run the boat over to the depot.

"Need I remind you that I have people in your homes! Now do as I order!" screamed Jose.

"Need I remind you that to get a message out to those people, you have to use the radio on one of my helicopters," replied Greg. "If you keep threatening my family and friends, you better find another way out of here."

"You're mine to do whatever I want with, you remember that. I have four people that will kill you on sight, if I order it. Now get over here!"

"Go ahead, Jose! Send them over, but you lost your pilot when Snooper Two went down. Keep pushing, you'll find that even a mouse will fight for its life. Then you'll still be walking home."

Greg turned the radio frequency before he said too much. If Jose thought for a moment that his grip on him was final, then he had better start thinking again. If his plan worked, his family would be safe.

After two hours of pacing around the fuel depot without Jose's men showing up, Greg climbed into the Snooper. Once more, on the private setting Greg keyed the microphone. "John, where are you?"

After a few long seconds, John answered back. "I called my home, Greg. Sandy told me she just saw your wife and kids at the grocery store. They looked fine to her."

"Good news. Thanks, John. How about the rest of the list that I gave you?"

"I'm at the hangar now; I should be in the air in about thirty minutes."

"Come to the fuel depot when you get back this way."

"Roger, Greg."

Taking the handheld radio, Greg climbed out of the Snooper. The loss of a Snooper and one of his men was more damage than he wanted. He was just trying to make a living for him and his family. Look where he is now: *One crazy medium-size drug lord, seven idiots dressed in black, plus four killers in berets*, Greg thought.

He adjusted the radio frequency, getting nothing but static. After making a few more adjustments he finally found the correct settings.

"Everyone check in," came a familiar voice. "This is Red."

"Brown here."

"Blue here."

"This is Green standing right next to you, Red."

"Okay, people, the radios work," said Red.

"There are only three gangster wannabes here," stated Red.

"My mutt and I are heading out. Green gets the three clowns."

"This is Blue. Brown and I are splitting the four here up evenly, then starting out right away."

"Gentlemen, it's going to be dark soon. Let's move out," commanded Red.

"I don't want three of these idiots following me around, Red," Green whined to Red, his complaint coming across the radio.

A gunshot came through Greg's handset.

"This is Brown. What are you doing over there, you two?"

"Shit! Red just killed one of the guys here," said Green.

"Stand down or die right now, you choose," came Red's voice.

"You can stay alive too if you do as you're told."

"Red, I think you better leave before these two also end up dead."

"You two listen up. We're here by someone else's orders. We're not friends of Jose's. So I recommend you contact him for instructions. Me, I'm headed away from Red. It's just good for all of our health."

"Hurry up and talk with your boss. I want to get an hour away from here; too many animals around to stay."

"Take your finger off the radio key!" yelled Red.

Greg turned off his handheld radio. "This isn't going to help at all."

Getting back into Snooper One, Greg contacted Bob in Snooper Three. "Snooper Three, find a place to land and call it a night. We'll start up again first thing in the morning."

"Okay, Raptor, I have a nice mountain top right behind you to land on. See you in the morning, Snooper Three out."

Greg climbed into the back of Snooper One then laid down on the bench. His eyes closed and in a few moments, he was asleep.

He woke at the sound of a helicopter coming in close, quickly realizing that it was the landing lights of the Raptor. Greg shielded his eyes from the strong lights filling the Snooper. Getting on the radio, Greg called out. "Welcome back John."

"It's good to be here, Greg," answered John.

Greg walked over to the Raptor then reached into a small compartment behind the seat. He pulled out the tent and sleeping bag that were kept there.

He saw John jump out of the Snooper with his own tent and bag also. Greg set up his tent under the blades of the two helicopters then threw in his sleeping bag. He was going to get a good night's sleep knowing that his family was safe. Jose had lied to them about that, he wondered what else Jose may have lied about.

Greg watched John finish putting his tent up. "I have a surprise for you Greg," said John. He walked back to the Raptor and opened one of the empty missile compartments. Reaching up inside John pulled out a cooler.

"A little something to eat and drink," stated John.

"Yep." Greg was going to get a good night's sleep.

CHAPTER 5

The next time Greg opened his eyes the sun light was barely showing through the dark clouds. In another hour, the fuel depot will be covered in cloud filtered sunlight. Greg's head hurt a little from the alcohol last night. He stowed his tent and bag then he turned his attention to the day ahead. Greg woke John, "You feel like doing some more flying John? Let's get some coffee brewing then we can start this revolt sooner."

An hour later John was back in Snooper One flying off. Greg watched Snooper One turn into a dot in the cloud-covered sky. Not a good day for flying, but we had to make things look good for Jose.

Greg cleared his mind, "Snooper Three are you awake? This is Raptor."

In a few minutes, Snooper Three answered back, "Awake, but still tired, Raptor."

"I want you to come into the depot, so we can check Snooper Three. I don't need you going down out there, okay?"

"Roger, Raptor" came back across the radio.

Within five minutes, Bob was back on the air. "Raptor, I'm getting a strange heat signal on the other side of this mountain. I have one object without a GPS signal, but it seems to have a smaller heat signal following it."

"Could it be a dog, Snooper Three?" Greg asked. "One of the trackers is out there with only his dog."

The kids and I stepped out from under the rock. My old bones ached, and the knees made popping sounds as I walked. We rounded the first ridge; I could see a brown bear not that far away.

The bear seemed to notice us at the same moment and roared at us. "Quickly, you two—back to the rocks. RUN!" I yelled.

I knew the bear would outrun us, but maybe we had enough distance between us. The kids scrambled back to last night's campsite. My aching body would only let me go so fast in the early morning.

Dropping my pack, I ran, hoping it would slow the beast down. Falling to all fours, I crawled under the slab. Charles and Amanda were in the center of the rock lean-to. We didn't have to wait but a few seconds before a big foot with long nails reached inside.

The bear couldn't get inside the opening far enough to reach us. I could smell it as its claws flew about trying to grab something. Then the leg disappeared, but the bear's breathing could still be heard.

Without warning, the bear's paw came shooting in from the other side. He had no chance to reach us, as that side of the slab was too close to the rocks. The bear returned to the entrance, sticking his big head into the opening.

He vanished once more, but we could hear it walking around trying to figure out how to get to us. I got the Winchester out of its sheath then worked the lever. If he stuck his head in here one more time...

The sound of a dog growling was added into the mix. Both the bear and dog were now in combat with each other. I was hoping the distraction would let us slip away. Two more noises made me stay.

First the yelp of pain from the dog, second of a rifle going off. The bear roared in pain, then in anger. I heard a man's voice. "Damn it, get up here!" then another blast from the rifle sounded. "Shit!" Nothing but someone's screams. In moments, there was only silence.

Yet another voice filled the air. "Shoot! Shoot!" yelled the man. Rifle shots mixed with the roars of the bear. A scream reached into our hiding place. "God, no!" said a different voice. A rifle went off again, then the heavy thud of something hitting the ground.

Looking into the kids' frightened eyes, I signaled them to try to be quiet. My heart was beating hard as I wiggled my way toward the entrance. I couldn't remember being this scared before. I stopped right before the exit. The kids and I looked at each other for what felt like forever.

"Shit! I'm bleeding," an angry voice shouted. "God damn it. Here I am in the middle of fucking nowhere bleeding to death. This damn tracker better still have that radio. What a bloody mess you are, dickhead."

We sat there listening to this man move about—not like we had much choice for now. "Hey! You trackers! One of your men is dead and so is one of ours. I'm bleeding all over the place here."

"Why are you still alive, asshole?" came from the radio.

I guess he found the radio and called for help, I thought.

"Your friend's dog found a big bad-ass bear for us. Then your friend pissed it off real good by shooting it. That's how he died, shithead."

"Peters, get Jose to get me some help. You hear me?!" shouted the man at the radio.

"Ha-ha, looks like you're a dead man to me. Have a nice day."

I slowly climbed out from hiding. The lifeless dog was only a few feet away from me. The next body was a man still wearing a brown beret, perhaps the first person that the bear had killed. The bear lay several feet farther. I could see its sides rise then fall. It was just barely alive.

Crawling on my belly, I made my way behind the bear. I could now hear the labored breathing of this great animal. This bear unknowingly gave its life to save us.

Slowly, I rose up to peek over the bear. I could see yet another blood-soaked man lying on the rocks. Sitting with his back to me was the last man, rocking back and forth in a small pool of blood.

I rose to my feet with the 9mm in hand. Taking slow, careful steps, I passed the bear then the other dead man. Finally, I stood behind the last live one.

"Put your hands were I can see them now," I said.

The man jumped at the sound of my voice.

"Hands were I can see them. now!" I yelled.

He turned looking at me while raising his hands. "You're not Tony Carroll," he stammered.

"No I'm not," I answered

"Look, guy, I'm bleeding here; can I put my hands down?"

I took a step to his side when he made a move.

His hand flashed to his lap then started to come up with a gun. I fired one shot to his temple and red spurted out the other side of his head. His body went limp, then rolled forward down the mountain, hitting rocks and trees as it went. I watched him come to rest against the base of a tree. He didn't move. He just stared back up at me. Even though I couldn't see his eyes, I knew they had to be open.

The sound of the bear pulled me away from those eyes. It was still alive but still breathing hard. I moved closer to the bear with its eyes watching my every step. I sat down next to him and touched its head. If it had the strength, it would rip my throat out easily.

"I'm sorry, big guy. I never meant for you to get hurt, just wanted you to leave," I whispered into his ear. He breathed once, twice, and then I watched the life slip out of him. I got an idea how to get the dogs off us for a while longer. I cleared the area of the two other men, then called the kids out.

I had to convince them that it was safe to roll on top of the bear. I went first. The body was still warm, the pelt was soft, and I could almost feel myself sink into it. If the smell masked our sent for twenty minutes, we could be far enough away before anyone found this site.

We started down the path once more. I was surprised to find my pack barely damaged. The tarp was completely unharmed when we got to it. I also noticed that my joints didn't hurt anymore nor did my knees pop.

The kids followed me like zombies; both were silent as we followed the animal trail again. With the tarp over our heads we left the bear savior behind us. The trail rounded the mountaintop, and then headed back down to the tree line.

After what seemed a lifetime, we put the tarp down. We had walked for hours without food, so I got some more energy bars out of my pack. "Here, eat these even if you don't want to," I commanded them, "and drink some water."

"Why is this happening to us?" Amanda asked as I watched a tear form and roll down her cheek.

"Why does the sun shine, Amanda?" I asked back. "Why did that bear show up? Was it just coincidence? On the other hand, maybe God sent it to help us. I don't know, Amanda. We have enough going on right here," I said without a smile.

"Amanda, if you get a negative answer to your question, don't ever believe it. It'll only eat you up inside. That's one thing I do know. If my life had been different, I may not have been here to pull you and your brother out of the lake. Maybe that's why I was pushed to be here.

"Not all people are evil, young lady, but the ones that are always hurt others because they enjoy it. As to why bad things happen to people—I think it's to push them into a direction that they don't want to go in. That's the best I can do for you now."

"What direction do you think we're being pushed, Mr. Hampton?" Amanda asked.

I stopped and stared through the trees. She called me Mr. Hampton, a sign of respect unasked for, not ordered respect like the military demands from its people. It was a surprise to me that Amanda thought that much of me.

Without looking, I pointed. "For now, Amanda, we're being pushed this way. Toward the river that's out there some place." I turned to face both of them. "Come on, you two, we still have a long way to go." *Really, I had no idea where I'm being pushed*, I thought.

Charles ran ahead of Amanda and me, but he stayed in sight at all times. The trail would lead us to an overlook where I could see a river flowing down a ravine. Since we changed the plan by going over Menatuline Peak, we were now looking at the Inklin River. This ribbon of water also flowed to the Nakina River—all we had to do was follow the Inklin.

About mid-morning, the first raindrop hit me. It was a sign from above to take cover. We wrapped the tarp around a tree and crawled under it. The sound of the rain increased as we settled in order to wait it out. The clouds continued to release their cargo of water in the forest below. Water from the sky in the form of rain or snow was the lifeblood of the forest.

The day was half over when I finally emerged from under the tarp while the raindrops fell. The light rain that now encompassed the forest was busy cleansing the air. The forest glistened with droplets of water clinging to everything.

I allowed myself the time to look out at this new world. The fresh air filled my lungs along with the smells of the landscape. The birds started sounding off again.

The kids stepped from our temporary shelter to peer out. This clean vision of a freshly watered world held their gaze.

"Wow!" exclaimed Charles. "It looks new."

I took a few steps forward and looked down at the river. It flowed a bit faster but presented no more danger than before. "We have to move, you two. Let's get our packs on."

Once again, we were headed down the mountain toward the Inklin River. Following the animal trail, it only took a short time to reach it. The river now looked to be flowing much faster than from above.

We continued walking downriver, looking for a crossing. Up ahead was a place that looked safe for just that. I hoped all would turn out well as we drew near to the river.

I dropped my pack and weapons then had Charles climb on to my back. Taking the first step into the icy water, I fought for my footing. I placed my other foot into the river and made my way out. I moved into deeper water while Charles held his sister's pack on his head. The current grabbed at my legs as I worked farther into the water. Carefully, I went on as the water got deeper with each step I took.

We finally found ourselves halfway across the chest-deep river. I fought to keep my footing and brave the numbing effect of the cold water as I continued. The water level soon started to decline, and in a short time Charles and I emerged on the other side. Cold and wet, I stumbled up on to dry land.

I had to get Amanda across the river, so once more I entered into the icy water. Somewhere near the halfway point I saw another person walking down the riverbank. I plunged into the river, but as soon as my feet left the bottom, the rushing water began to carry me away from Amanda. I fought hard to plant my feet, and fighting for each step I moved closer to the riverbank.

I looked for the man as I struggled closer to Amanda. I spotted a green beret bobbing among the trees. He was working his way behind her. "Amanda! Behind you!" I shook my hand in the direction I thought would be safer for her.

Amanda turned, looking behind her. "Run Amanda, run!" I yelled again.

She saw him and took off running down the river with the green beret behind her. She had a good start, but that was no reason for me to stop. I stumbled to shore, not knowing where either one had gone. I grabbed the Winchester and headed downriver.

Running in watersoaked clothes and shoes, I was desperately searching plus listening for Amanda. From a distance away I could hear Amanda yelling.

"Leave me alone! Help me!"

I headed off, chasing that cry for help. I had to find her now. Neither she nor I even knew what these people wanted. I ran on through the forest almost in a panic.

If that son of a bitch hurts her, I thought.

Her screams were louder now. My heart was pounding heavy from running. She screamed once more. I was terrified.

I came around a tree to see them both up ahead. The green beret was on top of her laughing at her flaying arms. He was reaching to undo her pants.

"Yeah, the prize is mine. Get ready to become a woman now, girl," I heard him say. Then he drew back his fist, and the sound of him striking her filled the air.

Still running, I lifted the Winchester by the barrel. I swung it like a club as he turned to see me. The shoulder stock connected with his upper lip, knocking him off Amanda. I was sure he was going to be missing some teeth when he woke up.

As he rolled off Amanda, I grabbed her arm and pulled her away from him. I was surprised how fast he recovered from the blow I had delivered to him. He looked at me with the hate of the world in his eyes. I had seen this look before in other men.

Still dazed, he grabbed at the knife connected to his belt. I levered a round into the rifle. Raising the rifle to hip level, I fired as his knife left his hand. Pain shot through my left shoulder as he jerked backward, landing on his back.

I levered another round into the chamber as he tried to get back up. My shot jolted him to the ground, where he stayed this time. I sank to my knees breathing hard, exhausted from the river crossing and running to catch up with them. I noticed bloodstains on my shirt as the pain kicked in. Through clenched teeth, I slammed my fist into the ground. Tears filled my eyes as I worked through the pain. From somewhere I could hear Amanda.

"Wade!" I heard her scream. "Be alright, please, be alright," she pleaded. "Charles and I still need you."

I reached out with my right hand, touching her. "I'll be okay, young lady. I still have to get you out of here, don't I?"

As the pain leveled out some, I noticed the knife was lying on the ground. My right hand came up to my wounded left shoulder. As I felt around I figured the knife had hit the shoulder bone then fell out. The pain was nothing more than me imagining the worst. I crawled over to the dead beret to remove his backpack. Amanda helped pour the contents of the pack on the ground. I picked up the small first-aid kit that had fallen out.

Luck was still with me, but would it be enough for my wound? I removed my coat and shirt then gently pulled my arm out of the T-shirt. I applied some antibacterial cream to my wound. With Amanda's help, we used the bandage to wrap it up. Slowly, I put my T-shirt back on then pulled on my shirt and coat. I got to my feet and leaned heavily on the Winchester. Amanda helped as best as she could to get me off the ground. I got a little lightheaded as I stood.

Without me asking, Amanda repacked the dead man's stuff and threw it on her back. On the way to the crossing, we found the sheath for the Winchester. Finally reaching our crossing place, I was happy to see my equipment still there. I looked across the river, but Charles wasn't to be seen.

Amanda put the food and first-aid kit from the dead man's pack into mine. I picked up the dead man's pack and launched it into the river, then watched it float out of sight. I helped put my pack on Amanda's back.

After running the Winchester through the gun belt and shoulder harness, I handed both to Amanda. She could hold them over her head, keeping them out of the water. With her on my shoulders, we began to cross the river.

Her left leg was wrapped tightly around my wounded shoulder, but the pain helped me focus on making my way across. When we reached dry land once again, I let Amanda down then quickly started looking for Charles.

The sound of a barking dog came across the rushing water. Grabbing the Winchester and sidearms from Amanda, I pushed her toward the trees. Moments after I reached the safety of the trees I looked to see a dog run downriver in the direction of the dead green beret. As the dog disappeared from sight, two men appeared up the river, trying to chase after the dog, which was now out of sight. They slowed to a walk and continued down the riverbank, calling out for the green beret.

Amanda and I both dropped down, hoping they hadn't seen us. We backed slowly deeper into the forest. My head began to spin and my body started shaking from the cold river. I think I heard a whispering voice.

"Amanda, over here." It was Charles.

"Charles!" called out Amanda. "Come here."

Brother and sister were back together again.

I woke to the sound of raindrops on canvas. The kids erected the tarp as a lean-to. A small fire burned close by heating the enclosure. Amanda and Charles sat staring out on the world.

I started to sit up then found myself almost completely naked under the kids' tarps. "Amanda," I said, "water please."

Both heads jerked around in total relief that I was awake. Charles shot over to my side. "Amanda, he's alive!" he exclaimed.

"I see, Charles; thanks for telling me," she answered.

I spotted my clothes hanging close to the fire. "Are they dry yet?" I said while pointing at my clothes.

"No, those aren't ready yet. But the ones in your pack should be dry," Amanda answered back.

She started pulling stuff out of my bag. As she found my extra pants and shirt, she threw them to me. The cold water's effect, combined with the knife wound, made it slow going getting dressed.

I put on my wet boots then packed up our gear. The day was almost over as we started following a different trail. We all began looking for a place to spend the night. Heading deeper into the forest, we climbed up another mountainside looking for a cave.

Thankfully, we didn't have to go far, and I didn't think I could have walked much farther after today's close calls. The entrance to the cave was small, but it opened up nicely once we got inside. The ceiling was at least ten feet with a width and depth of about fifteen feet. Not huge, but better than anything we'd seen so far today.

Charles got some wood from outside to start a fire. Amanda busied herself repacking the backpacks. "Amanda. How are you doing? I mean, after what happened out there?" I asked her.

She carried the first-aid kit over to me. "I was really scared; I had no idea what he was going to do to me. Then I saw you running toward us. That's when he hit me. Thank you for saving me."

As she handed me the kit, I shined my light on her face. I could see the bruises on her. "You remember how many times he hit you?"

She pushed the light away. "I don't remember. I was just afraid that he was going to take me back to Jose."

I took hold of her arm. "Amanda. You don't have to hold the pain or fear inside. It's okay if you let it out. I've held a lot of emotions inside, and it hasn't helped at all. The memories are still there, always there. Now I don't think I could cry if I wanted to."

She fell onto my wounded shoulder crying.

"There are times to stand strong, and also times to be gentle. Now it's time to let it all out so you can go on tomorrow. Don't ever let anyone tell you that you are weak; don't let people—those kinds of people—stay in your life if you can help it. You hear me, young lady?

In a shaky voice, I heard her say, "I hear you, Wade."

Charles brought in some firewood; Amanda pulled away and went back to repacking the backpacks. I opened the first-aid kit to redress my knife wound. The wound went to the bone but was clean for being out here. I put more cream on it then rewrapped it.

"Come on, Charles, let's see if we can find some more wood for tonight," I said as I made my way outside.

I felt like giving Amanda some time alone—I mean, here was a girl becoming a woman. What did I know about that? Not a darn thing.

This creepy person thought he had the right to destroy her. Now she had to work out an outlook on life, a life that included people like that green beret and Jose.

Any people who would harm a child for their own pleasure are surely sick. Pedophiles, rapists, murderers, and stalkers are truly ill people in my view. I found living in my cabin and not hearing about this kind of filth quite relaxing. One of these monsters finally made it out here. Somebody had to stop him, and right then, I had two kids to keep safe.

Darkness was almost on us when Charles and I returned. We stacked the wood away from the fire. Together the kids and I pulled some branches in front of the cave entrance to block the firelight.

I passed out some homemade beef jerky, hard biscuits, and more energy bars. I washed my meal down with cold water, then felt really tired. The day had taken its toll on me and I was ready for sleep. Before closing my eyes I prayed for the first time in years.

"To the one or the many Gods that exist, I pray. Watch over these two children; they are innocent yet. Help me lead them to safety while showing them what I have learned about living."

Somewhere in the night I jerked awake with a cry of "NO!" echoing off the cave walls. Sitting up that fast made the pain shoot through my shoulder, which elicited a loud groan. Once again, I heard the call of "NO!" This time, however, I knew it came from Amanda. I shined my light in her direction and saw her siting up with a frightened look on her face.

"Amanda!" Charles called out. "Sis! Are you alright?"

Charles was already at his sister's side before I got to her. They held each other in an embrace. With my light on them, I felt a tear build up in my eye. Maybe there was hope for me yet.

Charles seemed to know that something had happened to his sister, but he had no idea what. "I'm here," he said to her. "I'll protect you, Amanda."

Both were growing up faster than I thought they should have to. Maybe in days gone by, kids had to grow up way before their ages. Only in modern days has the idea of a childhood come into being.

They curled up together and soon fell asleep. After putting more wood on the coals I laid back down. Staring at the wood catching fire, a feeling of loneliness swept across me. I wanted something to hold on to for the night. However, this crazy idea of manhood made that impossible. *Suck it up, Wade,* I thought. *What S.O.B thought up those rules?*

So I held on to life itself—another heartbeat, another breath of air, another sunrise to watch. I kept going because of those things. I keep clawing my way to somewhere. Perhaps tomorrow I would find the answer, but for now, I slept.

CHAPTER 6

Bob set Snooper Three down at the depot, shut off the engines, then jumped out. "Hey, old man," Greg called out.

"Don't get smart there, you young whippersnapper," Bob replied in an even older-sounding voice then he really was.

Bob had already checked most of the engine fluids before starting the Snooper this morning. He had only to check a few more while the engine was still hot.

Greg jumped into the cockpit of the Snooper to check out the electronics. While there, he made some changes to the Snooper's radio settings. He had done the same with Snooper One when he had it here at the depot last night. Now everything that went over the radios would be recorded by the Raptor. Being paranoid wasn't one of the things Greg liked—it left him feeling all alone—but he had to make sure that Jose didn't find out what he was planning.

It only took a few minutes to reconfigure the radio, and then he went on to check the equipment. By the time he had finished Bob was at the small fire drinking coffee.

"When you finish that, get back to searching for those targets, okay?"

Bob looked Greg's way. "Sure thing. We're having fun now, aren't we?"

"I'm going over to see Jose."

"You be careful over there, Greg. Jose, as we both know, is not all there." Bob smiled at his joke then raised his coffee mug in the air.

Lifting off, the Raptor did a 180-degree turn then headed across the lake. The flight was way too short for Greg. No time to plan anything to say to Jose. He'd just have to make it up as best as he could. The Raptor landed on the small beach at the trailhead leading to the cabin. Anybody living out this way was nuts or a tough-as nails-kind of person. Greg just couldn't imagine living way out here, in nowhere land.

Before the blades had stopped, Greg opened the canopy to climb out. There were only inches of clearance between the canopy and the blades. His feet touched the ground. "Damn it" was all he said as two of Jose's guards stepped out to greet him.

The guards followed Greg all the way to the cabin door. Reaching to push the door open, he looked over his shoulder one more time. The guards were gone as fast as they had appeared.

Jose looked up to see Greg walk in. "Where are my prizes?"

"Damn it Jose, we're doing everything we can to find them. Please go home and let us handle this," answered Greg.

"I don't trust anybody here. Everyone would put a bullet in my back if they thought they could get away with it."

"Yeah, that's right! Blame this on everybody else. We weren't the ones who hired, then threatened this Tony guy. You wave that gun around so many times that someday people aren't going to duck for cover. Just like those trackers you confronted yesterday."

Jose stood up from the last remaining chair. The cabin had been torn apart by a madman. "One of those trackers is already dead, in addition to two more of my men."

Greg acted surprised; he didn't want Jose to know that he could listen in on their radio calls.

"What, you have your own radios out there?"

Jose shrugged. "I have my ways of keeping one step ahead of you at each turn."

"It seems that one of the dogs chased a bear and got itself killed along with its owner. I can't say that news saddens me at all," said Jose.

Jose passed by Greg, going out to the small front porch. He sat down on the wooden chair and propped his feet up on the stump. "Just imagine what kind of person would choose to live out here. Must think he's a real mountain man, a Davie Crockett kind of person. Maybe even a Daniel Boone. Whatever, I want you to find him. If the Carroll's or the kids are with him, I want him dead, and them brought to me. You got that?"

Greg stood at the doorway. "So, Jose, you're not done killing innocent people yet?"

Jose laughed "You Americans you think you're much better than most of the world—is that it?"

"We don't go shipping out death like you Jose. We, for the most part, honor the laws of our nation," retorted Greg.

"Bull!" said Jose angrily. "The United States ships out more death than all the drug cartels in the world. It enslaves more people around the world than others with sweatshops for the great corporate America around the world. They are nothing more than high-priced thieves and death merchants." He paused. "I, on the other hand, am upfront about my product. Let's see the pharmaceutical companies of America be totally honest about their products. Nothing gets into the way of profits; not even the death of their fellow Americans. Your rich and your government bully everyone else in their country and in the world. However, you call me and my kind criminals. Look in your own backyard first.

"Your government interferes with other countries all over the world. It's the largest arms dealer also. They are the cartel's greatest competition in building empires. Your great CEOs take all they can for themselves; they only care about their own and no one else. Oh, they donate lots of money—but take away the tax benefits and see how much they give then."

Greg watched as Jose's face reddened with anger as he spat out his remarks.

"No! I'm the honest thief here. They hide behind laws that they make. They hide and steal your country blind. Yours is not a country by the people, for the people—it's big business, for big business, and the politicians keep feeding that monster. That beast will only serve itself with the blood of young Americans.

"Now get out there and bring me Tony Carroll, or you'll go home to an empty house."

Greg swung off the doorframe to face Jose. "I told you not to threaten my family again—and there is a big difference between your kind and the United States. With all our faults, with all our mistakes, we still come to the aid of those in need. We have pumped trillions of dollars into the world. Where has your kind been?"

"Chaves called us the devil—where was he when disaster strikes around the world? I know where he is now: dead! Just where were people like him? Yes, we're just normal humans, but at least we try to make the world better in some ways, which is a far, far cry from what you do."

Not listening to anyone but the pounding of his blood, Greg turned and stalked away from Jose.

"Come back here, now! I order you to come back!" shouted Jose.

A gunshot sounded. It echoed throughout the valley. A small cloud of dirt rose up by Greg's right foot, the thud of the bullet striking the ground then a nearby tree. Greg turned around and he felt his brow curl as he marched back to Jose, halting only inches from his face. Greg knew the guards were standing close by, but he'd had enough. He grabbed the gun out of Jose's hand then slapped him with his free hand.

Jose stood there stunned that anyone would lay a hand on him. Greg unloaded Jose's gun as he once again walked away. He tossed the magazine in one direction and the 9mm chambered bullet to the other side of the trail. Greg stopped and without looking at Jose he said, "Next time don't shoot into the ground."

"Shoot him!" Jose yelled.

Greg looked at the first guard to appear. "You want out of here? Shoot me, and good luck figuring out how to get out of here."

Jose jumped from the porch, running to the nearest guard. He pulled the rifle out of his hands. "Jose," cried out the guard. "I will kill, if that's what you want! If I do that for you, how will we get out of here?"

Greg could see Jose's hands shake with rage. For a moment, he was sure it was over—he and his family were dead.

Jose lowered the weapon then advanced on Greg. "If you ever touch me again I will make you suffer. You will beg for death." Jose stepped even closer so he could whisper in Greg's ear. "I won't, though; I will keep you alive for days, for weeks. I will make your life a living hell."

Jose turned away from Greg but pivoted around, swinging the rifle. Greg dropped low, and it passed over his head. When he stood back up, they were once again face-to-face. Greg took three steps backward, not letting his gaze leave Jose. They just stared at each other, then Greg took a few more steps back. Reaching a turn in the path Greg, lost sight of Jose. Knowing all four of Jose's guards were now behind him, he wasted no time getting back to the Raptor.

As he lifted off, two guards came out into the open. Greg flipped a switch, and two mini-guns folded out of the nose of the Raptor—one on each side of the nose aimed toward the guards.

The two men on the ground moved back behind the trees. Greg rose then pivoted the Raptor about, flying away from the beach. He had pressed the trigger for the mini-guns, but nothing had happened. Greg knew it had been a rush job installing them, but was still surprised they didn't work.

He returned the mini-gun switch back to the off position. The guns returned to their hiding place, unseen from the human eye. Upon landing he rolled out the guns once more. When everything finally shut down, the Raptor just became a piece of metal, a huge paperweight, maybe a bad idea. But it was his baby.

Greg remembered the huge celebration when the Raptor was completed. Then the day it first flew, when the missile doors opened, the cradle assembly dropped down. When the .50 caliber mini-guns first rolled out of their hiding place, showing the teeth of the Raptor, his dream came to life. His future was right there in front of him. Life was going to be great for his small company.

"Snooper Three, this is Raptor. Come in, Snooper Three."

"Raptor, this is Snooper Three. What do you need, young one?"

"I need you back here at the depot."

"Roger, Raptor, I'm on my way."

It was only minutes before Greg could hear the blades of Snooper Three cutting the air. It seemed like hours to him.

Bob saw the mini-guns on the Raptor as his craft set down at the depot. "All right!" said Bob as he began shutting things off.

When Snooper Three was completely still, Bob jumped out and walked over to Greg. "Wow! You didn't tell me you installed them. Are we going to war?"

"No, not now; the guns aren't working," answered Greg.

"I have something for you to do, Bob. I have this recording of Jose's voice. I want you to set up the Raptor so when I need it, it'll sound like Jose's on the radio, got it?"

"Sorry, Greg; can't be done on the Raptor, but the Snoopers have the right equipment to do that."

"Then get it done on yours only. Don't tell John, you hear me?" Greg lightly slapped Bob on the shoulder.

"I have both you and John doing different things. I don't want one of you accidentally letting Jose know what we're up to. Okay?"

"Once you have your Snooper set up, I have an errand for you."

Greg turned back to the mini-gun problem. He had been heavily involved in its design. He knew it was only a matter of time before…

"Damn it, John!" yelled Greg to the open air. "Bob! Get over here now, please."

"You find the problem, Greg?"

"Yeah, the motor assembly's main gear is missing on both guns. So I have more for you to do."

"I need you to fly the Snooper to the hangar in Juneau as fast as you can. Find the gears then get them back here. Try looking at the test guns we used; there should be some in there. Don't talk to anyone on the radio unless I ask you to, understand?"

"I also want you to call my house or yours. Find out if they are safe or not, got it? Use your imagination Bob, but find out if they're safe!"

Bob hurried over to the Snooper. "Greg! Are they all supposed to be safe? Tell me now please."

"That's what you're going to find out for me."

"Now go, bring me back good news if you can."

As Bob left for a fast trip to Juneau, Greg broke out the tools he had at the depot. It wasn't going to take long to get the guns out. This move was more of a waiting game.

After the guns were laid out on the ground, Greg sat in the Raptor. With the radio on, he leaned back to shut his eyes.

"Raptor, this is Ground Force," came out of the speaker.

"Ground Force, this is Raptor. What do you need?"

"I need to talk with Jose; can you contact him right away?"

To Greg's surprise, Jose's voice came through the speakers.

"This is Jose! What do you want?"

"That damn green beret tracker left us in the middle of nowhere. He said something about spotting the targets then gave his dog a command and left. The dog held us back while he disappeared from sight. Just as we were going to shoot the thing, it turned and ran off."

"Get off your butts and follow them, you dumb shits!" screamed Jose.

"We did, Jose! And we found him dead, shot twice, plus that damn dog is nowhere to be found. Good riddance.

"We're going to cross the river then set up for the night. How about having one of those copters bring us some supplies? That damn tracker took ours at gunpoint. We'll have a fire going."

Greg cut into the conversation. "Roger, Ground Force, I'll have you resupplied just as fast as I can."

Greg turned off the radio as Jose started to talk again. He packed the supplies into the now empty gun compartments. He had moved the guns away from the Raptor, but now he needed to cover them to keep the dust off. Greg stopped to look at the tarps, and in seconds he knew how the targets disappeared.

Greg got back on the radio. "Need a GPS reading from who called for the supplies."

CHAPTER 7

The sun had set only an hour ago when I heard a helicopter outside of the cave. The embers from the fire cast a soft orange glow on the cave walls. Bright lights found the gaps in the cover I had put up over the entrance. The helicopter was still some distance from the cave we took up residence in. I pulled back a small part of the covering to look out.

Slowly, the helicopter worked its way toward the river, shining its landing lights as it descended lower. I finally saw a small fire burning by the confluence of the river that we crossed and the Inklin. I retrieved the goggles from my pack then turned on the battery.

Holding the goggles to my face, the world lit up in black-and-white images. The helicopter was landing close to the campfire I had seen earlier. The heat from the engines and strong lights covered the burning wood from the goggles. I could make out three smaller dots moving back and forth between the helicopter and the camp.

I scanned the area below the cave with the goggles, seeing multiple heat signatures. While most of what I was looking at was wildlife, some of them could be other men searching for us.

I backed into the cave, sitting by my pack. I wished I knew what was going on down there. "Charles," I called out softly.

"Yes, Wade?" Charles answered back.

"How's your sister doing?"

"She's asleep again."

"I need you to watch out for her, okay?"

"Why; you're here to help both of us."

"I'm leaving for a short time. But in case I don't get back before the sun comes up, I want you two to stay here. If I don't get back by tomorrow night, I need to know you can get out. So listen up. If the time comes for you two to leave, you take a left turn out of the cave. You will see the big river out that way. When you get to the river, turn left again, then follow it. In five to six days, you'll get to a lodge that's out there. Think you can remember that, Charles?"

Charles rushed over then threw his small arms around my neck. "No! Don't leave us alone." Little tears formed in his eyes but none fell. Little Charles already learned that boys don't cry. That was a shame because they should all know how to cry.

"Charles, I have to look at something down by the river. I can't take you two with me this time. I need you to stay with your sister. She needs you to be the strong one for now. Protect her while I'm gone, okay?"

Charles pushed back away from me. "I'll always protect Amanda," he asserted.

"I plan on being back before dawn, but just in case I don't make it, you know what to do, right?"

Standing there in front of me, I saw his shoulders square up. He tried to make himself taller. "Yes, go left out of the cave, then left at the big river."

"Good; keep the fire low. If I don't get lost, I'll be back soon."

Leaving the Winchester in the cave, I only took the two handguns. With goggles on, I made my way down the mountainside. The rocks were still wet from the evening rain, and the ground was soft and damp. It took longer than I planned to get close enough to hear the Inklin and Taku Rivers collide into each other.

Continuing along toward the Inklin River bank, the helicopter started back up. From the trees, I watched as it lifted above the landscape. It flew off in the direction of my lake, my cabin, my life.

It was soon well away from my night's hunt. I moved out toward the campfire, slowly taking care where I set my feet. The fire came into view, casting its light in a small circle. I watched the two men move about the firelight. Each one was preparing to settle in for the night.

One of the men took guard position just out of sight of the fire. I slowly lay down on the wet ground. My clothes sopped up the water, leaving me cold. I began crawling closer to the fire. Finding a good spot, I got comfortable to wait for the right time.

The fire died down after the first hour, allowing me to use the goggles. I could see the man by the trees clearly. His head was slumped forward as if asleep.

Quietly, I stood up and edged my way through the shadows. Finally, I was about fifteen feet away from the guard. I carefully lifted one foot, then shifted my weight as I gently placed it back down. I practiced this step many times while hunting. Everything needed to flow, balance, from one foot to the next. Close to fifteen minutes later, I was standing by the one lying down. I picked up his weapons—one rifle plus a handgun. I then slowly picked up his boots, which to my joy, his socks were stuffed inside. Taking my time, I returned to the trees to hide my haul.

I made my way back to the sleeping man's backpack. Opening the side pocket, I pulled out the nylon rope he had. I set off again and approached the guard from behind. I grabbed my revolver, holding it sideways in my hand, fingers wrapped around the cylinders.

When I was less than an arm's length from him, I let out a "psst." Nothing happened, so I touched him. The man jumped while turning to face me. That's when I hit him in the forehead with the revolver.

The guard dropped to the ground, out cold. I glanced over to the other man—nothing; he was still asleep. I quickly tied the guard's hands and gagged him. I removed his shoes and socks, then tied his feet. If, for some reason, one of them tried to attack their bare feet would slow them down. I smiled at that thought and almost laughed.

Gathering up his rifle, handgun, plus boots and socks, I made my way back to the tree were I had stowed the other items I had collected. I approached the sleeping one of the two men. "Get up!" I yelled. I then kicked him hard in the shoulder. "Get up!" I repeated.

He reached out for his handgun before he even looked up at me. I stood over him, revolver cocked, ready to fire. "Spread your arms out now!" I ordered him. "Palms up! I want your nose to the ground." He was still staring at me, not sure what was happening.

"Put your arms out! Palms up! Put your nose on the ground now!" I ordered again. Slowly, the situation became clear to him. He extended his arms, palms up, then he placed his nose on the ground. Stepping away from him, I holstered my revolver, then pulled more nylon from my pocket, and fashioned a loop on one end.

I moved in front of him. "Left hand in front, palm up," I ordered. As his hand touched the space in front of me, I placed my foot on it, pinning his left hand between the ground and my foot. "Right hand in front, but don't let it touch the ground."

I slipped the loop around his right wrist then pulled it tight. I dragged his arm behind his back as I stepped around him. "Left arm behind you," I ordered as I wrapped the rope around his left wrist, then pulled both arms together and tied them. "Now get out of that sleeping bag."

When his ankles emerged, I stepped on his legs hard. "That's good; now just stay still." I fed the rope around his legs then secured them together. He wasn't going anywhere right now.

I dragged the other man closer to the fire. It was time for a heart-to-heart talk with these two.

Using water from their supplies, I doused the unconscious man. This always surprised me on how fast people wake up when this was done to them.

"You," I said while pointing at the now wet-faced man. "You are going to have one big headache, mister. However, I'll let both of you live if you answer my questions correctly.

"This is what's going to happen. You play right, then I'll leave you a knife to free yourselves. If you're very good, I'll leave your shoes. If you're bad, I'll just leave you like you are. Some bear or wolf would like a free meal maybe. So tell me now, how are we going to play my game?"

"Look, Mister Carroll, we don't know anything but to find you for Mr. Hernandez," said the wet face.

"What's your name?" I asked in a calm voice.

"Russ."

"Okay, Russ, I don't believe you so you're out the shoes." I paused. "By the way, I'm not this Tony Carroll guy ether. My name isn't important at this moment. Why does this Hernandez guy want me for?"

"If you're not Tony Carroll, he doesn't want you," answered the man to the right.

"Your name is what?"

"Bill," he replied

"Okay, Russ, Bill, tell me what Hernandez wants with this Tony Carroll."

"Carroll stole from him."

"Now Bill, that answer is way too short. What did he steal? No, better yet, just tell me everything you know, okay?" I smiled at them, acting like we had been friends for a long time. We would be the only ones who know they blabbed.

The two of them looked at each other for a few moments. "Hernandez is a drug dealer from Mexico," stated Russ. "Tony Carroll got hold of all his private bank account numbers. He wants the Carroll's kids, which we know are with you."

"If you give us the kids, we'll just say you disappeared. Then you can go about your life, like we never were here," reasoned Russ.

"Ha-ha; I don't think this drug dealer would ever let me just walk away. So the bargain on the table is the one I gave you. So keep talking. Who are the guys in the berets, and how many are there?"

Russ spoke up. "There're four of them out there. Two that I know of are dead. They belong to an associate of Hernandez's who wants his drugs or his money back."

"Ahh, without the account numbers, no money right?" I asked.

"Yeah, Hernandez is getting scared. If this guy doesn't get one or the other soon, Hernandez's world crashes."

"Almost done with the questions. What's with the helicopter landing out here tonight?"

"It was a supply drop for us. The main pilot Greg told us to up the sensitivity of the heat sensors. He thinks you're hiding your heat signal somehow, possibly by holding a tarp over your heads, breaking up your heat patterns."

"Okay, this is what's going to happen now. I'm going to get your shoes, put them right here where I'm standing. Then I'm going to plant a knife in between them. You're going to wait ten minutes, then you're on your own."

"I'm taking your firearms with me. So you can keep going down this river or head back to my cabin. Any questions, you two?"

Neither man spoke up. "Now stay here," I said, laughing.

I retrieved the boots plus one backpack with some food inside. I placed everything in front of them. Then I embedded the knife into the ground. I stood back to look over the scene in front of me and snickered to myself.

"I'm taking the radio, goggles, and of course, like I said, the weapons. Good luck, gentlemen; really, I wish you bad luck." I turned away from them, walking toward the trees.

My eyes adjusted before the two got themselves free. Carefully, I made my way from the campfire. Gathering up the equipment I had from those two, I headed toward the riverbank. The river would make a great place to hide their equipment.

After disposing of the weapons, I picked up my pace. I had a strong need to get back to Amanda and Charles for some much-needed rest, but I took the time to cover my trail from man and dog.

Far away, there in the sunshine are my highest aspirations. I may not reach them, but I can look up and see their beauty, believe in them, and try to follow where they lead.

Louisa May Alcott

CHAPTER 8

Amanda and Charles woke me up the next morning. I could easily see the sunlight making its way around parts of the tarp. Beams of sunshine on the cave walls produced patterns as it bounced around from wall to wall.

The cold morning air made my joints hurt again. I could hear the slow drip of rain outside. In addition, the late-night recognizance had left me feeling tired from the lack of rest. I reached for my water container and felt the frigid liquid run down my throat.

"Have you two already eaten this morning?" I groggily asked.

"Yes," Amanda said. "Charles the pig had two bars this morning," she said, then stuck her tongue out at him.

Charles returned the gesture, then laughed.

"Good; I hope we find the time to catch something soon. I'm getting tired of those bars. Nevertheless, cooking whatever we find may be out of the question. The smell of cooking may lead them right to us. So for now keep eating the bars, okay?"

I slowly worked my way to a standing position, feeling the mileage of my life starting to catch up to me. In all the years I'd spent in the wilderness, the mornings had been the worse for my joints. Maybe I was just one of those people who needed a warm setting in which to live. If so, I picked the wrong place for sure.

I pulled back the tarp to see the sky full of dark clouds. Rain had been falling for some time now. It seemed to be the rule to this day. The thunder cracked. The lighting flashed and commanded us to stay. But we had to move.

"Come on, you two, we have to leave now."

"But it's raining out," whined Charles.

"Yep, it sure is. Now get your packs on; we have to get going. This isn't going to stop those guys out there looking for us."

We headed to the left at the cave entrance toward the Taku River. The rain made the going slow, but we had to put some more distance between this Jose person and his men. We couldn't wait for good weather to move on. I couldn't see the helicopters searching for us in this storm. So I was hoping we only had to watch out for the men on the ground.

It didn't take long before we were all soaking wet. Our jackets helped keep us warm. Our pants and feet were drenched, however. The hoods in our coats helped, but hiking in the rain had a depressing effect on us.

We marched on to the sound of raindrops on our heads and thunder in our ears. All this had the feel of what Chinese water torture must be like. After some hours of hiking, a new sound made it through the rain. It was the Taku River, our guide out of here. It better be the Taku River.

As we emerged from the trees, the river came within full view, an eight hundred foot wide ribbon of water rushing its way to the pacific. The trees, mountains, and Taku were a reminder of the beauty that the wilderness offered. It also reminded me why I left the ugliness of the manmade forest called cities.

I know lots of people would disagree with that statement. They would have that right, but for me, man couldn't ever match this picture in front of me.

"You two take the time to look around, let nobody steal this from you. This is where humans grew, where they learned to live within nature. Don't try bending nature to your will, hear me? Always let nature bend you to its will.

"Someday, someone will want to mine the land here. They will destroy it for money. Others will want to cut down the trees for money. Then others will want to fence people out so only they can enjoy the view. Don't let them do it. Don't let the rich buy the land, and don't let others ruin it for everyone else. They'll say all kinds of things to get in here and strip or sell the land that belongs to all people."

"It's amazing, Wade," said Charles.

"Yeah, I feel it deep inside whenever I see something like this."

Amanda stood by, looking at the pure beauty that now surrounded us. The rain dripped off my hood, but the sight before me held tightly, not allowing me to move. The roar from the river rushing past us filled the air.

At last I broke away, aware we were standing in the open. We needed to continue moving along the tree line. At places, the trees grew right up to the river; at others it was hundreds of feet away. However, we stayed close to the trees for cover.

I knew fishing in the rain wasn't the best. However, all I could do was try, perhaps fail, so why not. Besides we all could use something besides those energy bars.

"Amanda. You and Charles build a lean-to then build a small fire by it. When you're done, come on down to the river for a fishing lesson," I told her.

I slipped off my pack and opened the side packet where the fishing line was. As I made my way to the river, I picked up some fallen tree branches, stripping the small limbs of the branches with my knife as I walked. Opening the handle, I removed the fishing hooks that I kept inside.

I had thrown the line in about four times when to my surprise, a fish hit the bare hook. I pulled in the line with my gloved hands. I now had some bait, plus most of all, some food for tonight.

I sat in a small cove covered by trees. Deep water lay below the rock cliff where I fished. I put bits of fish meat on the hook then dropped it down into the water. To my astonishment, I got another bite in just a few moments. Maybe things were starting to turn in our favor.

By the time the kids showed up I had four good size fish already waiting. Now a fish is a fish to me, but from my time there, I'd learned to recognize some. These four rainbow trouts were going to lift our spirits this rainy day.

I apologized to the kids about not waiting for them. They both poked their lower lips out at me and looked sad. They both laughed as they ran back to the shelter. I tried calling them back, but they ignored me. Guess it was up to me to carry the fish back.

I made my way to the water's edge between two good-sized boulders. With water and dirt I created mud wraps for each fish. On the third one I looked across the river. There on the other side I saw three men and a dog moving in and out of the tree line. I moved behind one of the boulders, being thankful I saw them first. They continued on downriver, disappearing back into the trees. The day was going so well until now.

With my four fish encased in mud wraps, I made my way back to the kids. I found them sitting under the lean-to warming up by the fire. After breaking up the logs into coal, I placed the four wrapped fish in the middle. Using tree limbs, I pushed the coals onto the mud wraps. With each fish now covered, we sat back to wait for a real meal.

Charles was exploring the area looking for anything that would interest him. Amanda was looking out through the trees to the river. She watched the water flow pass for a few minutes then moved on to the treetops. She watched the birds fly in and out of the branches. I tended the coals of our lunch while watching out for Charles.

After about twenty minutes, I broke open one of the mud wraps. The smell of cooked fish filled the lean-to. As the mud came off so did the scales, and as if by magic Charles was standing beside me. I used my knife to cut off bits of fish, piling them on large parts of the broken wraps.

After I finished the first fish, I passed the mud plate to Charles, who wasted no time in attacking his meal. I broke the next wrap into larger pieces for a better plate. After I cut this one up, it was Amanda's time to eat. My turn came and went before I even realized it. I almost felt like I had just shoved the whole thing into my mouth.

I placed the last fish aside, still encased in the mud. I picked up the broken mud wraps that smelled of fish. All it would take is one bear to get a whiff of it and come investigate. We all carried these pieces down to the river cliff then threw them in.

I glanced across the river to see a very large bull moose staring back at us. His antler span was near six feet. This grand animal must have stood seven feet tall, if so he had to weigh around fourteen hundred pounds. The kids watched this wonder walk to the riverbank for a minute or two.

"Come on, we need to get moving," I said, then turned, heading back to camp.

The rain started up again as we made our way to the camp. When we arrived, Amanda started tearing down the lean-to, while Charles worked on making sure the fire was out. It was now my turn to relax and look out at the world. That, of course, was when we all heard the growl of a dog wearing a green collar.

It stood upriver from us about thirty feet. It ears were flat against its head. The hairs on its shoulders were raised. All its white teeth showed as its lips curled back. The dog moved forward then stopped only twenty feet from me. I started to move very slowly to my holstered revolver.

My hand closed on the handle while my thumb pushed the leather strap off the hammer. The revolver slipped comfortably out of the holster. I slowly cocked the weapon, knowing the dog would hear the sound. Its eyes locked on me as it made up its mind on what to do.

From behind, I heard footsteps on the wet ground. Just as I was going to fire on the dog, Amanda showed up beside me.

"What are you doing?" I sternly asked her, not taking my eyes off the dog.

"It's hungry," she said while passing me up.

In her hands, she held the last fish still in the mud wrap. She started breaking the mud shell, peeling more of mud off the fish. Slowly, she bent down to place the fish on the ground, then took a step backward. When she was even with me again I stood up, and together we retreated.

We reached the tarp where I grabbed a corner while continuing to back away. The revolver was still in my hand with my thumb riding on the hammer. Charles was suddenly in front of his sister, fully aware of the danger. "I'll protect you, Amanda," he whispered.

When we were a comfortable distance away, the dog moved toward the fish. Feeling safe, it sniffed the fish then began eating. With all our gear on the tarp, we dragged it farther away so not to disturb the dog. The temporary campsite became lost among the trees before I put the revolver back in my holster.

"Good eyes there, Amanda, but let's not push our luck too many times, okay?"

She smiled at me. "Like you and Bear," she answered, "and the wolves too."

Not having a quick reply, I stuck my tongue out at her. "Let's get everything packed up then put some distance between that dog and us."

As the hours slowly passed, we put many miles behind us. I called for a short rest, which both Amanda and Charles signaled their consent by collapsing on to the ground. It was almost time to find us a place for the night. After a short time, we continued on our departure from this timber-covered world.

I had been a part of many wondrous things in the past five years. I had never thought much about the danger of Bear or the wolves. I knew that they were wild animals and could have attacked me anytime. However, until Amanda stepped up, putting herself in harm's way to feed that dog did I really see how dangerous that looked. I knew I had been lucky when I first met Bear and the wolves. I had grown to trust them to a certain point, but now I was feeling just lucky.

I wasn't pushed to go anywhere; maybe Amanda and Charles were just lucky that I picked that spot to live. Perhaps, this was a random set of circumstances, but then maybe not.

The same question that had followed me through life still haunted me that day. Was there a God or not? I have stood in the forest many times listening to the sounds of the trees, the flow of the creek water, the wind as it blew across the lake. The bellowing of moose, the howling of the wolves, the screech of eagles as they flew over the treetops. The smell of the pine trees, the taste of wild berries, and the cool air on a hot day.

These miracles of God or evolution would have a hold on me forever. I guess it didn't matter whom or what created this, I would be a part of it until I die. Thank God.

We continued to walk on, following the river. I knew that this route would make it easier for the enemy to find us, but the chance of coming upon some campers or fisherman was also much better.

CHAPTER 9

Bob was waiting for Greg at the depot area when the Raptor landed. Sighing heavily before getting out of his dream machine, Greg hoped Bob had some much-needed answers.

It was late in the evening, and he was tired of sparring with Jose. He saw Bob sitting by the fire pit away from the fuel. Bob turned to face Greg as he approached the camp.

Even though Greg wanted to hear about his family first, he put it off for now. "Did you find the gears, Bob?"

Bob looked away from Greg while picking up a coffee mug, then retrieved the coffee pot. "You want some of this, Greg."

Greg sat down in a folding chair next to Bob. "Yes, I could use some. It's not been a good day, so I might as well be up all night."

"No, I have a special additive that I stopped and bought before returning. Greg, meet my old friend Jim bean. I haven't talked to him for a long time."

Bob poured a little coffee into the mug then filled most of it with the bourbon. "Here is to old friends, Greg," said Bob as he handed over the mug to Greg while raising his own mug in a gesture of friendship.

"The gears are in the Snooper," stated Bob. "I had to remove them from the test guns. I also found the remains of two gears in the trash. What's going on?"

Greg took a drink of the now hot bourbon. "What about the families, Bob? Are they safe?"

Bob stood up then walked closer to the fire. After pouring out the contents of his mug, he replied, "No, they're still being held. I used Jose's voice pattern to call yours and my house. Both times some guy answered. I gave them some run around about everything going to plan. When I called John's home, his wife answered."

Greg lowered his head into his hands. "I don't know who to trust, Bob. I thought I could trust you and John, but now I'm not sure. My family is in danger. Jose is getting out of control, and maybe you or John is lying to me. Could be even both of you; I just don't know anymore."

"Greg, my wife is in danger also. It's John's wife who doesn't appear in any danger to me. I've been flying this damn helicopter all over the place trying to find these people. I've left you to handle Jose. I've trusted you to solve this problem."

Bob ran his finger through what hair he had left. He then smiled. "I've even given you the hair off my head. Look, I don't know what to tell you, but you have to decide who to trust. I don't think me standing here talking at you will convince you who to believe."

Greg said, as his eyes held on to the mug, "Bob, I sent John to the hangar to install the guns." Bob started to talk, but Greg continued. "No, just listen please. I also asked him to check on our families while he was there. He told me he had called his wife, and that she had seen my wife out shopping just that day, alone. I set up his and your radios to record all conversations then send them to Raptor. That hasn't helped me one bit."

"You spied on me?" questioned Bob. "Look, just to let you know, John contacted me while he was at the hangar."

Greg stood up, spilling some of his drink. "He did what?"

"Hey!" called out Bob. "Now it's your turn to keep quiet and listen, okay? John called me on that stupid handheld radio. He didn't want you to know that he had no idea how to install the guns. We met on some mountaintop while I aligned them and bolted them down. Remember, you and I were the only ones who played with the guns. For whatever reason, John never touched the mini-guns or the missile bays. So how in the world would he know how to install them?"

Annoyed, Greg said, "And you didn't notice that the gears were missing?"

"The guns were in the Raptor's bays. All I had to do was line up the bolts. Tighten them down and connect the wiring. Think about it, Greg. I never got to see if the gears were there. I didn't lift the guns out of the bays to see. They lined up perfectly the first time. Now I know why it went so easy—no gear teeth to match up."

"Are you losing your trust in me, Greg?"

"I don't trust myself, Bob. But I know that two kids out there are in danger. I don't plan on seeing any harm come to them. First, they have to be found, and then if Tony Carroll isn't with them, we have to locate him and his wife. Right now, I don't think the kids are with their parents. The Carrolls are smart people but whoever the kids are with isn't stupid. He's been using a tarp or something to cover their heads to evade us. I need you to turn up the sensitivity level on the heat sensors. Report any bizarre readings you come across.

"One more thing I want to hear, John—tell me why he didn't just come here and let me finish installing the guns. So please leave him to me, okay? I keep saying to let me handle the problems. This time I mean it—let me talk to him first." Greg walked over to where Bob stood. "At this moment, I'm not sure what's going through my head. Maybe I'm just getting paranoid, or I'm right to think something is wrong with one of us. Perhaps I should go jump into the lake here and soak my head for a while."

"Thanks for the coffee, Bob," said Greg as he walked away. "I guess I did need it."

Greg once again got his tent out of the Raptor and wasted no time setting it up then climbing inside. Before long, this was going to be over—that much was true. For now, however, he had to keep playing along. Jose was going to lose his hold over him real soon. Before sleep took him, Greg heard a raindrop strike the tent.

Greg woke with the sound of thunder blasting through the air. The light of a cloudy day was already illuminating the outside. The problems of the past nine months came roaring back into his mind. Greg felt like he hadn't slept at all, but there was sunlight out there. The sound of rain brought him the rest of the way awake.

Climbing out of his tent, Greg looked to the sky. A lightning bolt flashed between the clouds and earth. The thunder sounded seconds later. The Raptor and Snoopers shouldn't be flying today. However, maybe this was just the right time for them to be flying. This weather could be good for everyone but Jose.

Bob still appeared to be sleeping in the Snooper. Greg put more wood on the fire then stoked it. A few red-hot coals could still be seen. If this didn't tear the company apart, it would be a miracle, thought Greg. Maybe breakfast would help clear things up a bit.

"Raptor, this is Snooper One," came from Bob's Snooper radio.

Bob sat up, wiping his face with his hands. He made his way to the cockpit when John called out again.

"Raptor, this is Snooper One, reply please."

Greg was standing at the open bay of Snooper Three when Bob responded. "What do you need, Snooper One?" Bob groggily asked.

"Hey Bob, oops sorry, Snooper Three. How's it going buddy? I need to talk to Raptor please."

"He's climbing in right now; hold on, okay?"

Bob put down the microphone then turned to leave the cockpit. "The possible traitor calls."

Greg ignored Bob's remark as he sat in the copilot's seat. "Go ahead, Snooper One, what do you need?"

"I'm out here on a mountaintop, and the weather isn't looking good right now. I figure I could come down to the depot and relax with you two. How about it, Raptor?"

"We can't fit all three ships here at the depot. Meet me at the north end of the lake. You got that, Snooper One?"

"On my way in just a minute, Raptor," came back over the radio.

When Greg got back to the fire pit, he saw that some coals were still hot but the wood he had laid in them had not caught fire. He added some small tender to the fire then softly blew on the coals. He watched them glow a brighter orange each time. After a few moments the wood tender started to burn.

"Sorry, Bob, looks like you're the cook this morning. I'm going to move the Raptor then come back with John."

"If he is a traitor, why bring him back here?" Bob asked.

"Keep your friends close, but keep your enemies closer. This way we can watch each other plus be paranoid together. Just try to be friendly until I talk with him."

Greg walked away, not really listening to Bob but thought he heard, "He'll be luckily I don't tell him to go to hell."

Greg climbed in the Raptor, started it up, and was happy to be alone with his thoughts for a short time. The lake passed underneath him as he headed to meet John. Another lighting flash lit up the sky to his left. This wasn't the best thing to do in this weather, but he had to keep his two friends talking. One of them may be lying. He didn't know which one it could be. Right now, John looked guilty to him. Then again, neither one looked like a traitor to him.

Greg put the Raptor down on the far side of the clearing. He would leave the Raptor here for the night; if all went well Bob would bring him back tomorrow. Greg sat in the Raptor waiting for John to show up. If he couldn't trust his closest friends, he would have to go to Juneau himself. If Jose found out, things could get even crazier.

The sound of John's Snooper broke into Greg's thoughts. The Snooper landed just moments after Greg had exited the Raptor. After the runners touched the ground, he boarded the craft. He then made his way to the copilot's seat.

"Don't lift off yet, John. We need to talk for a bit," announced Greg.

Greeting Greg with a smile, John said, "You're looking awful serious there."

"I have what could be a major problem here. You or Bob—maybe both of you, or neither of you—are lying to me. I don't know which. I'm hoping neither, and that it's just me getting on edge about hunting people. But I have to ask you some questions."

Looking John in the eyes, Greg asked, "Who installed the guns into the Raptor?"

John stared back. "Bob installed them. Why? What's happening?"

"I tried to use them on two of Jose's men. While they rolled out of the bay, they failed to spin. Now Jose knows that somehow I've gotten them installed. I could have freed us from this mess if they had been done correctly," Greg answered sharply.

"I sent Bob back to base last night to get the spare parts, so I could fix them," he continued. "I also had him check the families, which he reports that our families are still being held. Your wife, however, answered your phone at home. Now I don't know what's going on, but if I have to fly into Juneau myself, I will."

"I tried to do this so I could surprise Jose, but that's a failure now. When we get back to the depot, don't talk to Bob but to say hello. I'm not sure if you or Bob are or are not lying to me. My head is starting to spin trying to cover every angle right now.

"Now tell me the whole story this time. Where and when did Bob install the guns? How did you check if everyone was safe?"

John shut down the Snooper, then made his way into the cargo area. He sat down on the bench and looked out the open bay door. "If you think that I'm a traitor, you're wrong, Greg! I put my heart into this company; my future, too."

"John!" Greg spoke loudly. "I'm not calling anybody anything yet. You got that? Bob has put a lot into this company also, but right now, I have a mystery that I need to solve. Hell! Think about it, I could be the traitor trying to get you two at each other's throats. Who came up with the idea of testing the Raptor by flying out to that ship?"

"I did, Greg, but I didn't know Jose was a drug dealer."

"John, I trust you and Bob. I trust you are telling me the truth, but look around—we're hunting people now. When this is over, we'll be smuggling drugs again if Jose doesn't have us killed. Just tell me when, where, and who installed the guns. Furthermore, tell me how you checked the safety of our families."

"Damn it, you and Bob were the ones that played around with the guns. I loaded them up in the bays then closed the hatches. I called my wife, and she told me that she had just seen your wife and kids downtown. So I figured that everything was okay.

"I called Bob on the handheld when I got back into range. We met up on some mountaintop where he bolted them down plus connected the wiring. I then flew over to the depot where you were. That's the whole story, I swear."

"Okay, remember when we get to the depot, don't say anything to Bob. I want to see how he tells me his story to me again. Right now, I don't know what to think. I hope none of us are hiding anything from each other. There is still a chance that we can get Jose out of our lives for good."

"Once I talk to Bob again, I may have to ask you more questions, but if I get good answers, I'll be sure to let everyone know that we're safe to continue with a plan I have to free our families. Now let's head back to the depot."

Greg once again watched the lake waters pass by as they headed to the depot. He was adding people to his list of would-be traitors. He also kept hoping that he was just being over imaginative about the whole thing. He wasn't sure how much time he really had to make his plan work.

The Snooper landed before he was ready to talk to Bob again, but he had to try to find out if he was right or way off base, or maybe even just plain crazy.

Greg and John climbed out of the Snooper. "Greg, you really think one of us is stabbing the company in the back?"

"My hopes are that I'm wrong, but I just keep adding more people to my list. I'm starting to see spooks in every corner in my life. It's time to get answers to all those questions that nag the edges of my mind."

"I'll play it your way, Greg, you know that," added John.

"Yeah, I really can't see you or Bob as my enemy, but someone is doing us dirty. I just don't know who it is. I need to start somewhere. This is as good as a place as to start."

"Hey, you two, breakfast is getting cold. So come eat up," shouted Bob.

"Sure smells good, Bob, but before I eat I need to talk with you again in private."

"Sure, Greg," Bob said, then followed him.

Greg walked past the food and warm fire. He continued until he thought he was far enough away from John. If Bob's answers brought up questions, he didn't want to give John time to make up answers.

Greg stopped then turned to Bob. "Why did John have you install the guns? Please don't tell me because he didn't know how. He could have come here and let me do it."

"He knew you were upset with him, Greg. You keep telling him not to antagonize Jose. So he came to me for help."

Greg sat down on a small patch of sand. "This is it, Bob; we're getting out from under Jose before this is over. You hear me? Before it all tears me apart. Go tell John to come over here, please."

Greg continued sitting on the ground with light rain falling on him. He would be overjoyed when this was over, one way or the other.

"Bob said you wanted to talk with me. What questions do you have now? I told you the truth."

Greg stood up then brushed the sand from his pants. "Don't ever think that I'm mad at you or Bob. You two are like the brothers I never had. Don't ever think for a moment I wouldn't have helped install those guns, okay?"

"Sure, Greg; I thought that you had enough on your plate at that time. I didn't mean to add to it."

"I still don't know who removed the gears in the first place, so I have to ask. Did you remove them before you put the guns in the bays?"

"No I didn't, Greg; when I got to the base, the guns were sitting on the bench in the cage. I just set them in, closed the bay doors then left. If I'm not the traitor and Bob's not, then who is?"

"From my viewpoint, John, I know it's not me. I believe you, and Bob didn't remove the gears. So that leaves Freddie, who's dead now." Greg lowered his head into his hands. "I also have one other person in mind, but I think it's better to keep that to myself for now. I don't want to point a finger at someone until I can talk to them."

"Come on, I'm hungry. Plus, we still have some planning to do."

Greg made his way to breakfast, and after filling his plate, he got Bob's and John's attention. "I hereby bless both of you as friends, and neither of you as the enemy. I apologize for even thinking that of you."

Bob interrupted Greg. "Don't you go apologizing for any of this Jose stuff. You were set up somehow, but we'll get away from him. I know it."

"So you have any idea who took the gears, Greg?" asked Bob.

"Like I told John, I'm thinking Freddie took them. Other things I've learned over time added up now. There is someone else I want to ask some questions too. But I'll have to wait for now."

"Who else are you suspecting?"

"He's not saying," John said.

"I don't want to accuse anyone again until I get the chance to question them. I'm still feeling bad about suspecting one of you two."

John spoke up again. "Hey, as I said before, you're the boss. Ask all the questions you want to, okay?"

"I guess I should do some 'I'm sorry' stuff too," said Bob. "I thought it may be you, John. However, I kept thinking about it. After all these years we've spent together, I just couldn't completely convince myself. But why do you believe Freddie is the one, Greg?"

"I'm afraid I'm not going to even try and answer that question right now, Bob. I need to talk in person with somebody before I get to blaming people again. Now eat up, gentlemen; today we get our families to safety."

They sat in silence now, quickly devouring their breakfast. After cleaning up the area then stowing away the cooking equipment, Greg sat down and explained his plan to them.

It only took moments for them to climb into Snooper One then leave the area. Lightning still lit up the sky, rain fell lightly from the clouds. John flew Snooper One out over the lake heading toward Juneau. Bob sat in the copilot seat watching all the instruments. Greg sat on the bench with the cold air rushing into the cargo hold. He needed to work out a few more parts of his plan. Hopefully, no one would get hurt. Greg wasn't sure if he could live with himself if one of them got killed.

Greg watched the mountains go by; he looked at the trees trying to hold just one tree in his sight as they rushed by. This was it—freedom or death, maybe even jail if it went really wrong. But today Jose's control over them would come to an end. If all went well, Jose himself would be completely out of the way for good.

It was past nine a.m. when the Snooper set down outside of Juneau International. They left the Snooper on the landing space just outside of their hangar. Greg went inside to his office safe. In a few minutes, he emerged with three .38 handguns along with four M-26C Tasers. He also carried a daypack with extra .38 ammunition plus three replacement cartridges per Taser.

He bought four of them just for the novelty of it. Greg never thought he would have to use the damn things, but right now he was happy to have them.

As he got into his SUV, he left there just a few days ago. He then handed out the weapons. "Don't shoot yourselves with one of these. No shooting me either, you two. If we make it out of this mess I may give you your chance to get back at me for getting involved with Jose."

Greg smiled while letting out an uneasy laugh. Both men looked at the weapons that they played with when Greg had bought them, and then looked at Greg. "Spoiled sport," muttered John.

They laughed at that, but quickly fell into silence. "Anybody who wants to back out, now's the time to do it," Greg said.

"I'm in," said John.

"I'm not going to cut out now," answered Bob.

Greg started the SUV up. The windshield wipers skidded across the glass as he turned on to Renshaw Way. They had agreed to head for Bob's house first since it was the closest to them. It was going to be too short of a ride. Greg made his way to Glacier Highway, made a left on Egan Drive, then headed to Mendenhall drive. Here Greg turned the

SUNSHINE: THE INTRUSION: A NOVEL

SUV to the right, continuing north for a short time. He made his way onto Glacier Spur Road. About a mile past Gladstone Street, he pulled the SUV to the side of the road.

They could barely see Bob's house on the left side of the road. It was a well-kept single level home. Bob's wife Caroline was a great gardener; she loved working in it whenever she could, but in the winter months she was confined to the indoors, which she kept pristine.

Greg led the way through the trees to one side of Bob's house. "Bob, you go to the back door; John go with him. I'll go to the front. If I can, I'll grab Caroline and I'll run. If not, I'll wait to see you in the hallway before I make a move. It's play it by the ear time, guys."

Greg left the .38 in the SUV on purpose. Holding the Taser behind his back, he approached the front door. He paused, then knocked on the door. When it opened a man stood at the doorway. "Hi, my car broke down almost in front of your house. I was hoping to use your phone to get help. I forgot my cell at home," Greg said while smiling. "It's just not being a good day for me today, huh?"

"Go away," spat the man. "I can't help you."

"Just let me use your phone, please," pleaded Greg. "I'll stay right here outside. All you have to do is bring the phone to me."

The man stood there in thought. "Wait here," he said, then stepped away from the door.

Greg caught a small glance of Caroline sitting upon the couch by herself. The man reappeared with a cell phone in his hand. Greg raised the Taser, firing it point blank. The man collapsed to the floor, motionless.

Greg stepped over him while looking at Caroline, who was on her feet headed over to him. "Is there another one, Caroline?"

"There was, but he left just a while ago. He could be back at any time. He went to the store," she informed.

Bob and John walked down the hallway. "Caroline!" called out Bob.

"Oh, Bob!" cried out Caroline, then ran to meet him.

The two gray-haired people met and embraced each other. They cried tears of joy at being together again. "I was so afraid for you, Caroline. I couldn't sleep at all," Bob said while holding onto his wife.

"John, can you find something down there to tie this guy up with?" asked Greg.

John pushed his way past Bob and Caroline. "Think this rope will do?" he asked, holding out his hand. Greg dragged the unconscious man into the living room. John closed the front door on his way to help Greg. They tied the man then added a gag across his mouth before he could regain consciousness.

Bob walked into the living room with his arms around his wife. "We'll have to wait for this other guy to show up," said Greg.

"Heavens, why?" asked Caroline. "Just call the police, let them take care of these two."

"These people have Greg's family and John's wife held prisoner also," said Bob.

"Who are these people, anyway?" Caroline asked her husband.

The sound of a car pulling into the driveway cut the conversation. "You hear that?" Everyone nodded yes.

"Bob, get your wife into the other room now," ordered Greg. "John, get behind the front door. Be ready to stun this guy. Go!"

Greg took a seat on the couch in plain sight. He now wished he had brought the .38 along.

The door opened up, and a large man stepped in. When he saw Greg, he dropped the bags he had in his arms. He reached inside his coat for the weapon that hung in his shoulder holster. John's arm came out from behind the door. The man went down hard, just like his friend, as John tazered him.

With both men tied up, Greg and John hauled them out to the driveway. "We'll dump them into the trunk of the car, then head to my place," announced Greg.

John got inside the car while Greg, Bob, and Caroline got into the SUV. Together they made their way back to Egan Drive. Turning left, they headed toward downtown Juneau. They rode the eight miles to the Juneau-Douglas Bridge then crossed over the Gastineau Channel. Turning right onto the North Douglas Highway, they continued for a short time until they came to Evangel Drive. At the end of the road, Greg stopped the SUV.

John parked the car on the passenger side of the SUV. "Caroline, I would like you to stay here," Greg said.

"Hell no!" retorted Caroline. "I'm not letting Bob out of my sight. Besides, you may need help with the kids before you're done."

"Alright, but stay back please. I don't need anything to happen to you," said Greg.

"Don't worry about her, Greg. I think she can kick your butt," said Bob jokingly.

Caroline let out a playful growl. "Grrr."

Everyone was thankful for the levity. Greg reached out and touched Caroline's face. As he felt himself start to choke up, he exited the vehicle. Greg made his way to the front of the SUV then waited until the others joined him.

Leading the way, he worked his way past the trees, trying to stay out of sight of his home. Making his way to the side of the two-story home, the group split up. Bob and Caroline headed to the front door while Greg and John accessed the backyard using the fence gate. Greg noticed the family dog right away. It laid out in the yard—but he could see something was wrong. It didn't dawn on him what was so odd. It finally came to him the dog was dead, left here to rot. Greg liked the female Queensland blue heeler mix. The dog had never hurt anyone in all the time it had been part of his family. She didn't deserve to be shot then discarded like this.

They moved on to the utility room door. Greg tried the doorknob and was glad that it turned, opening the door. The two of them stepped in but left the door open. The next door opened into the home's kitchen. Slowly turning the knob, he barely opened it. He looked back at John and a nod of his head told Greg he was ready. Greg lowered down to one knee. John stood right behind him, prepared to charge in.

Tasers ready, Greg pushed the door open fast. No one was there. It was strange to be sneaking into his own home knowing that Jose's men were here. The kitchen was a mess—unclean dishes, pots, and half eaten meals scattered around. Marlene was going to go nuts when she saw this. Greg didn't want to be near her when she walked in.

"Man, Marlene is going to want these guys dead for this," whispered John. "We all better duck for cover when she finds out."

Greg half smiled then moved farther into the kitchen. The two of them worked their way to the living room without running into anyone. The sound of the doorbell made Greg jump. Bob and Caroline made it to the front door. Greg and John stayed close to the staircase wall that led up to the upper level. Moving slowly, they made their way to the foot of the staircase so Greg could see the front door. A strange man answered the door.

"Wow! Doesn't Greg and Marlene Woods live here? I swear we have the right place, honey!" said Bob.

"This is the address they gave us, look here!" answered Caroline, holding a piece of paper for Bob to see.

Bob looked over the paper then the house number. "Yep. This is the right place."

The man at the door interrupted. "They went on a small vacation to Hawaii. I'm just watching the house for them."

The downstairs restroom door opened up as the toilet flushed. "Hey! Who are you?" the man exiting yelled as he went for the weapon on his belt.

John turned then shot him with his Taser. The fifteen feet of line sprang out of the weapon, both lines striking the man. The one at the door turned to see his associate go down. Greg turned to Taser the one at the door when he fell straight to the floor. Standing in the doorway was Caroline with Bob's Taser in hand and a smile on her face.

"Dirtbag!" she said.

Greg stepped over the dirtbag, taking the stairs two at a time to the second floor. He quickly scanned the hallway for his wife and kids. John showed up right behind him when Greg started for the master bedroom.

If they've hurt any of my family, someone is going to pay, thought Greg. John turned the other way to check the kids' room. But as Greg moved toward the master bedroom, the door opened. Marlene walked out stiffly, followed closely by a man with a gun pointed at her head. The look on her face scared Greg, so he pulled the trigger on the Taser, accidentally shooting Marlene. Marlene became dead weight, which the man couldn't hold up. Marlene crumbled out of his grip, and just as her head passed the gun barrel it discharged, making a hole in the wall. Greg pulled the trigger on the second Taser he had. Two more lines shot out, imbedding the metal hooks into the man's clothes. Almost at the same time, John's hands appeared by Greg's, head firing his Taser as the man fell.

Greg rushed over to his wife, pushing the unconscious man away. He quickly changed the Taser cartridges. Loaded once again, he stepped into the bedroom. Greg was attacked by two small children screaming "Daddy!" He fell to his knees hugging them with tears falling down his cheeks.

John checked Marlene. "She'll be okay, Greg. However, I think she's going to be very mad at you for a while."

With a shaky voice and tears in his eyes, Greg answered, "She can damn well divorce me if she wants to! But they're all alive, that's what counts right now."

John reloaded his Taser then checked out the rest of the second floor. Bob got busy securing the two men downstairs. Caroline ordered Greg to let her have the children. He lifted them over Jose's man, not wanting them to touch him.

The kids saw their mother lying on the floor and started to cry loudly. "Mommy!" both cried out.

Greg took hold of both of them again. "Mommy will be okay, I promise," he said to them. "Now go with Caroline, please."

Caroline held each kid by the arms. "And your mommy is going to be very angry with Daddy when she wakes up, very angry."

Greg stood up, but his eyes were locked on the man at his feet. This man dared to put a gun to his wife's head. The anger boiled up in him, too fast to control. Greg turned the face-down man over, then launched an all-out attack on the unconscious intruder. He repeatedly struck the helpless man's face. Something grabbed Greg, pulling him past the bedroom door. Greg rose to his feet, turning to face this new threat.

John raised both hands while backing away. "Whoa there, Greg. If you want to be like these asses, okay go for it, but I know you're better than any of them. Hell, the only attention people like these get is when they hurt unarmed or weaker people. It makes them feel big time when they're really small." John paused. "Come on, man, we have a lot to do before we can let loose. There's still some guy out there with two kids we need to find. Now get Marlene downstairs and comfortable, because she's going to be one pissed-off woman when she wakes up," demanded John.

Greg slowly relaxed. "Yeah, that's one of the reasons I keep you two around. You help keep me sane. But don't you dare step between Jose and me. I just changed my mind. I'm going to kill him."

"No, Greg; we're going to kill him. You, Bob, and me," stated John.

"Good; when do we start that part?" asked Bob from the hallway.

Greg watched John help Bob finish securing the three men. Caroline was keeping the kids busy outside. He sat on the couch waiting for the Taser effects to wear off his wife.

"Greg, you're home," whispered Marlene.

"God, Marlene, you're awake!" shouted Greg.

Marlene looked at him, then hit Greg in the shoulder as hard as she could. "You shot me!" Just as quickly she asked, "Where are the kids?"

"Caroline has them out front. Just a moment," said Greg.

Marlene grabbed Greg's arm. "You shot me with that stupid Taser, didn't you? I told you not to buy them, but no, you had to have your toys."

"I can untie these three then leave if you want me to."

"You better shoot yourself if you leave," she retorted.

The kids ran into the living room. Greg and Marlene stopped talking as the kids ran into their parents' arms.

After too short of a time John interrupted, "I hate to sound selfish, but we need to check Sandy. You remember her, right? That's my wife, just in case you've forgotten."

"Yeah, John's house is next," added Bob.

Greg stood up, looking at his two friends. "Let's get this done, then we can head back to Canada and finish this."

Marlene tried to jump up, but lost her balance. "You're not leaving us again!"

Greg sat down with his wife. "We have to check John's house next. Sandy could be in danger, just like you and Caroline were."

"We need to put these three someplace safe. Any ideas, people?" asked Greg.

"They have a car outside in your driveway; we can do the same thing as before, put them in the trunk. After we get Sandy, we'll figure out what to do with them."

Greg smiled. "How far is Kodiak Island?"

"Well that's over six hundred miles, Greg. I'm sorry, I couldn't do that to the bears there. But we could set them down in Canada then call the Mounties," suggested Bob.

"We'll come up with something. Let's get Sandy," said Greg.

Greg had Caroline and Bob go get the other vehicles while he and John put the three men into the trunk of their own car. It was a tight fit, but they got them in. Greg didn't care if they suffocated or not.

"Marlene, I need you and Caroline to take the kids to the hangar. Take the key, stop somewhere, and get food on your way. Everything for cooking is there," said Greg.

"I need to know you're safe before I can put a stop to what's going on. Soon, we'll be safe for good, okay?"

"Don't go doing something stupid, Greg. You hear me?" answered Marlene while wrapping her arms around her husband.

"Too late for that, honey. Now I have to get all of us out of my doing something stupid."

"Are you going to tell me what's going on?"

"Mar, when I get back I'll tell you all there is to know," said Greg. "Bob talked with Caroline on the way over here. So for now she's the one to ask that is until this whole thing is finished."

Greg took his wife's face in his hands then kissed her. "You're my dream, my life, my everything. If I lost you, I would be better off dead." He kissed her one more time then turned to leave.

"I'll see you at the hangar before the three of us leave again. Now take your car and go, please."

With Bob driving one car and John in the other, Greg followed in his SUV. John's house was not that far away it would only take minutes to get there. This didn't offer much time to think of the day. They turned right onto Douglas Highway and headed back toward the bridge.

They continued pass the bridge, staying on Douglas. They soon came to E street in Douglas, Alaska. Turning right, and passing up 5th Street, they went about two miles more. Pulling to the side of the road, they got out of the vehicles.

"Okay, you two, this is the last stop for now. So far, no one has been injured. Let's try keeping it that way," said Greg. He then turned to start the half-mile hike to John's place. The only sound heard was of the footfalls of the three of them. The light rain could be heard hitting the leaves of the forest around them. In silence, they walked while each one dealt with their own thoughts.

Greg could only hope that he was wrong about the other person he suspected. That's why he left John's home for last. He would have his answer for that question soon. When John's house came into view, Sandy was sitting out front on the porch. Clearly she was alone.

Just too be sure, Greg made his way to the side of the home. "Let's check the inside first," suggested Greg.

John's place was a single-level home. The layout was simple enough for being out in nowhere. John led the way through the backdoor then into the kitchen. Quietly, they searched the house finding no one else. They then stepped out on the front porch.

Sandy jumped. "Shit! John, you scared the bejeebers out of me. What are you doing?"

"We're all here to save you, Sandy! That's what!" John said. "Bob's wife was being held hostage. Greg's wife and kids were too. But I get here, and you're relaxing on the porch." John turned to Greg. "I don't understand."

Greg looked at his friend. "You remember me saying that there maybe somebody else working against us."

"What are you saying, Greg? That my wife is helping Jose?"

Sandy's hand shot to her mouth. "No!"

Greg looked at Sandy. "How long have you known Jose Hernandez, Sandy?"

"She doesn't know Jose! Do you, Sandy?"

Before Sandy could answer, Greg spoke up. "John, you're the one who suggested we needed to test the stealth capabilities of the Raptor. In fact, you insisted that we test. Where did that come from? You also brought Freddie in. You pushed me to hire him. Who introduced him to you?"

Greg could see fear in Sandy's eyes. So he asked his next question. "Did you have an affair with Jose?"

Sandy leapt to her feet then quickly went past her husband. She entered the house with John close behind her. John reached out, grabbed her arm, and spun her back toward him. "You were the one that kept asking about the test." His voice was tight. "You introduced me to Freddie." John's hands tightened around Sandy's arm.

"Stop it, John, you're hurting me," pleaded Sandy.

"Why Sandy, why did you betray me?" John spoke in almost a whisper.

Sandy jerked her arm away from John. Standing up straight, she looked at all three men, then back to her husband. "You were spending all your time with your friends and that damn helicopter! You didn't have any time left for me! Do you know how many nights I spent alone out here? Waiting for you to step through that door with a 'Honey, I'm home.' Do you know how much I wanted you to touch me, hold me? Do you, John? Huh, do you? Well, I met a man who paid attention to me. Who was there to listen to me, being what you were not at that time. But when I found out he was just playing me. It was too late."

John's hand shot upward above Sandy's head. She tried to back away from the blow that was coming her way. Greg reached out, grabbing John's arm. Bob quickly moved in between John and Sandy.

"If you're going to strike someone, start with me, John," challenged Bob.

"Remember what you told me at my place, John?" Greg told him. "I believe it was something about being an ass like those other guys out there. You also said something about being better than they were. Well, I know that you're better than anybody the likes of Jose. We still have a man out there with two kids we have to find."

"Your wife didn't."

"Hey! Listen up!" Greg broke in. "I've made the biggest mistake of all of us. I, not you, not Sandy, not Bob, not anybody but me decided to make the run out to that ship! I made the decision to hire Freddie! Hell, Mar almost left me back then. You didn't know, that did you? It could have been Mar who Jose had targeted. I know it wasn't. However, it could have been. It doesn't help John, but we're all human. We all make bad decisions. One of the many things that make us human is that we can forgive ourselves and others."

"It may take time friend, but we can do it together," added Bob. "Now let's get Sandy to the hangar then find those people. Once that's done, we take care of Jose."

Through the tears that left their paths down her cheeks, Sandy said, "I don't understand—what did Jose do to you guys? What did Freddie do? What did I do?"

John began to relax and let go of his anger. "You didn't do anything wrong, Sandy. You needed something I wasn't giving. I'm sorry."

John turn toward the door, then walked out. "I'll make it up to you Sandy. I promise."

"Sandy, listen to me." Sandy couldn't place the voice at first. She wanted to go to John. "Sandy!" It was Greg who spoke. "Get into your car, drive to the hangar. Caroline and Marlene should be there by now. The other girls will fill you in to what's happening."

Greg and Bob followed behind John, leaving the house behind. They slowly made their way back to the road. More than halfway back to the vehicles, Sandy pulled up next to John. Greg couldn't hear what they said to each other. After a few moments John reached in the open window and kissed his wife.

Greg got into his SUV, thinking to himself, *We're all going to have to work on our marriages after this is over.* Bob started up one of the cars while John climbed into the other. Off they went back to the hangar—a caravan of sad, angry people, along with the five men tied up in the trunks of two vehicles. It was three in the afternoon now. Time went somewhat smoothly for them. The rain was still falling, but the lighting had stopped.

Sandy led the way in this four-vehicle procession, back across the bridge, then north on Egan. *Where are the police when you need them?* thought Greg. They all arrived at the hangar together.

Greg watched Bob and his wife cuddle then laugh. He watched his kids running around the hangar while holding his wife. He watched John and Sandy start to mend their lives while reaching into the future for comfort. Perhaps they would make it work.

"Come on, you two, we have to go," announced Greg.

Greg turned toward his wife, putting his fingers to her lips. "Don't say a thing, just listen, please. When this is over, we're going to renew our wedding vows, then go on a long vacation. I will change the business to a tour company. We'll live quietly for the rest of our lives if that's what you want. I love you, lady of mine, never forget that."

Greg walked away but still heard Marlene say, "I love you too."

Bob and Greg pulled the cars up close to the Snooper. With Tasers at the ready, they popped open one of the trunks. Picking up one of the men, they placed him in the Snooper. Bob climbed in, and then began tying him to the bench. They repeated the same steps with the other four men.

Sandy walked up to the Snooper. She stared at the five men. "Are those Jose's people?" she asked. "They're the ones who invaded your homes?"

"Yes, that's them," answered John.

"What are you going to do with them?"

"Not a clue, Sandy; that's for Greg to decide."

"Greg, Bob, I'm sorry for what Jose did to you. I can't believe how much of a fool I am."

Greg looked at Sandy. "Already forgiven, lady. As I said I could have stopped it all. I was just too caught up in my dream."

"Come on, you two, let's get this over with," called out Greg.

"Hey Sandy lady, don't worry about a thing. Here we are, all unharmed now. Only two more things to do on the list," assured Bob as he moved to the copilot's seat.

John held his wife close. "We have lots to do, Sandy."

"Yes we do, John," responded Sandy.

John made his way to the pilot's seat; he then started the rotor engine up. Sandy backed off from the Snooper, waved at John, and turned to head to the hangar. John lifted off after getting the go-ahead from Juneau International. He flew away from the runway flight path then set a heading back to the depot.

Greg sat on the bench watching Juneau pass by the open door. "God, I hope this works out," he said to no one. The five men looked at Greg, probably thinking something closely to what Greg had just said.

It was past six p.m. when the depot finally came into view. John lined up Snooper One to land next to the other Snooper. He gently set it on the ground.

"Where the hell have you been?" came Jose's voice from the radio.

"Ignore him," said Greg.

Bob got out of his seat and made his way past Greg. He exited the craft with the rotors still going full speed. Greg followed Bob, trying to come up with a plan on how to topple Jose's last hold on them.

The downdraft from the rotors increased as the Snooper lifted up. Greg and Bob both hit the ground, covering their faces. The wind blew what sand was on the rocky beach. When it lessened, Greg jumped to his feet running. "Damn it, John!" he shouted. Greg made his way to Snooper Three, and once in the pilot's seat he threw switches for the radio. Dialing up the private frequency, he yelled, "John, what are you doing?"

"I'm going to kill that son of a bitch, Greg. This is the last time he screws with anybody's life again. I don't expect to make it back, so tell Sandy I love her for me, okay?"

Greg kept keying the microphone. "John don't do it. He'll be waiting for you. We have to go after him together. Come back, damn it!"

"Sorry, Greg, I can't do that. It's not your wife he took advantage of. Jose's a dead man today. I'll see to that."

Greg started throwing more switches. Snooper Three came alive. The rotors started turning. The lights from the dash were on. A hand came into view—it began shutting down what Greg had just started.

Greg turned to see Bob continuing to shut down the Snooper. Enraged, Greg shouted, "What the fuck are you doing? Get the hell out of my helicopter now!"

Bob spoke softly. "Greg, by the time you get there, he'll be dead, you know that? Don't go getting yourself killed too, okay? Right now, Jose would murder us all when he sees those men in John's Snooper."

"I can't just sit here. I can't do anything to help John. If you're such a coward, then go! Tuck your tail between your legs, go on!"

"Greg, after all this time, is that what you think of me?" Bob paused for a moment. "I asked you a question, Greg! Do you really think I'm a coward? You can't help him. You have Marlene to think about. What's she going to do with your kids? What are your two kids going to do without you?"

Greg sat there staring at Bob. The anger drained from his face for the second time today. Bob was right—all he could do would get himself killed. He just sat in the pilot's seat waiting. The faint sound of two gunshots came from across the lake. Three more rapid shots came from near the cabin area. Some automatic weapon sounded off. Now there was only silence to fill the night air. The rain started up again.

CHAPTER 10

We found a ledge to call home for the night. The path leading here was narrow enough to keep large predators away. Using rocks and tree limbs, we created a shelter using the tarp. The hard rock beneath me pulled my body heat to it as though the rock hungered to be warm.

I woke the next day feeling stiff. The cold air during the morning cut through me, making me eager to get started. Standing outside of the lean-to, I saw dark clouds filling the sky again. The weather would make it hard for our hunters to find us. It also made it difficult for us to find them first. After breaking camp, we headed west toward Juneau. I figured we still had ten days of hiking to reach safety. That meant ten more days of being hunted by Jose's men.

The ground was wet with dew; it covered our shoes, making my feet cold. The animals of the forest went quiet. I stepped into the trees, waiting for the forest to come back alive. It refused to accommodate me by staying quiet. Something was out there, but what I had no idea. The forest remained quiet as I looked at each tree, each bush for anything.

After minutes of watching the landscape, I decided to move on. The kids stayed silent as we made our way through the river valley. Then a raven filled the air somewhere behind us. The raven squawked up a storm, warning everyone that danger was present. After some time, the forest sounds came back alive. The question of the quiet still required an answer.

I picked up the pace to put more distance between whatever and us. In all the years out there, I'd never run into this feeling of strangeness. The closest was when the male wolf surprised me while I was spying on his mate. The air itself had a smell to it that I somewhat recognized. The ground at my feet felt shaky. I was uncertain of each step I took. This was different. Something out there was watching us. That was the only answer I had.

We continued our walk to freedom in the river valley. Now and then, the hushed wooded area would try to tell me something. It kept whispering words I couldn't quite hear. Throughout the morning, I tried to decipher the woodlands sounds, but all I got was danger, danger. Was that warning for us or was there someone else nearby?

We came upon a rock out crop just above Amanda's height. I lifted Charles up onto the rocks then had Amanda climb on my shoulders. "Stay here, Charles, I'll be right back." I carried Amanda down the trail until we found another rock formation. After she had gotten atop the rock, I removed my pack then headed back for Charles.

Whoever may be following us would find only one set of footprints. When I returned to the rock where I had left Charles, he was gone.

Panicked, I searched the rock area until I finally located a partial footprint of a kid's shoe. It was a fresh print, only minutes old, pointing up the mountainside. Why would Charles leave this spot? What made him head up? I followed his trail, which was not hard once I had a starting point. I would have to go get Amanda soon, so she wouldn't panic about where we were.

A roar of a mountain lion cut through the trees. The sound wasn't far away, but it was still a ways away. I hurried on, looking for any sign of Charles. The lion roared again, and this time I heard Charles' voice. I couldn't make out what he was saying, but it was him. I moved faster in his direction. The trees started to thin a bit, but I still couldn't see Charles or the lion. A dog started barking while the cat's noise changed to more like a hiss. I finally saw the lion, ears back, teeth showing, swing one claw-loaded paw at something.

In a few more steps, the whole scene opened up for me. The dog was standing in front of Charles, challenging the cougar. He snapped at the cat then withdrew, staying out of reach of the claws. Both seemed to stay just out of range of the other. Both animals were looking for a weakness or a mistake to take advantage. I called out, "Stay right there, Charles."

I could see Charles relax a bit at the sound of my voice. The cat, now facing two threats, turned to run off. The dog moved closer to Charles, appearing to be protecting him. It was the green-collared dog that Amanda had fed yesterday.

I approached slowly, unsure of what to expect. Charles, on the other hand, wrapped his arms around the dog's neck. "Good dog," he said. The dog stared back at me, wagging his stubby tail wildly.

I walked over to stand by Charles then reached down and scratched the dog's head. "Good boy," I said, not sure if I should trust him.

"Come on, Charles, we need to hurry. Your sister will start worrying soon. Tell me what happened as we walk."

"Can the dog come with us?" asked Charles.

"The dog can go wherever it wants to," I answered.

Charles' story was short. He had seen the cougar and moved behind a nearby tree. He next saw the lion as it jumped onto the rock he had been sitting on. Crawling slowly, Charles moved farther up the mountain in hopes of escaping. The cougar saw him retreating and began to chase. In seconds, the lion was right behind Charles, only moments from pulling him down. That's when the dog charged out from the brush, ramming the cougar while it roared it swung its paw, claws extended at the dog.

The two animals seemed to circle each other for a long time. The dog kept the cat's attention off Charles while they both tested each other. Trying to stay close to Charles the dog stood its ground. Then I had showed up, adding to the number of threats to the cat.

"Where you scared, Charles?"

"Yes, but I knew it wasn't going to help. So I tried to hide."

"Good to know that you can think under pressure."

Instead of heading straight to the trail, we worked our way through the brush. Finally, we came across the trail we had been following earlier. With Charles on my shoulders, plus the prints of the dog, we made our way along the path. I would hope that the hunters would think the prints were one of their own.

Amanda came into sight, still sitting on the rock. "I was worried about you two," she said.

"Look what I found!" called out Charles.

Upon seeing Amanda, the dog promptly stood in front of her, wagging its tail. Charles proceeded to tell his story of the mountain lion to his sister. Amanda scratched the dog's head. "Good boy," she praised. His stub was just a blur now as it flashed back and forth.

The dog followed us as we made our way along the Taku River. We stopped to put up the tarp. A long-overdue rest was needed after this morning's close call with the native wildlife. The kids sat down under the tarp out of the drizzling rain. The dog stayed close to Amanda, joining the kids under the tarp's protection. I took some fishing line and went out to find lunch. I saw some animal burrows along our path. Now the trick would be to find one that was occupied. It took longer than I hoped to locate one that felt lived in.

I set up a small loop of fishing line in front of the tunnel, anchoring the loose end to a tree. I then positioned other traps in the surrounding area to snag whatever may come along. I didn't want to be reliant only on the snares. I found a thin branch to use as a fishing pole, then made my way to the river.

After a short time, I had a hook in the water and was settling in to wait for a nibble. I watched the river flow past, thinking about all the life it provides for. I watched the treetops sway in the gentle breeze, the dark clouds that covered the sky above the river valley. The light raindrops that hit the river surface, causing the water to ripple. The cool air felt good after the long hours of walking up and down the valley floor.

I almost could forget about the outside world, but the hunters kept pushing toward the front of my mind. I had to get these kids to safety before I could enjoy the quiet solitude of my cabin again. The branch I had connected to the line bobbed. Lunch was near.

I finally caught two trout as the sun broke through a hole in the clouds for a few moments. I shielded my eyes with my arms as I stared toward the light. The slight warmth of the sun touched my skin.

On my way back to camp, I checked the traps. I found a rabbit with the loop of the line tightly around its neck. I cleaned the fish then went to work skinning the rabbit. All I needed now was a fire and twenty minutes—can anyone say lunchtime?

"Lunchtime," said a voice. "Come on, Wade. You haven't forgotten me, have you?"

I spun around looking for whoever was talking. "Wade! It's me. It's been over six years since we last spoke. I like the way you killed that man the other day. It woke me up. Just think; you and me back together again."

I killed him in self-defense, I countered in thought. *Now go away!*

"Yes, I saw that. Perhaps we can continue with our conversation that you rudely interrupted."

"I've been doing fine without you. I've lived out here for five years just fine," I said.

"You without me!" the voice exclaimed. "Now that's funny. I'm the reason that bear didn't kill you. The wolves also let you live because of me."

"That's not true! They knew I meant no harm," I argued. "I don't have time for this. Go back to the dark corner of my mind and stay there!"

"Let me loose, Wade."

"No! Not now! Not ever again. You're the reason why my father and brother are dead. They were coming to that mental hospital to visit me. You're the one who put me there, more than once!"

"Ah, now isn't that too bad. LET ME OUT!" the voice screamed. "Free me, free me, free me, Wade. I'm part of you. Stop denying it."

"Wade, is something wrong?"

My eyes shot open. Amanda was standing in front of me.

After six long years without the voice inside my head, now it's back.

"No, Amanda, everything is fine. I was just lost in thought," I answered. "Let's go cook lunch."

"Ha-ha, 'everything's fine,' now that's a good one, Wade. Hey, she's kind of cute. Come on, Wade, let me out, pretty please."

The voice was just trying to stress me out more. *That's how it works*, I thought to myself.

"I can hear your thoughts, Wade. I'll just sit back, waiting for my release. Soon I'll taste freedom once again. You're going to need me before long."

Go to hell, I thought back.

"Only if you go with me," said the voice. "Ha-ha."

I pushed the voice back so its sound was barely there. I had too much to do. It whispered once more to me. "We are one."

I cooked the fish then gave the rabbit to the dog. I no longer liked this spot, so we broke camp and continued on our way to Juneau. I couldn't run away from the voice but if walking could keep it quiet, then I'd walk.

The rest of the day was uneventful. We put four more miles behind us. Finding a group of boulders, we stretched the tarp over the top of them, forming a small room. The dog was nowhere in sight when we started down to the river. I found some berries for us to eat plus use as bait.

In a few hours, we caught three fish for dinner. Amanda wrapped them in mud while Charles played in the mud. Nature minded its own business, and the hunters weren't to be seen.

When we returned to camp, the dog was waiting for us. It had killed a baby goat and dragged it back to camp. I looked at our three mud packed fish, then at the goat. "Show off," I whispered to the dog.

Charles got the fire ready some thirty yards from the camp. I hauled the goat back down by the river. The dog followed me with its tongue hanging out of it mouth. "How about we call you Troll? You like that name? It has to be better than Dog," I told dog as he followed me.

I had a dog named Troll a long time before. But his time had come to an end many years back. I missed him to this day still.

I skinned the goat, throwing the unusable parts into the river. If I were at the cabin, I would have used most of what I was discarding. Being on the move the way we were, I couldn't use the entire animal.

The dog and I made our way back to the fire. Amanda and Charles had cooked the fish, plus had eaten some. I cut a large piece of the meat off for Troll then made two small piles of rock on each side of the fire. I added two branches across the rocks. I then placed the rest of the meat on the branches to cook. Charles and I went out looking for more firewood while the meat cooked. It was going to take a while for dinner to be ready.

The dog stayed with Amanda, not wanting to give up on his meal. It didn't take long to collect the wood that we would need for now. Before dark, we would all go back out again. It was good to see all the fallen trees and branches lying on the ground. It signaled to me that mankind had not made it here yet. The smell of the cooking goat made me hungry. It also made me worried about who else may notice it.

After a while, I turned the goat meat over then remembered that I had not thanked it for its sacrifice. The dog watched me closely as I knelt by the fire. "To all the Gods that have been, to the one God that is. To the young goat whose life that was cut short so we could live, I thank you."

Charles now knelt down by me, Troll was sitting up watching, forgetting his meal. A bird squawked repeatedly as it flew overhead. In the distance, a goat bellowed. "I'm sorry I wasted so much of you, small one. I promise to honor you and your kind for the rest of my life. Thank you once again."

"Thank you, little goat," said Charles.

I heard a soft sniffle from behind me. Turning, I caught Amanda wiping her eyes. "I will also try to remember sooner to thank those that die so I may live. I wish to thank the fish and rabbit whose lifeblood we took. Go now, young spirit; take those that we have forgotten with you to the next life."

I stood and walked away, ashamed that of all things I had forgotten on this journey was to be thankful. "How touching," said the voice. "I really mean it, Wade. It's the part I don't have; it's the part I need." Perhaps the voice was right. We were one. A tear slowly rolled down my cheek.

I lost so much in my life. So much pain until I got here. The peace that I found filled my soul as if I was always meant to be here. My new mother was nature, and she watched over me answering my questions.

I returned to camp and sliced up a little meat for the kids. Amanda noticed that I didn't take some for myself.

"Wade aren't you going to eat?" she asked me.

"Tonight I'm going to pay a small penance for forgetting a rule of mine," I answered while smiling at her, "I'll make up for not eating in the morning. I promise."

The dog went back to gnawing on its bone. The kids ate their meal. I finished carving up the goat meat. I packed it up with the rest of our food then hung the bag from a tree some distance from our camp. Lying down, I pulled my pack under my head. I kept playing the small conversation I had with the voice.

In a low voice I heard, "Goodnight, Wade."

Shut up, I thought.

CHAPTER 11

Greg had to know what happened across the lake. He also had to get John's Snooper out of Jose's hands. Using the thermal-vision goggles, he and Bob started the walk around the lake. Bob also had two Tasers. He also had the two .38s on him. When Greg got to see Jose, he didn't want to be carrying any weapons. Bob would put one of each on the pilot's side of the Snooper for him.

They had been walking for some time when Greg finally recognized the distant silhouette of the Snooper. As planned, Bob stepped into the trees and disappeared from sight. Greg kept walking while making noise to attract the guards' attention.

One of Jose's guards stepped out where Greg could see him. He proceeded on to the Snooper to look inside. The five men he had helped Bob tie up were now gone, of course. Greg climbed into the Snooper, preparing it for a fast getaway.

As he jumped out of the Snooper, two guards were waiting for him. Part one of his plan's had worked, he was now in Jose's control. Bob should have an easier time getting to the Snooper without these two catching him. One of the guards waved his rifle toward the cabin trail. Greg took the command. The two guards followed him up the trail path. Step two of his plan was working.

Halfway up the trail, three of the men who they had Tasered in Juneau showed up to escort him. The two armed guards fell back into their positions.

Greg walked up to the three. "Hi, How's your day going?"

One of them smacked Greg in the side of his head. Another one kicked his feet out from under him. The third one planted his foot into Greg's stomach. The breath went out of him with that last blow, and then the beating really started.

Somewhere in the fun he was having, Greg must have passed out. He was now looking at the roof of the cabin above him. As he tried to sit up, pain shot through him from all over. Slowly, his eyes focused even more, and he could see John.

"Hi Greg," greeted John.

"You're fired, you know that?" replied Greg. He could see the bloody bandage on John's leg; he had ropes on his ankles. Greg guessed that his wrists were also tied because his arms were behind his back. A gag hung around John's neck.

"Ah, the worm awakens. See your friend is still alive. I don't just kill everyone," said Jose.

Jose rose off the bed to stand in front of Greg. "Your man comes here to kill me, but I let him live. I'm not the monster you think I am."

Greg grabbed the table for support as he stood to face Jose. "Then you have no problem letting us both go, right?" asked Greg.

"Why would I do that? Your families are free for now, so he stays here. You need to understand once again." Jose moved closer to Greg. "I own you! If you fail me he will die."

"No, Greg, don't listen to him. I got myself here, me and my temper. Get in the Snooper and fly. Don't look back ever!" yelled John.

A fourth person that John had had in the Snooper stepped on his wounded leg John screamed in pain. John's cry of pain came to a quick halt when the guard removed his foot.

Greg tried to stand on his own but his legs just weren't ready for that. He stumbled into Jose, who pushed him away. Greg made a slow circle, trying to catch his balance. He took a few steps in John's direction then toppled over. As Greg fell on to John, he saw John's arms move, it looked like he placed his hands to get ready for the impact.

Landing on John's upper body, Greg rolled down next to John. As he settled on the floor, Greg's hand hit John's wounded leg. This wasn't planned, but he noticed that John didn't move.

Greg made his way to his knees while looking straight into John's eyes. The look he received told him what he needed to know. John, however, sat there pretending as if nothing had happened between them. *Whose side are you really on, John?* The thought crawled through Greg's mind.

Getting slowly to his feet, Greg turned facing Jose again. Taking two wobbly steps, Greg now stood an arm's length away from the drug dealer. Blood dropped from his lip as his gaze moved from Jose's eyes to the floor, staying there.

"Now that's better," said Jose. "Now, you see who the master here is. You'll do as you're told from now on, my little mule. You could never have beaten me. I had you from the beginning, but not until now do you see it."

"You have until the end of the day to find the Carrolls or their kids. Two of my men will stay with you until you do. Two others will watch over the other pilot also. Another one will stay at your depot." Jose gathered five of his men together outside the door for a private conversation.

"Believe what you want, Greg, but I'm on your side," said John. "Jose has been using Sandy's past against us for some time. I've been trying to play Jose for a while now, but he keeps on about turning Sandy over to some mobster guy."

Greg turned his head to stare at John. The fire that burned in him showed in his eyes. "You listen this time Greg—so don't say a word, just listen. Sandy can tell you all the details of her past. I'm not asking for forgiveness, just a little understanding. Jose is mine, Greg. I'm going to kill him or die trying. That is the truth. Sandy can live in peace then."

Greg started to snarl something to John. "Shut up—here he comes," John said softly.

Greg was acting submissive as possible his shoulders slumped forward, back hunched over, his head still looking down. Greg wanted nothing more than to smash Jose's face in. He knew if Jose were to look him in the eyes, he would realize he was faking.

"Get out of my sight, dog!" said Jose. "Go find them now!"

Greg hobbled toward the front door then out to the trail. The five men pushed and tripped him all the way back to the Snooper. Greg looked around for Bob when they arrived at the lake. He was nowhere to be seen.

He slowly climbed into the Snooper then made his way to the pilot's seat. Greg was surprised to find Bob in the copilot's chair. "You look good and refreshed there, Greg," said Bob. "I see you brought some friends also."

"Fasten your belt tight Bob," said Greg as he closed the cabin curtain. "They're going for a short ride."

Greg reached down by the Snooper's collective control, where his hand touched the .38. Right beside it was the Taser. "Did you disable the boat?" asked Greg.

"Unless they have another battery, it's not going far using the engine. I also removed the paddles that were in it," answered Bob.

Greg went through the startup steps. The blades began to turn faster and faster. He turned the throttle control on the collective lever. The Snooper lifted while moving toward the trees. Greg pulled back on the cyclic controls to bring the nose of the Snooper up.

The five men could be heard bouncing around in the cargo area. Greg lifted the craft to about two hundred feet. He then did a hard left bank over the cabin. He thought he saw two objects fall out. He quickly brought the Snooper around to past over the cabin again. This time he did a right bank staying in a tight turn until he saw a body crash through the trees below.

Greg leveled out the Snooper, unfastened his harness. "Bob take over the controls then head back to the depot. Don't land unless I say so." Greg grabbed the .38, checking to ensure that it was loaded. He stood in the cockpit doorway of Snooper One. There was only one of Jose's men still there—holding onto a bench leg for his life. Greg raised the .38 then aimed. "Don't you people know how to use seatbelts?" The man's eyes flashed with fear as he saw what was coming. In what was slow motion for Greg, the gun jumped in his hands. The man's grip loosened then he slipped out of the Snooper and disappeared. The helicopter cargo hold was now empty of Jose's men. He had missed seeing one of them take the big plunge. This wasn't how he had planned this part; the person who had to die was Jose.

Greg returned to the pilot's seat, putting the .38 back by the Taser. He sat there while Bob flew the Snooper toward the depot. "Bob, take me to the Raptor, then follow me. We're moving the supplies."

The Snooper banked right to a northern heading. Greg just stared out the window as Bob headed to the Raptor. The next step would be to get the fuel plus the supplies out of Jose's reach. The sun didn't even illuminate the whole valley yet. He also needed to take care of his wounds and rest.

Greg left the lake area with Bob close behind. He flew to the Inklin River area. Greg landed the Raptor where he had met two of Jose's men the other day. As the rotors came to a stop, Greg could hear the river flowing close by.

Soon Greg and Bob were back again at the depot loading barrels of fuel into the two Snoopers. It would take most of the day to get this all moved. If Jose wanted to he could walk around, and then just wait for them to return. From this point on they would only fly one Snooper, plus the Raptor. If Jose wanted to fight, Greg would be ready.

Attaching a host above the Snooper door, Greg and Bob cabled the fuel barrels one at a time. Once both Snoopers were loaded, they hooked nylon barriers across the doorways. They then loaded each copilot's area with food crates. Climbing over the barrels, Greg knew the Snooper could lift the weight. After all, that's how they had gotten the stuff here. He still worried if the crafts were up to it. Once he made it to the pilot seat, he got the rotors up to speed. He couldn't really see Bob because of all the food crates blocking the window. He pulled lightly on the cyclic control, turned the throttle a little more. When the Snooper didn't lift up, he gave it some more fuel. Pulling back farther on the control, the Snooper lifted and moved away from the depot. He worked the controls until the Snooper lifted farther into the air.

They worked well into the afternoon Greg and Bob flew back and forth. Once they had most of the fuel and all the food supplies, Greg stopped the move. Getting his tent out, he threw it to the side and reached in one more time, wrapping his fingers on to his sleeping bag. "Wake me in a couple of hours, Bob," said Greg.

He placed his bag under some trees where the sun wouldn't find him. The pain came back to the surface as he relaxed while lying down. Sleep swept through him quickly as the hours passed by.

CHAPTER 12

I woke at the sound of nature whispering to me: "Danger."

I lay on the ground listening to the outside world. The breeze blowing through the treetops, the river flowing over the rocks was all I could hear. The silence of the wildlife spoke nothing but trouble. For whom it spoke to, I had no idea.

The warning cry of a hawk overhead reached me. The kids still appeared to be sleeping, even though the sunshine poured in through the open spaces of the tarp. Hunched over, I left the shelter to look around. A heavy weight landed on my shoulder blades, knocking me to the ground.

Dazed, I felt a hand grab my wrist, pulling me out into the open. Fingers intertwined into my hair, lifting my head up.

"You're not Tony Carroll. Lucky me, I get a punching bag."

All I could focus on was the red beret that he wore. Then a blow to the side of my head sent me to the ground again. I forced myself into a kneeling position only to get a boot in the mid-section.

At the sound of a growling dog, the man issued a set of commands. The dog lay down. In that small amount of time, I was able to get my feet under me. As he turned his attention toward me, I launched myself his way. He sidestepped my attempt to even things up. I ended up rushing passing the red beret. I didn't stop to face him. I kept running away from the shelter. I finally circled a small tree, striking out blindly. The hope was that he would be trying to cut me off by going around the other side of the tree than I. It paid off. The heel of my palm met his face.

Slowly, I was regaining my balance. I still had a chance against him. He countered with a left that I was expecting. Dropping down into a crouch, his fist passed over my head then into the tree. To my surprise, he came up with a right upper cut catching me in the forehead. I stumbled backward but managed to stay on my feet.

I saw him shaking his left hand, so I charged once more. I was able to encircle his waist from the sides while lifting him up. His feet came off the ground as I leaned forward toward the tree he had hit with his fist. The red beret fell backward against the tree scrapping the back of his neck on his way to meet the ground.

Placing my hands on the tree, I brought my knee up to strike him. Even though my knee connected with his head, he managed to wrap his arms around my legs. I then started to push down with my weight, hoping to force him farther onto his back. He in turn brought his left foot up to strike me in the back. I relaxed the pressure on him from the blow. He turned on his right side, forcing me to follow or injure my leg.

I was now on my back with my legs wrapped around his waist squeezing as hard as I could. Red began trying to strike my head with both fists. I used my arms to protect my head as much as possible. I was losing the battle. Then I heard a gunshot.

Red straightened up a bit with a surprised look on his face. One hand went behind his back for just a second, reappearing with blood on it. There was the sound of another shot, and this time Red's body jerked. He turned, looking at who had shot him, and started to laugh.

The next shot made Red fall toward me. I braced my hands on his right shoulder, while gravity plus his own weight sent him to his left. As his upper body stopped blocking my view, I could see Amanda. Arms out, locked in place, eyes wide open with that piercing stare of hers. The .38 in her hands cocked ready to fire again.

"No!" I yelled. "Drop the gun Amanda. Drop it now!"

Amanda just stared at the red beret, moving the pistol to point at him. I got to my feet then slowly walked over to Amanda. I placed my hand in front of the gun's hammer, just as she pulled the trigger. Charles stood by with the Winchester in his hands. If not for the past few minutes, it would have been funny.

"Amanda, it's over; you can let go of the gun now," I told her.

"No I saw him move," she replied.

"He's been shot three times Amanda. He's not going to hurt anybody now."

Her hands slowly let go of the .38, which fell into my hands. "I killed him," she said.

"No, he killed himself, young lady. Don't ever think of it any other way. He tracked us. He attacked me. He could have just walked away, leaving us alone. No—he brought this on himself."

"No, little girl, you killed me alright," said the red beret, coughing up some blood.

"Don't listen to him; he's just trying to hurt you. It's the only thing he has left. People like him never take responsibility for their actions. It's always someone else's fault," I countered.

"No, Wade, he can't hurt me, but…" Leaving it at that, she turned and ran.

The sound of laughter came from the red beret. "Come on, finish me off. Come on, be responsible Wade." He laughed again.

"I don't think so. You can stay right there for now," I told him.

"What, another coward too scared to kill someone?" he taunted.

Holding the .38 to his head, I removed the weapons he had on him. "No, you caused a lot of pain and harm in other people's lives. Now it's time for you to pay a little for it. Also when you get to hell, ask your green beret friend who is afraid." I then went after Amanda.

As I passed Charles, I relieved him of the Winchester. "Stay away from him, Charles, he's still looking to try and hurt someone. I don't want it to be you." This wasn't a man. He didn't deserve any respect he wasn't even on the level of an animal. He was just a heartless piece of human trash.

All the drug dealers, gang members, and religious nuts in the world are the trash of mankind. If only we could just eradicate them all, leaving those who would live peacefully. But where do you stop? What do you do with the new ones that show up later on? Yes, there are real monsters in this world and they're free to move about the planet. This monster, however, won't hurt anyone again.

I found Amanda a short distance from camp. "Hey, you okay?"

Amanda looked up at sound of my voice. "I hate this. Ever since those men showed up at your cabin, we've been running. The world has gone mad!"

"No, Amanda, you're just starting to learn about the world sooner than some. Charles is learning even sooner than you have. Think of all the children in drug-infested areas; they learned how to live on the streets way before you, No, the world has always been insane."

"I've never seen it like this, Wade. My world hasn't ever been this destructive," said Amanda.

"They still have news on TV?" Amanda nodded her head yes. "When you make it back to the real world, try watching it for a while. I saw the madness, even before I left—African genocide, the disappeared of Argentina, Pol Pot of Cambodia. Those things happened before you were born Amanda. If you look, you'll find atrocities all over the world now."

"Why do people let this happen, all the death and suffering?"

"I can only give you my reasons why. You'll have to work out your own. So here goes—freedom isn't free, and we the people let the government plus the military, along with law enforcement with the lawyers, convince us that they could protect us. It took some time, but the criminals figured out that they couldn't cover everywhere. They found out little by little that some would be caught, but most would get away.

"Then the lawyers and the government passed laws hoping to slow down the criminals. In doing so, they tied the hands of good honest folks. No longer could you protect yourself. You had to run away, escape your own home. Anything else would find you standing in front of a judge. They then let the families of the criminals sue the victims for wrongful injury or death. Lawyers twisted the law to fill their own bank accounts. Don't get me started on gun bans. The only thing gun bans do is un-arm the honest law-abiding people.

"Before I start repeating myself, let me say this: It's everyone's fault for the condition throughout the world. Rich, poor, religious, non-religious people across the earth are to blame. Greed comes in many forms, Amanda; you can be highly religious and be greedy. Greed isn't just love of money. You can be so greedy to save souls that you lose your own.

"When do we, as the intelligent life, form of this plant start working for each other? When do we stop being so self-absorbed and become stewards of this planet? The good people of this world have fought from the beginning of time. They had a better vision for all life on this small rock in this vast universe.

"I may have truly lost my mind, Amanda. Maybe I've been living too much in my head. I know that most of the people I call evil don't see themselves as evil. What I call evil may be good to others.

"You'll have to search your own life to answer the questions about the world. Remember to never stop questioning, especially those people in places of power.

"Make a difference! Amanda, make a difference." I paused for a moment then continued. "Okay, I've said a lot and nothing at all. Hopefully I've put an idea in your head that won't leave you alone for years to come.

"Now I have to get back before Charles gets himself in trouble. If you want to talk more just ask, and I'll do my best not to ramble on and on. Okay?"

"Thanks, Wade, for taking the time. I'll think about what you've said." After a small pause, she looked at me. "I'll catch up with you shortly." She walked up to me, wrapping her arms around me and we both just stood there.

"Great, but don't take too long; we have to get moving." I turned then headed back to camp.

I could see that the red beret was still alive as I arrived. He had moved himself to a boulder that sat close by. Charles was sitting well away from him, studying the man.

I squatted down by Charles. "What are you thinking?"

"He's been trying to get me to go over to him. All I could think about was how much he is like Bear right now."

"What do you mean, Charles?"

"You said never to trust Bear. If we obeyed the rules that you two had made, we could enjoy watching him." Charles pointed at the red beret. "I don't trust him. He's more dangerous than Bear. He would hurt people for no reason. "

"He doesn't know any better, Charles. It's what he has learned from his life. Now go find your sister, and tell her to wait for me wherever you find her. Okay?"

"Okay, Wade," he answered, then went back the way I had come. Charles called to the dog, which jumped up with tail wagging. He ran ahead of Charles, looking like any other dog out with its boy.

I busied myself breaking down the camp under the watchful eye of the red beret. In a short while, I had all our gear packed up. Putting my pack on, I moved the kids' gear away from the campsite. I then made my way to the red beret.

"What am I going to do with you?" I asked.

"Kill me now! Get it over with," he spat.

"Well I thought about just leaving you here. Let you starve to death or some animal find you still alive. That's what your kind of person deserves, left to think about how they got in this situation. Maybe you'll even ask for forgiveness. I doubt it, though."

His stare never softened. "You can't leave me here like this. I'm a warrior! I deserve a warrior's death. Kill me!"

"Don't you worry, I won't leave you like this. That's something you would do and Lord knows the one thing I'm not is you," I managed to say. "As I see it, one of the rounds hit your spinal cord. Can you move both of your arms?"

"Come closer and find out!" he answered in a weak voice.

I climb the boulder behind him then pulled my revolver. I removed five of the rounds from it. I spun the cylinder so that the remaining shell would be in the firing position when the hammer was cocked. I then dropped it in his lap.

His hand shot to the weapon. His thumb pulled back the hammer and he leveled the gun at me.

"I would think very carefully if I were you. There is only one round in the gun. It's in the firing position right now. You can waste it by trying to shoot me or end you own life. Up to you. I can wait for some time. How about you?"

After what seemed minutes, I saw the barrel disappear under his head. I dropped down behind the boulder when the sound of the discharging weapon echoed across the river valley. I retrieved my .38 then reloaded it. Turning away from the red beret, I left him sitting there with blood splattered on the rock above his head.

Amanda and Charles came running around a tree as I made my way to them. Sometimes doing the right thing is hard to do. Also, at times, doing the wrong thing for the right reason is hard to do.

"We heard the shot!" exclaimed Amanda with a look of worry in her eyes. "You didn't kill him, did you?"

"No, Amanda, I didn't kill him. I only gave him the means to kill himself. Now take your packs. Let's not talk about what happened back there, okay?" The morning had only just got started as we walked on in silence.

"You're a better man then I, Gunga Din," said the voice. "But then we are the same man. Free me, Wade; we'll end this game."

"It's not a game. In games people don't really die. Games are for enjoyment. I'm not enjoying this at all," I answered.

"What did you say, Wade?" asked Charles.

"Just thinking out loud, Charles," I said. "Keep walking there; we still have a long way to go."

I looked downriver watching the water swiftly moving toward the ocean. *Shut up*, I thought to the voice.

"Okay, I won't say a word," it answered then laughed. "Whoops."

CHAPTER 13

We walked on for about three more hours when we came around a corner where we could see an angler in the distance. As we got closer, I spotted a canoe not that far away. I unsheathed the rifle while pulling the hammer back as we approached the man from behind. I saw that he also was armed with a shotgun close by, plus a handgun on his hip.

One of the kids stumbled over a rock, filling the quiet with sound. The stranger started to reach for his handgun and turn at the same time. "Freeze!" I yelled at him. He looked our way, locking his eyes first on the Winchester then me.

"We're not looking for trouble, mister," said Amanda.

I followed up with, "I don't want to shoot, but I will if you pull the weapon, Sir." The man just stood there with his hand almost on the butt of his pistol.

"Please, move your hand away from the weapon." Still not saying anything, he put both of his hands on his head. He then turned his back to us waiting.

"Please help us," said Charles. The dog's hair rose at its shoulders and it bore his teeth at the man.

I slowly walked up to the fisherman. "What's your name, mister?"

"Tim," was his reply.

"Okay, Tim, we have some real-life bad guys after us. They'll kill anybody to get to these kids. We've been on the run now for four days. I'm tired. The kids are tired, and started our day by being attacked by one of them.

"I need to get these kids to Juneau fast. That canoe would help out a lot." I placed the rifle barrel on the base of his neck, removing his weapon from the holster. Backing up quickly, I stepped over to his shotgun. I placed the Winchester beside it, still cocked. I pointed his own Glock semi-automatic at him.

"Turn around. Tim." He did as I ordered. "You out here all by yourself?"

Tim was just a little shorter than I was, a little potbellied too. "I have a satellite phone in my canoe. If you need the police I can call for help."

"Sorry, but I'm too jumpy to let you get it. Tell me where it is."

"You're not a trusting soul, are you?" he said.

"Not today, Tim. My name is Wade. If you want to take a swing at me after these kids are safe, I'll let you have a free one."

I unloaded the shotgun then threw the shells in the river. I picked up the Winchester while making my way to the canoe. "Charles come here; don't step in between Tim and myself."

I waited for Charles to arrive before asking, "Okay, where is this phone?"

"It's right there, Wade," said Charles, pointing at a small black object. Things had really changed over the past five years.

"I really have to get out more," I said to no one.

I reached to pick it up when the sound of a rifle let go. A hole appeared in the canoe, kicking up some sand at my feet. I grabbed Charles by his shirt, pulling him down behind the craft.

Another rifle shot went off; I saw Tim fly backward then lie still on the sand. *Great, now what*, I thought.

"Raptor, we have targets in sight; answer me, Raptor."

"This is Raptor, come back," shouted Greg through the walkie talkie.

"They're on the southeast side of the river from us. I'll set up smoke when I hear you coming," came from the Raptor's speaker.

Greg put down the microphone. "Showtime," he said to himself.

"So what's the plan, boss?" Greg turned to find Bob standing next to the Raptor.

"You follow me, but stay a ways back. Try locating that guy and the kids. Don't land until I say so, okay?"

"I'm going to get more blood on my hands, Bob. These kids are going to be safe before today's over. Maybe we'll have time for Jose, also."

"Let's fly," answered Bob as he turned, heading for the Snooper.

"Bring them to me right away," came Jose's voice over the radio. "I want the guy who's been trying to keep them away from me. I'll make him beg for death before I kill him. Go get them!"

Greg struck his head. If only Jose knew what he had planned. "We're in the air, people," said Greg over the radio.

I lifted up over the canoe, firing a wild shot. No answering shot came back, no way to try to pinpoint their location. "Okay, Charles, when I start firing. you run to your sister, understand?"

"Yes, Wade," he said.

I heard Amanda scream and the sound of dogs fighting. "Run!" I yelled at Charles. I rose to one knee, firing the Winchester as fast as I could. Getting to my feet, I made my way to where Tim was.

All I found was an empty spot where he had been. I noticed that his shotgun was also missing. I felt the wind of a round fly past my head. Turning, I ran after Charles, who I could see going into the trees.

As I entered the forest, I heard a helicopter approaching. "Damn it, Lord, a little help please," escaped my lips as I sprinted on. Amanda screamed again, which gave me a direction to go in. I came upon a small clearing where Tim was guarding Amanda with his shotgun. Charles was standing between Tim and his sister doing his best to protect her. Two dogs battled each other in the opening. One had a red collar on it the other with a green collar. I raised the rifle, took aim at the red-collared dog, then fired.

The dog dropped dead to the ground, ending that fight. Not sure if I had another round in the rifle. I worked the lever action on it. I pointed the Winchester at Tim and yelled, "Drop the shotgun, Tim!" I ordered.

"He was helping us!" answered Amanda, anger piercing her voice.

"I don't care right now!" I spat out the words with my own fury.

"Let me out, let me out!" echoed through my mind.

"Put down the damn weapon, now!" I screamed.

Tim slowly set the shotgun on the ground.

"Amanda, pick up the shotgun then bring it to me."

The dog growled at me. It seemed to show its dislike for my actions. "Shut up, dog, or you're next," I said, feeling almost out of control.

Amanda carried the gun over to me as I muttered to myself, "You're scaring me, Wade." She gave me a look that said just that—fear.

I took the shotgun from her, and once more I unloaded it. Taking a deep breath, I relaxed a little. "Listen, Amanda, do you hear the helicopter? We don't have time to be nice!"

I turned to Tim. "I thought you were hit?"

Tim looked at me before answering. "Heard the bullet go by, thought faking getting hit was the right thing to do."

"Please understand, these kids are in my care. I'll do whatever it takes to get them to safety."

Greg followed the Taku River, leaving Bob behind. He was approaching the GPS location the Ground Force had sent him. He started to let up on the speed while looking for the smoke signal. The Raptor was at tree level as it traced the river.

Looking to his right, he finally saw the blue smoke. Greg brought the Raptor to a stop, hovering over the river. He looked the riverbank over, spotting his targets lying in the brush along the bank. He flipped a switch. The mini-guns rolled out into the firing position one more time.

Greg rotated the Raptor to the right, then opened fire on the target's location. He could see the dirt jump through the air. The brush was being chopped down one round at a time. The guns spoke their strange tune, the whirling of the mini-guns, and the impact of the firing pin on the round. Right now, Greg found those sounds to be magical. One figure jumped up then tried to run to the safety among the trees. Greg quickly brought him in line, taking the man down. A round struck the Raptor. Greg moved the pedals toward another person boldly standing in the open. Pressing the trigger, Greg put an end to his life.

Sparks started erupting from the main rotor blades, raising the Raptor up, backing halfway across the river. Here he finally saw the last of Jose's Ground Force personnel several yards away from the other two.

The Raptor tilted forward while picking up speed. It headed toward the last target. Greg opened fire, covering the area with death. The man cartwheeled as a round hit him

Lifting the Raptor higher and still looking for any more men within the area, Greg asked, "Where are you at, Bob?"

"Coming up on your location now," announced Bob over the radio.

"I need you to scan my location for more of Jose's men, then go find the targets."

"Got it, Greg; I'm scanning your area now." After a few moments, Bob came back on line. "I only get three readings. None of them are moving."

"Okay, go find the targets."

"Already done: I have them on the other side of the river moving south. There seem to be two adults now."

"Keep them on your screen if you can. I'm going ahead of them," said Greg. He flew the Raptor low over the three men he had just killed. A blue beret laid by the second man he had taken out. The other two were Jose's men.

"I also see a large group of signals close to six miles ahead of them."

"Great job, Bob. Let's get this part done."

Greg turned the Raptor downriver looking for the right place to land. As he passed over the far side of the river, Greg saw a canoe. This could be where the other person came from. Great, now all he had to do is stop them from shooting him.

Tim spoke up. "I have friends about five to six miles downriver from here. I'll make sure you get a canoe from them."

"I'm sorry to drag you into this, Tim. But you see now that we really do need your help."

The sound of rapid fire drove me to the ground. The kids followed my move and dropped to the earth as well. Tim went down, trying to make a smaller target. I started calming down enough to think clearer.

I reloaded the shotgun while making my way to Tim. "Here, take this back." I handed him the shotgun along with his Glock. Without saying any more, I headed toward Juneau. The sound was still going on by the river. I wondered what they were shooting at.

Tim led us toward his friends. I pulled out the radio, pushing the power button. All I got was static, so I thumbed through the channels until I finally found the right one.

"Think Jose is going to be mad that you took out his men?" said Bob.

"Don't care, Bob. This is the best chance we've ever had to get rid of him. We get these kids to safety, then Jose only has John as leverage against us."

Greg found a clearing that ran from the water's edge to the mountainside. He landed the Raptor and shut down the engine. Grabbing the hand-held radio, he stepped out into the rain. He found a place under the Raptor and sat down to wait.

"How far are they from me, Bob?

"About a half-mile until they reach you. They're not even trying to hide their heat signal, Greg." After a small pause, Bob added. "You be careful down there. I don't need to lose a good boss."

"Ha-ha, thanks, Bob. But this whole mess with Jose is still my fault. I hired Freddie plus made the decision to fly out to the ship."

"Stop knocking yourself, boss. You didn't know Freddie was working for Jose. I also don't remember anyone trying to talk you out of going to that ship. We all thought it would be fun pulling one on the military. Let's get these people to safety, take care of Jose, get drunk, then shoot each other, okay?"

"I like that idea Bob, except the shooting each other stuff. I'll have to get the wife's permission first. We also need to get John out too. Jose can rot up there, but with the way things have been going, he'll find a way out."

Greg sat under the Raptor sheltered from the rain. He wondered what the two men would do when they made it to the clearing. Waiting for the present to catch up to the future was never easy.

"Hello, Greg," a strange voice came over the radio.

"Hello back, whoever you are," answered Greg. He was surprised that the voice came over their closed frequency.

"I have a rifle pointed at your head. If you don't do as I say, you won't have to worry about anything anymore, understand? Have your friend Bob land. I want to see the two of you together."

"Look, we're here to help you get out of this place," replied Greg.

"You and those helicopters have been hunting us for days now. Don't think for a moment I trust you. Now, get that 'Snooper,' as you call it down here."

Snooper, thought Greg. *He's been listening to our radio conversations for a while.* "Greg, I'm coming in. We'll face this part together. You and I, got it!" said Bob.

"No, you stay there. If he shots, you just head back to Juneau. Hear me?" shouted Greg.

"Someone has to take the first step, Greg. Let us be the ones to put our lives on the line with this guy. I've been flying around since this garbage started, and I'm tired of it. Besides, you can't stop me."

"You're fired, you know that?" said Greg.

"Won't be the first time you've fired me. Heads up, people, I'm coming in."

I lay in the brush with Greg in my sights. The kids, along with Tim, were about fifty yards back in the trees waiting for me to signal them. I watched the second helicopter come into sight then land behind the first one. One person emerged, jumping to the ground. He walked over to Greg then sat down.

The new person, Bob, pointed my way then motioned with his hands back behind me. He was telling Greg where we were hiding. I stood up, looking over the rocky area. While moving toward the two I continued to scan the area, being careful not to stumble on the rocks. *Damn heat detectors*, I thought.

As I got closer to them, I blew a whistle that Tim had loaned me. "The rest will be here soon. Sit quietly until they arrive," I instructed them. I saw no sign of fear, just the uncertainty in what was going to happen.

The first to show up was the dog. He came running up behind me, stopping by my side. I turned to see the others working their way to the helicopters. Some animals, no matter how they're trained, have more sense of the world than people. "You trust them, Troll?"

The dog walked over to Bob and wagged his tail while licking his face. He looked at Greg for a few seconds then licked his face. He then ran off to greet Amanda and Charles as they made their way to me.

CHAPTER 14

Tim and the kids arrived then began to settle in. "So why should we trust you?" I asked them.

Greg let out a small laugh. "You know where that dog comes from, don't you?

"Yeah, some dead nutcase with a green beret. I can tell by the green dog collar. The brown beret had a dog with a brown collar and the red-collared dog had a red beret guy."

"Had? You are saying the red beret is dead or just the dog?" Greg asked.

"Both are dead—the red beret early this morning, the dog just before you showed up at the river. Now, why should we trust you?" I asked again.

"Here we are, unarmed, at your mercy, and all our own choosing. Well, I am; Bob's here because it's what you wanted."

"Tim, would you go check the other helicopter for weapons please?" I asked.

Bob spoke up right away. "There are two .38s and two Tasers in the Snooper cockpit area. Look on the far side of each seat; you'll find them there."

Tim left to search the helicopter—Snooper, as they called them. "What was the rapid firing we heard a while back?" I demanded of them.

Greg spoke up this time. "This ship here has two mini-guns attached."

"I took out two of Jose's men, and also by my count the last beret. You did pretty well taking out three of them yourself," added Greg.

Wade followed up with "A bear got the brown beret who was on your radio. I only shot one of Jose's men there. I stopped the green beret with two shots to the torso." I looked at Amanda before going on. "She shot the red beret three times."

Greg and Bob looked at Amanda. "It may not seem like it young lady, but good for you," said Bob. "He needed killing."

I watched Amanda for a few seconds. She seemed to handle the reminder of this morning very well. I stepped closer to Greg. "You look like somebody didn't care about your face."

Greg reached up, touching his bruised face. "Yeah, five more people no one has to worry about anymore. That red's handywork I see on your face?"

"Would have been worse if not for the helping hand I got."

Tim returned with the handguns and Tasers. "This is all I could find in the helicopter right where he said they would be."

"We can use the radios on the helicopters to call the police," added Tim.

"That's not a good idea, at least for Bob and me. We would have to explain why we are here, loaded with the mini-guns in the Raptor. Then there are the three dead bodies back by your canoe. No, not my first pick, but you have the guns," stated Greg.

"Maybe we can take Tim back to his canoe, leave him there," said Amanda.

"The first shot hit the canoe; it probably has two holes in it at least," I said.

Tim spoke up. "Well, I may be able to patch up the canoe. I have a kit back there in it."

"If you get your canoe fixed, head back to your friends. I would really appreciate it if you don't ever tell anybody what happened here," said Greg. "I still have one blackmailer, I sure don't need another. If I have to go to jail, I'll go. Sure would be nice not to, though."

I hear that," added Bob.

"Let's go see if his canoe is fixable first," I suggested.

"Sounds good to me," said Tim.

"Bob, take them all back to the clearing. I'll meet you with the Raptor," offered Greg.

"No, you'll leave this thing here for now. We'll all stay together a while longer. For the kid's safety, let's say, okay?" I said while smiling at Greg.

We all climbed into the helicopter. Greg and Bob sat in the cockpit area. The four of us buckled ourselves in for a hopefully small ride. The dog sat between Amanda and Charles, who held on to him. The helicopter ascended slowly to treetop level then headed upriver.

In minutes, the helicopter was setting down where we had first met Tim. When the blades had completely stopped, I spoke to Amanda. "I want you to get off with Tim. Take Charles and the dog with you. If all goes right, I will be back real soon, no questions okay?" Amanda nodded her head yes.

I turned to Greg and Bob. "Stay right there, you two," I ordered.

"Look, we've been trying to tell you that were on your side. What do we have to do to prove it?" asked Greg.

"Just a little longer, guys, then I'll make up my mind. Now, when they're safely away, show me these three men you took out."

"You're going to leave those kids with him? You just met him," said Greg.

"I trust the dog to protect the kids, and Tim hasn't been helping anybody to kill us. Start it up—let's go see those dead bodies."

Greg was getting annoyed—was this just another bad decision on his part? He had them both in what seemed a dangerous spot again. He started up the Snooper once again, lifting the craft into the air. He crossed the river to where he had gunned down three people.

I sat by the doorway, watching the river pass under us. Greg brought the helicopter around for me to see the riverbank. I made out the one body in the open. The helicopter moved slowly up to the river.

I kept looking for another body to show up. The copter lowered close to the ground, moving upriver.

I saw a blue beret caught in the rocks not too far away. I stuck my head in the cockpit. "Set it down, please."

When the blades came to a stop again I jumped out onto the beach. I slowly walked over to the blue beret's body. I could see several large bullet holes in him. I flipped him on his back. This man wouldn't hurt anyone again either. I look to see Greg and Bob standing by me. I walked over to the man's hat and picked it up.

"We need to hide the bodies someday," I said.

"Okay, it looks like you're here to help. Let's go see the other two before we leave." With that, I started walking up the shoreline.

I paused at the next body, taking his backpack and weapons. I stared into his face, not wanting to forget the waste of life I've seen in the past few days. I handed the weapons to Greg, who slowly reached out to take them.

"Does this mean that you trust us now?" he asked.

"To tell you the truth, I never had any choice but to trust you. I've listened to enough of your radio talk to know a few things about where you stand. I need to get these kids to safety before I go take my home back.

"One thing I've learned throughout my life is to trust an animal's instincts," I continued. "It will let you know if it means to harm you or not. They have to live by their instincts of knowing what or who is set to hurt them. If the dog had growled or bark at you, then things would be different."

"You mean that dog decided our fate," asked Bob?

"That, plus your radio conversations."

Greg led the way toward the last body. "He should be right around here somewhere. Damn, don't tell me he faked me out."

"No, he didn't fake you out. I found some blood over here." I started following the trail I had spotted.

It didn't take long before we saw him. I drew the 9mm this time, ready for anything. I could see him trying to lift a handgun he had. No matter how many times he tried, he just couldn't do it.

With the 9mm aimed at him, I approached the wounded man. I could see blood in the corners of his mouth. I had watched far too many people die lately. The first thing to do was remove his weapon. I reached down to pull it away from him. He just sat there looking at me with sad eyes. "Let's leave him and go," said Greg. "I'm sorry, but I've had it with these people today."

"I've felt the same way earlier, now I'm happy I stayed. We can be like them in some ways. Even so, in the end, we are very much different," I said. "I still care about the difference I see right now." I sat down next to this man, placing my hand on his.

Bob stepped up, knelt down, then placed his hand on the man's shoulder. "Think we can get him to a hospital before it's too late?"

Greg studied the man gauging if he could make the trip. "If we take him in, the police will be called. You want to go that way, Bob? Once again, it could be jail time. I can always take him in myself—that would keep you out of it."

"Bros forever, Greg. If you go, I go," said Bob, still watching Jose's man.

"I'll bring the Snooper closer, and then get a bench seat for a backboard." Greg ran off toward the Snooper.

It didn't take long before the helicopter landed close by. Greg soon showed up with the bench. The man grimaced in pain as we moved him on to our homemade backboard. Bob took one side while I grabbed the other; together we made our way back to the helicopter.

Greg talked as we made our way. "We need to pick up the kids and go. Maybe Tim will also need a ride, so let's not delay too much."

We slid the wounded man into the cargo bay of the helicopter. We strapped him down as best as we could, and I sat beside him holding his hand once again. Here was a man who had hunted us, who also had shot at us from across the river. Why was I being so nice to him now?

Maybe because he was helpless or was it because I still had to prove that I wasn't like them.

"You're really a wimp, Wade. You know that?" said the voice. "You should have just left him there. Let the animals have him. I would have done it."

I thought back to myself, *That's why I won the last battle, and you lost. I still care about life, unlike you.*

"Touché there, Wade, you got me with that one."

The helicopter took to the air then sat down on the other side of the river. "I'll be right back. You hang in there," I said to Jose's man. Climbing out, I found the kids ready to board. "We have a wounded man with us. So be careful in there, you two."

I then made my way to Tim. "How's the canoe repair going?"

Tim looked up at me. "I almost have it completed. It'll get me home."

"Look, Tim, I want to apologize for the way I treated you at first."

"No problem—now that I see what you're going through, I don't think I blame you for being an ass," he added with a big smile to his face.

"The world needs more understanding people like you, Tim. I have to get going now. We may be coming back this way later on. I'll look for you." I offered my hand. "I still owe you that punch."

Tim gripped my hand tightly. "No, you did right; keep it up. I'll have to let the glue dry, which should take some time. Besides, I still have some fishing to do here. I have my phone if I can't get back to my group."

I started back to the helicopter. "You take care of yourself," I called out. "And don't let anybody sneak up on you."

Tim laughed then waved as I climbed aboard the helicopter. Troll was lying next to Jose's man with his head in the man's lap. I sat down on the deck, taking hold of the man's hand. "What's your name?" I asked him. The blades started up at the same time I saw his lips move.

I moved so I could keep Troll from sliding out, never letting go of the man's hand. Once I was sure of Troll's and my safety, I put my ear close to the man's mouth. This time I heard "Buddy." He weakly smiled at me. I seem to recall that the name meant brother, though I wasn't sure.

When the Snooper landed behind the Raptor, Greg jumped out then ran over to it. Before he could get the canopy open, Bob lifted off, heading to Juneau. Both men knew the Raptor would catch up easily.

As Greg started up the Raptor, he calculated the miles back to the hangar. It was about fifteen miles to the Canada-Alaska boarder, fifty-one more miles to Juneau. In less than an hour, he and Bob would be home. Jose could wait awhile longer.

I watched the terrain change as we left Greg behind. The helicopter stayed close to the treetops, which flashed past the open doorway. Off in the distance, I could see mountains slowly move across the horizon. Soon the kids would be safe, and then I could begin to liberate my home.

The voice started up its chatter. "Come on, Wade, just push this guy out the door. You know, it's what he deserves after the past few days."

No, you don't stand a chance in convincing me to do that, I thought. *In fact, I don't think you stand a chance in taking control over this situation ever. I will win. You will lose.*

"Keep thinking that, Wade; I'm learning to wait. Soon I'll take center stage. There's nothing you can do to change that."

I can choose not to go back to the cabin, can't I? I countered.

"No! Free me now!" the voice screamed inside my head.

Or what, you'll die, leaving me in peace? I shouted inside my mind.

Greg could see the Snooper. "Bob, I'm going ahead. I'll meet you at the hangar. When you land, get the kids out. I'll take Jose's man to the hospital."

"I can stop at the hospital on the way in. It would be faster, Greg," replied Bob.

"No, that would involve the kids, Wade, and you. As your boss, I'm taking responsibility for this problem. When you land at the hangar, get everyone out."

Greg flew on past the Snooper on his way to whatever was coming. *This could be it*, he said to himself. Then again, he had pretty much said that almost every day lately. "A little help now, Lord, would be nice."

The dog's head came up. The man's hand relaxed. Looking at his eyes, I could see that no one was there. It's a strange thing that you can tell just by looking in someone's eyes that there is life or not. Troll laid his head back down while looking at me. I reached out to scratch his head. "How's Buddy for a name? Think you would like that?" I asked the dog. He simply wagged his tail. We rode on in silence—just the voice, Buddy, and me flying over the earth with a dead man.

The rain blew in through the open door, whipping around me. I didn't want to look away from Buddy the dead man. *What did I know of this person? Why did he pick this kind of life?* I was left with more questions about why people pick their lifestyles. What would push a person to be so hateful, uncaring, and heartless?

Parts of Juneau came into view on the left side of the helicopter. A glacier was visible on the right side. It had been years since I was last there. Hopefully, it would be a short visit this time. I could see that man was taking more and more land for his own use: Juneau had grown. It would still take years, but man would eventually find a way to overload the balance of nature here.

When the helicopter landed, I could see Greg making his way under the spinning rotor blades. "Everyone out; I've got to get this man to the hospital!" he yelled.

The kids made their way to the door. I looked for the dog, then ordered him to follow the kids. "Protect them, Buddy, I'll be back real soon." The dog jumped on to the landing pad. Bob exited the cockpit following the kids.

Greg helped the kids out of the Snooper then waited for Bob to lead them away. He saw Wade wasn't moving to exit the craft. "Take them into the hangar, Bob. Make sure they're comfortable please. I think they earned it."

Greg climbed into the Snooper and knelt by Wade. "You're out of here, mister." Wade looked up. Greg could see that something wasn't right. A tear rolled down Wade's cheek. "Is he okay?" Greg asked.

"Depends on how you define okay," I said. "He won't be feeling any pain anymore here in this world." I shook my head. "Too much death for no real reason lately."

Greg sat down on the cargo bay floor. *How could he shed a tear for this person?* Greg thought. "Not long ago this man was trying to kill you. How can you cry for him?"

"If not me, who will do it for what I think was a wasted life? I've been pushed and pulled on for most of my life. I thought I found a place to live until that plane crashed into the lake. This is not what I wanted in my life. I'm sure he wasn't looking forward to dying. He won't hurt you or anybody again, so I can show some sorrow at his passing, can't I? It's the least I can do."

After a brief pause, I asked, "What do we do with him now?"

"Lynn Canal is a big place, and it's not far from here," offered Greg.

"Yeah, I guess it's the best thing for all of us. Let's get to it then," I said.

Chapter 15

Greg had to talk to the control tower now and then, but all I heard was the sound of the helicopter. We finally sat down outside of the hangar after dumping the body out over the water. As I left the helicopter, alarms were going off in my head. Something just didn't look right, but I couldn't say what it was.

Greg opened the door to see his family standing in the far corner of the hangar. Bob and Caroline were there with them also. He stopped in the threshold of the doorway. "What's going on?"

Greg started to step back, bumping into me. That's when I heard a woman's voice. "Get over there with your family, Greg!" The door stayed open as Greg disappeared into the hangar.

"What are you doing, Sandy?" Greg could see the gun in her hand pressed to the young girl's head.

"What I was told to do. What I have to do to save John and me," she answered.

"Get over with your family now, Greg!" she screamed. "I don't want to hurt any of you. Why couldn't you just do what Jose wanted? Everything would have been okay if you only listened."

Greg made his way to the corner of the hangar. He hoped Wade wasn't going to follow him in. He was relieved not to see him in the doorway. Maybe, there was still a chance.

"Give me the key to the SUV, Greg," she ordered.

"Why, Sandy?" Greg questioned.

"You can ask them when I'm gone," she countered.

Sandy started to move toward the doorway. "Move it, boy! Stand in front of your sister," she commanded of Charles.

When they got to the door, Charles stepped out first. "Wade!" he yelled.

I grabbed him by the shirt then pulled. "Run!" I yelled at him. "Run now!"

I pointed the 9mm at the woman's head as she stepped out. Charles took off running like I had told him. The woman turned, whipping Amanda out of the hangar to stop her right in between us.

"Come back here or I'll kill her!" she shouted at Charles.

"Shoot her and I shoot you, and then this John is dead too," I told her.

She backed away from the hangar entrance, dragging Amanda with her. Buddy emerged from the hangar growling. Teeth exposed for the woman to see. "Buddy, go protect Charles!" I commanded the dog. To my surprise, he turned and raced off in the direction that Charles had run.

"Hi, Amanda," I said while keeping my weapon trained Sandy. "How is your day going?" I asked.

"Stay back; this kid is the only way Jose will let me live."

"Not if he's dead," I said.

"No, you don't understand. He has friends who'll come," she retorted.

She backed up to a large white truck opening the door then shoved Amanda into the vehicle. She kept the gun pointed at Amanda all the time.

"Sandy, please don't do this; we can help," came Greg's voice from behind me.

She slammed the door closed then started the truck. Putting the vehicle in gear, she drove off down the road with Amanda. I ran down the line of cars parked there. It had been years since I had driven a car, but that wasn't going to stop me.

"Wade! Over here!" called out Greg. He was already climbing into a car. I ran over to get inside. "She's headed to their float plane on the other side of the runway. It's the fastest way out of Juneau."

"Stop at the helicopter, I need the rifle," I said, looking straight ahead.

"She is my friend, Wade. No matter what, she's my friend."

"And Amanda is a fifteen-year-old, who is going to see sixteen. If your friend leaves me, no choice, she's dead. I'm sorry about that, but that girl means more to me."

When Greg stopped, I jumped out to grab the Winchester. I heard the tires squeal as Greg pressed on the gas. "Damn it!" I yelled. After getting the Winchester I started back to the line of cars.

The first sedan I came to had the keys in the ignition. The tires bit into the tarmac while I cranked the wheel. I pulled the shifter to drive while slamming on the gas pedal. I took off in the direction that Greg had gone, hoping I wasn't too far behind. I drove out on to the open runway area looking for Greg or the white truck.

I finally saw Greg's car speeding on the other side of the airstrip. I avoided crossing the landing strip, but I was going to cut the corners very close. Before taking the first corner, I spotted the truck. Greg had been right about where she was going.

I made my way to the road she was driving on. A small fence stood between the road and me, so I aimed the sedan straight at it. As the car rammed through the fence, I slammed the brake as hard as I could. The car came to a stop on the road.

I turned the wheel, hitting the gas hard. Smoke came from both rear tires as they fought to grip the road. I raced around a corner to see float planes lined to the right of the car. About five planes down I could see Greg getting out of the car he had ridden in. The woman was pulling Amanda out of the truck as I came to a stop. With the Winchester in hand, I started my way along the line on foot. I could not hear what they were saying, but I could tell Greg was talking. As I got to the third plane, I stood at the wing and rested the Winchester on the wing strut.

"Come on, Sandy, I'm tired. The kid is tired; we're all tired. Plus, Bob and I still have to go get John away from Jose," said Greg.

"You don't understand! If you kill Jose, the man he worked with here in the States will come after us." Tears were flowing freely down her face. "He's the one who put Jose on to us. We'll never be free— there is always somebody else."

Greg stepped closer to Sandy. "Don't make me shoot you, please," she pleaded. "You get into the plane," Sandy ordered Amanda.

Greg took another step as Sandy fired the gun, hitting the sedan engine compartment Greg had driven. I moved toward the end of the pier then onto the road, taking aim once again. As Amanda disappeared into the plane, Sandy grabbed the door handle to pull herself up. I fired the Winchester. The round struck near her hand, which made her jump. She fell off the small ladder of the plane onto the deck of the pier.

Greg rushed Sandy. He was almost on top of her when she rolled over, pointing the gun at him. "He's not going to let you take her, Sandy. Even if you kill me, he'll take you out. He's spent the past five days protecting those two kids. He'll do whatever it takes to keep Jose away from them."

"I'm sorry, Greg. I can't," she said, then moved the gun to her temple. The sound of the gunshot filled the air. Greg sat down, just staring at Sandy's now lifeless body.

I walked up to the plane. "Amanda, you okay?" I called out.

"Yes, Wade," she replied.

"Please stay there for now, okay? I'll let you know when to come out," I told her.

"I'm sorry, Greg; I tried to get her to drop the weapon," I said.

"Not your fault. She just didn't believe we could or would help," Greg answered.

"What do we do with her?"

Greg got up then open the trunk to the car. "Better make sure that thing will start first." After a few moments without a reply, I walked to the rear of the vehicle. Greg was just sitting there at the trunk opening.

"You want me to put her in there for you?" I asked.

"Have you ever seen somebody take their life like that?"

"Yeah. I started today that way. Greg, we have to move her. You want me to help?"

"No, I got it. Take the girl back to the hangar. I'll meet you there," said Greg.

"Wade! Is she dead?" asked Amanda, looking out the door.

"Yes, I'm afraid so," I answered. "Come on. Let's go find Charles. I'm sure he's worried about you."

Amanda climbed out of the plane, never taking her eyes off the dead woman. Slowly, she made her way over to Greg then wrapped her arms around his neck. "I'm sorry," she said. "You really did try to help her. You tried to help me also. Thank you."

Greg loosely put his arms around Amanda. "Thanks; now go with Wade. I have to say goodbye to a friend."

Amanda walked over to stand beside me. "Was she pushed to this point, Wade?"

"Yes, but for what end I can't tell. Maybe you can figure it out in the years to come. Possibly, we will never know why, but she was more likely shoved than pushed. Come on, let's go."

We walked back to the sedan I had driven here. I drove to the hangar using the road the woman had taken. We arrived at the hangar as Bob was climbing into the helicopter.

I stopped to talk with Bob. Standing by the cargo door, Bob came out of the cockpit. "Where are you off to, Bob?" I asked.

"Greg and I are going to take care of Sandy."

"I'm sorry it had to go that route, Bob."

"Not your fault; she picked her path, but she was a good friend. I wonder what John's going to do?"

"Are you sure she picked this path?" I asked, then got into the car, put it in gear, and drove away. Maybe it was a different way of thinking. I still think she was pushed. It could be something like a big chess game. All of us there were just the pawns.

When we entered the hangar, Charles and Amanda embraced and laughed with relief. Greg's wife guided all of us to the back of the hangar, where some cots had been placed. One of them was calling my name, but I couldn't sleep yet.

I walked to the restroom of the hangar, leaving the door open. I stared into the mirror. Turning on the cold water, I splashed it on my face. *This ordeal isn't over yet, but the kids are safe now.* I found a razor along with a pair of scissors. This time I started with the hair I had left on my head.

"Can I help you with that?" said one of the women. "My name is Marlene; Greg's wife."

"Not much to cut up there anymore, but yes you can. I'm pretty tired right now. I still have things to do before I head back to my place."

"The two men won't be back until tomorrow sometime," Marlene said.

Before she could start cutting my hair, I turned looking at her. "What's the date, anyway?" I questioned.

"Thursday, September 30, 2010," she replied.

"September," I repeated, "2010. Wow, the years are going by faster."

"Look forward now so I can cut your hair."

When she announced I was done, I already missed the feel of it brushing against my neck and shoulders. Looking in the mirror, I still didn't recognize the image; it had been such a long time. "Hi," I said to myself.

"Do you like it?" Marlene asked.

"It's like a new pair of jeans—you have to break them in first, then they fit great. Yes, I like the cut, thanks. Think the kids will know who I am?"

"Go get some sleep; whatever you have to do can wait until tomorrow. That's an order," she said, smiling.

I saw my backpack by one of the cots. "I'm sorry about your friend Sandy," I said while looking down at my feet. I looked to her feet then at her face. "I see why Greg waited so long to fight back against Jose."

"Why, thank you," she answered back.

I picked up the Winchester and left the restroom. Picking up my backpack, I moved to a cot next to the kids. I lay down, feeling my body relax. My muscles all screamed out, the bruises demanded attention. My brain wanted sleep.

"You'll be more comfortable if you take the guns off," said Marlene.

"No, I wouldn't," was all I remember saying to her.

Greg called Bob to tell him what happened to Sandy. He told him to get the Snooper then meet him where they camped last year by Muir Glacier. Greg didn't contact the control tower when he lifted off in John's floatplane. Staying low to the water, he banked hard to the right until he was headed north. Only when he felt far enough away did he raise to two hundred feet.

The camp was seventy-eight miles away. Greg would land the plane by the shore. He would put Sandy's body in the pilot's seat. Next to her, he would place the handgun she had ended her life with. Then Bob would pick him up for the trip back. Someone would find the plane. The police would investigate. Finding his fingerprints in the plane would be normal, so he didn't need to try wiping it down.

Then he had another thought. He opened the small cargo door, finding the extra camping fuel John kept there. He poured the fuel all around the inside of the plane. Then he sat down waiting for Bob to show up.

Greg didn't have to wait long for Bob. "Everything's ready; I just need to light the match."

"What's John going to say, Greg?" Bob asked.

"You'll have to ask his boss Jose or whoever she was talking about," answered Greg with a deadpan expression.

The Snooper flew away while the plane erupted in flames. Greg sat in the copilot's seat watching the smoke rise into the air. Sandy had been his friend. What could Jose or somebody else have had on her? He may never find out what it was. Greg's eyes closed and remained that way until the Snooper landed.

CHAPTER 16

When I woke the next morning, Charles and Amanda were not around. Sitting up, I could see Greg and Bob still asleep not far away. I unzipped a small packet in my backpack then pulled out my only form of ID. I had a few things to do before heading back to the cabin.

I left the Winchester, the two handguns, and knife inside the hangar. I stepped outside where I found Marlene. "I need to go to a bank in downtown Juneau, ma'am."

"You have one in mind?" Marlene replied. "Please call me Marlene."

"First National Bank in downtown Juneau. Also, do you have a phonebook? I need some archery supplies, if you know a place around here."

"There's a First National close by, unless you really need the one in town," said Marlene.

"I need the downtown one. That's where my safety deposit box is."

Marlene talked to the other woman who I learned was Bob's wife, Caroline. Marlene pointed to the white truck that Sandy had used yesterday. We'll take Greg's vehicle. He won't mind much," Marlene said while smiling.

We got inside the truck. Marlene powered down her window then spoke to Caroline. "We'll be back in about two hours," she said, then added, "You two listen to Aunt Caroline while I'm gone." She shook her fist playfully at her children. They shook their own fist back at her comically.

"So, Mr. Hampton, do we go to the bank first or the sports center?"

"Please, ma'am, if I am to call you Marlene, you can call me Wade. At this moment, I need the bank first; can't do much here without money."

As the SUV started off I looked back through the rear window. There stood Amanda and Charles. I turned to face forward—they didn't need to know yet what I had in mind. I looked out the side window watching this part of the city go by. "The hell they don't," I muttered to myself. "This Jose may come looking for them if he isn't stopped."

"Did you say something, Wade?" asked Marlene.

I smiled at her. "Must be living alone for so long. I'm thinking aloud, sorry."

I went back to looking out the window when Marlene pulled the vehicle to a stop along the side of the road. "I know Jose is a danger to my family, but I need Greg to come back alive." A small tear built up in her eye, threatening to move down her cheek. The tear, however, stayed there until she wiped it away.

"What am I going to with this business? I can't fly a helicopter."

I looked straight into her eyes and without any feeling in my voice, I told her, "I'll think of something, even if I have to wound him myself. Jose is mine even if it costs me my life. Jose will not be chasing Amanda or Charles much longer. That I promise."

I saw Marlene's eyes change from fear for her husband to something different. I wasn't sure what I saw there, but I continued to watch her knowing I was going to kill a man, perhaps very soon more than one man.

"I saw the same look in Greg's and Bob's eyes last night when they returned. It scared me then, and it scares me now," she confessed.

"Are you involved with Jose in any other way than your husband is?" I asked.

"Lord no!" she cried out. "I just want free of him."

"Well, you called out the right name there. I also believe you will be free before long, lady. We're wasting time. Let's get back on the road." I returned to looking out the window.

Are you still there, voice? I thought to myself.

"Oh yeah, I'm here," came the reply.

Your freedom may be at hand also. I went back to watch the world go by through the window.

Then in whispered words, I heard, "Freedom, freedom, freedom!"

The time passed quickly as we headed for the bank. I could see many different changes that had happened in five short years. Marlene turned left on to Front Street off South Franklin Street. There I could see the twentieth-century theaters written on the building with the Alaska General Store between it and the bank. Marlene pulled into a parking spot on the one-way road.

I climbed out of the SUV then slowly turned around, taking in the street. The post office was located across the street, plus the Ben Franklin Store next to it. Not much changed within the past five years. I pushed open the double glass doors to the bank, stepping in.

The marble, wood interior was as I remembered. With Marlene following me, I made my way to the service desk at the back of the lobby. The young man who was standing behind the desk had a nameplate that read Ryan.

"May I help you, sir?" asked Ryan.

"Ryan, I need to access my Safety Deposit Box. It's been about five years since I've been here."

"You have your ID and key, sir?" said Ryan while giving Marlene the once over.

I leaned in close to Ryan whispering, "Eyes front, boy."

Ryan looked embarrassed that I had caught him staring at Marlene. "Yes sir," he murmured.

I looked at Marlene myself. She had a big smile on her face. "Leave the young man alone," she said then laughed.

"Yes, Ryan, I have my ID and key," I said.

I filled out the card, writing down the box number in the space provided. I handed the card to Ryan, who walked off to check my signature.

After a few minutes of silence, Ryan stood in the doorway leading into the viewing rooms. I turned to Marlene. "Sorry, but you'll have to stay out here. I won't be gone long." Without waiting on an answer, I turned to follow Ryan.

The viewing room was small just enough room for two people to stand side by side. A wooden chair was pushed up against the shelf that held my deposit box. I inserted my key, then lifted the lid to reveal a box full of hundred-dollar bills. Also in it were important papers, some other IDs and three items wrapped in deer hide. As I lifted each wrapped item out of the box, I remembered what each one contained. The memories of my past now lay upon the table where I put them.

I pulled out three thousand dollars knowing I wouldn't be using it all. I stuffed the money into my pockets then returned the deer hides to their resting place. After locking the box, I stuck my head out the door. Catching Ryan's attention, I let him know I was done. He would return the box back to its cubbyhole between the other boxes.

"Thank you for your help, Ryan," I said.

"It's all part of the service, sir," he responded.

Marlene rose out of the chair she was sitting in. "That was fast," she said.

"When you only have a few things in there, there's not much decision making to do. Now on to the archery store—or, any place you know will do."

We stepped out onto the street once more. I again took in the street, trying to remember every detail. With any luck, it would be a long time before I would see civilization again. I opened the SUV's door and climbed in.

Marlene sat in the driver's seat looking out the window. Her hand positioned on the key to start the vehicle. "How do you feel about killing someone?" she asked.

"It's not about feeling anything. It's about knowing you're protecting something that means a lot to you. Amanda and Charles don't stand a chance against the likes of Jose. I mean to see that he doesn't hurt either of them." I looked at her. "From my point of view, your husband would die to protect you and your kids. He got involved in something and was waiting for the right moment to correct the problem. He waited for your safety. If he felt he could have taken Jose out before, I think he would have. Lady, your husband would die for you if he saw that as the only option.

"You asked earlier what you were going to do with this business. You'd said that you can't fly a helicopter. I suggest you have your husband teach you how to fly. Help him with the business. Get involved with him! Share his dream. Mold it into something that makes it yours too. Don't be an outsider to his life away from the home. Pull him into your world and also let him become part of your dreams—teach him, show him your dream. Then mesh the two together as best you can."

I pointed down the street. "Now, forward. Since it's a one-way street I suggest you should go that way."

"Where did you get so smart about life?" she asked.

"Smart? I'm not smart, lady. I've had some smart teachers along the way. Besides, I'm just making it up as I go along; so far it's worked most of the time."

"Now, before your husband leaves without me, let's go," I suggested again.

Marlene started the engine, put the truck in gear, then entered traffic. She made her way back to Egan Drive and headed north toward the airport. I closed my eyes, seeing the cabin in my mind. The landscape and the lake—I heard the birds, the wolves, and Bear. I wondered if they had the sense to stay away from the cabin. I imagined myself hunting people around the area.

The land moved as I stepped lightly through the trees. I saw the dark shadows of men roaming through the trees near the cabin. I worked my way toward the cabin, avoiding the guards, one slow agonizing step at a time. Finally, I could see the darkened image of a man standing at the cabin doorway. He raised a handgun, took aim, and fired.

Better to keep my eyes opened for now, I thought.

I watched as the waterway to the left stretched out of sight. Buildings went by that had replaced trees, roads where animal trails had been. Will the world be nothing but buildings and roads in a hundred years? Is man that blind to cover the whole planet with monuments to his misguided self-importance?

I watched a plane descend from the sky. The pilot's slow controlled fall to the runway below must have been successful. Though I couldn't see the plane land, no dark black smoke rose into the air. No fireball appeared over the tops of buildings that blocked my view.

It didn't take long to find the meanest-looking compound bow in the store. The Bear Archery Assault Bow and Bow Kit had everything I needed for one night's work. A five-pin sight with light came in the box. In addition, an Alpine Bear Claw five-arrow quiver was crying out for use. A Sims Mini S-Coil stabilizer and pro-hunter peep sight were included.

I next looked at ICS Hunter Arrows with some NAP Spitfire Edge broadhead tips. These razors had three sharp bladed expandable broadheads that open on impact. They would do the job I had in mind. The manufactures would not be happy to know what I had planned for their equipment.

I bought a pair of knee-high moccasins with real leather soles. When wearing them, you can feel the earth under your feet. They would allow me to approach the cabin without alerting anyone inside. Then I bought modern-day cameo long-sleeve shirt with pants.

Jose, here I come.

Once we were inside the SUV, Marlene spoke up again. "Do you really think you need that kind of stuff? You men are all alike when it comes right down to it."

I looked at her for a moment then answered, "Would you have me just ask them to leave and not bother you again? Look, I'm going back to my cabin to kill some men. Hopefully not getting myself killed while there. So I have to take them out silently if I can. I'm not thinking about much else ma'am; just what's best for the job I've elected myself to do. If you want to talk about the ethics of what I'm about to do, can we please wait until afterward?"

"Why not just call the Canadian police? Have them deal with Jose," she countered.

"And after the police investigation, the information will be turned over to the U.S. Government. Your husband will be extradited to Canada for trial. Bob could go on trial also. Is that what you're asking to happen here? Then when Canada is done with them, they get to come back to stand trial for drug trafficking in U.S. courts."

She just sat there looking out the driver's side window.

"Look, I don't want to do this," I said. "But if you come up with an idea on how to free everyone from Jose, please let me know."

"The police will understand. They'll see that Greg was blackmailed into helping Jose. They could offer some kind of deal for information to convict him. If you're innocent, you don't have to fear the authorities, right?" Marlene asked.

I could sense the panic in her eyes again. I could hear the tension in her voice. She was desperately searching for another way out.

"If it was just a matter of letting Jose go," I said, "I would be all for it. But he wants those two kids, and he's not going to let Greg go."

"But—"

"Marlene, how many innocent people are in prison because they put their trust in the police and the justice system? If a person is going to act like an animal, then let's treat him like one. The only people who will really know what happen to Jose will be us. Trust me. I can live knowing how scum like him died, can you?

"It's hard to know what the right thing to do is. Sometimes the right thing to do is just not tell anybody what you know. It may be against the law here also in Canada, but please believe me this is the right thing to do for all of us. As I said before, I will think of something to keep Greg out of it. He has much more to lose than I do. Now let's go, please."

Marlene started the SUV then headed back to the hangar in silence.

I hope I'm right, I thought to myself.

"Even if you're not, I'll be there to keep you company on death row," said the voice.

Cheery and helpful in the end, aren't you? I answered back.

I have nothing to ask, but that you would remove to the other side, that you may not, by intercepting the sunshine, take from me what you cannot give.

Diogenes

CHAPTER 17

eeling foolish, I stepped out of the hangar bathroom all dressed up in my new clothes. Camouflage pants, shirt, and my new moccasins. The pants and the shirt looked so clean and stiff looking. I made a pose for Amanda and Charles. They smiled and laughed. Greg's kids had a good laugh too. Greg, Marlene, Bob, and Caroline finally joined in siding with the kids. I was happy to let them poke fun at me. For just a few small moments, everybody forgot about Jose.

As I belted the holster around my waist, I began to tie the leather straps around my thigh. I remembered what it was I had bought all this for. The adults became quiet as they too remembered. Amanda and Charles also understood what was going to happen and fell silent. I tied my Rambo-style knife that hung from the belt to my other leg. I put my arms through the shoulder harness with the 9mm in it. I pulled it tight across my back, locking the snaps into place. I then tied the bottom straps to my belt. Even Greg's kids had gone quiet now—they knew something was going on.

Grabbing the box of arrow shafts and the broadhead tips, I moved over to the hangar workbench. Using a cloth rag, I wrapped it around the arrow shaft then lightly closed the vise that was connected to the bench. With the arrow secured I picked up one of the tips and hand-tightened it to the arrow shaft. Using a pair of pliers, I finished attaching the two together. I then repeated the process five more times. When I had completed this task, I looked around to find I was alone.

I opened the box with the bow in it. I made a few adjustments to strengthen the draw. When I pulled back on the drawstring of the bow, it felt good. I then attached the five-arrow quiver to the bow.

I stepped back from the bow, closing my eyes. What was I about to do? I was protecting Amanda and Charles from a monster pretending to be a human. It was best not to think, just do. Even if the law comes for me, Jose won't harm them. I didn't bring them here for some monster to destroy them. *They will live long lives, so Jose must die,* I told myself.

I reached out to pick up the bow. Close by laid the Winchester. I looked at the weapon then picked it up. "Not what I want to do, but what I feel I have to do," I said aloud. "Let's go finish this nightmare."

As I turned, Amanda was standing in front of me. She wrapped her arms around me. "Are you being pushed, Wade?" she asked.

I looked into her eyes seeing not a little girl but the beginning of a woman. "Not by you or Charles, but Jose is pushing really hard. You'll never be safe with him still around, and I want my home back."

I closed my mind off to the right or wrong, the Lord, or whatever may exist. I just held on to what I thought needed doing. I sidestepped around Amanda then headed toward the door. Everyone was watching as I exited outside.

I cut myself off from any more thoughts of events that I fell into. At the helicopter, I climbed in, secured my bow and the Winchester. Then I sat on the bench looking out the door. Charles stood looking at the helicopter with my backpack sitting by him. For a reason I would never understand, he stood straight then saluted me. I returned his salute back at him and almost collapsed inside of myself. Even Charles had some idea about what was going on.

Charles just stood there staring at me. I felt the weight of his young eyes questioning me. Caroline finally showed up, taking hold of Charles and guiding him off the landing pad. I was alone once again with only the voice for company. Three words—freedom, freedom, freedom—echoed across my mind. However, they didn't come from the voice—it originated from my own thoughts running wild in my mind.

Greg and Bob stood by the hangar door. Their wives stood by their sides, creating a picture I would have given most anything to be a part of. The two men didn't look around, nor did they look back as they made their way to the helicopter. Bob scooped up my backpack, sliding it into the helicopter. I sat in there watching every move of the two women being left behind. Amanda was nowhere to be seen.

After Greg sat down in the pilot's seat, I caught Marlene's attention. I gave her a thumbs-up sign then mouthed the words "They will come home." Marlene lipped back at me "Thank you."

The motor started up. The rotor's turning casted a shadow into the cargo bay. It was only seconds until they were going too fast to follow. The craft lifted up off the ground and banked left. After a few minutes, we banked to the right, heading out of town.

I watched the earth go by. The mountain peaks moved across the door opening. The cloud cover gave an oppressing feel to the world. The rain only deepened my depressed mood.

The Taku River was rolling out to the sea somewhere below me. The cold wind whipped around me from the open door. I pulled my coat closer, keeping my body warmth from blowing away. I quit smoking some thirty years ago, but right now would be a good time for one.

I closed my eyes while leaning against the bulkhead of the cargo bay. I let my mind wander back through the past few days. The running was over—now the hunted would become the hunter. I would violate some personal values before too long. Heaven or hell, or the vast nothing less of death, I was ready to pay the price.

Chapter 18

My eyes snapped open from the sound of Bob's voice in the headset I wore. "Wade, we're coming up on the lake in about five minutes." To my surprise, I had fallen asleep on the way here. I now felt more tired then I remembered at the start of this trip.

Keeping the headset on, I positioned myself to stand at the cockpit door. As I looked out at the Inklin River I realized it had taken the kids and me two days to walk this far. Now I was only five minutes away from home.

The helicopter rounded the mountaintop. "Home again," I said to no one.

Greg guided the Snooper toward the old depot at the base of the mountain. Bob was checking out all the instrument readings of the aircraft. "Greg, I'm getting a small heat reading south of here."

Bob made a few adjustments on the dash in front of him. "Can't tell from here, but it looks like a small fire—could be a campfire. We need a higher altitude or get a lot closer."

"John never made it out here, did he?" Bob asked.

"No, we picked up Wade and the kids before he got a chance to search this area," answered Greg.

I pointed, in the distance, at what looked like a wisp of smoke rising over the trees. "Now is a good time to check it out. Jose's not going anyplace," I added.

"Will going up another thousand feet will give you a better look?" Greg asked. The helicopter started to rise higher in the afternoon sky.

Bob studied the display as the Snooper moved higher. "I'm getting three heat signals: two people and a small fire. One person is trying to hide. The other one is lying by the fire."

"There is a small open field about two miles south of them," pointed out Greg. He banked toward the meadow only seconds away. Greg landed the Snooper and cut the engine.

Greg and Bob had their Tasers and .38s with them as we left the helicopter. Besides the firearms strapped to my body I carried the Winchester along with my backpack. Bob had taken a GPS reading before landing, and he now used a handheld unit to guide us back to the fire.

No one seemed to have any reason for talk, so we moved in silence. I could hear the footsteps of all three of us as we worked the two miles to the fire. The forest noise told me that at this time, no danger was near. The rain continued to fall on us as we made our way through the forest.

Bob led the way on the animal trail we were now traveling. Greg followed close behind. I trailed back a ways from the two of them, not wanting to bunch up the group. This also gave me time to plan on how to get Greg out of here. If by some chance it was the Carrolls, then they were out of here.

After about an hour, Bob came to a halt. He motioned for us to gather around him. "We're about a quarter-mile away," he informed us. "They are about a northeastern direction, that way." Bob pointed almost straight ahead but off to the right.

"Damn, we should have brought the goggles," answered Greg.

I dropped my backpack then reached inside, pulling out my goggles I had picked up days ago. "You two go near the edge of the camp, wait for me there. I will work my way around to the other side then come in from that way. We will have them in a crossfire if shooting starts."

I also pulled out the radio I had. "I'll call you when I'm ready to move in."

"Won't Jose hear any communications between us?" asked Bob.

"To hell with Jose; if we're lucky it's him out there," said Greg. "Bob and I'll work ourselves closer then wait for you."

Greg watched Wade turn then walk into the forest in an eastern direction. "We'll need to spread ourselves out. I'll go thirty feet to the right. After I get there, we'll start moving in. Keep your eyes open," said Greg.

Greg moved in toward the campfire hoping it was Jose, but knowing that wasn't going to happen. Jose was nothing without his backup. When it came down to it, he would run until there was nowhere else to go.

Greg slowly made his way forward keeping a tree between him and the campfire somewhere up ahead.

He soon started taking slow steps, placing his foot down lightly, rolling heel to the balls of his feet.

When he finally saw the fire through the light rain, he laid down. He crawled in behind some brush. From where he was now, he could see a man lying close to the fire's flame. Greg got his .38 in his right hand with the Taser in his left. Using the Taser in the rain may not be best idea he ever had, but he couldn't remember if the manual had a warning about such use. However, it beat using the .38 first.

He couldn't see Bob anymore, but he was sure he was doing the same thing Greg was. Peeking through the bush in front of him, he tried to find Wade.

After a few moments, he gave up. He fixed his eyes on the man by the fire. Greg watched him sit up and place a small log on the fire. Greg couldn't help but think the man knew he was being watched. He laid his radio down beside him. Greg let the drizzling rain soak his clothes. The cold air penetrated into his being, making him shiver. The events of the past days rolled past his thoughts as he waited to hear from Wade. He wondered if the others also thought about the last few days.

I left Greg and Bob behind while making a large arc around where the campfire was. I hurried alone through the falling rain. The clothes I wore were waterproof, but the cold air still made its way in. I was generating warmth by working my way around the campsite.

The battle between the cold outside air and my body heat continued as I worked my way through the forest landscape. I could feel each step on the soggy ground. At least the wet leaves wouldn't crunch beneath my feet and give me away.

I finally slowed down to a walk. The path I had taken around the camp was almost completed. Stepping with more care, I was attempting to silence the sound of my movements. Each step took several seconds to complete. I counted off each phase as I made them, first raising my leg, placing my foot gently one step ahead, heel first, then rolling forward onto the balls of my feet. For quiet, I slowed my breathing to the point I felt like I wasn't getting enough air into my lungs.

My senses had been on high alert since I left Greg and Bob behind. I could hear the flutter of wings. Small birds flew among the treetops, perhaps looking for the best advantage to watch the battle below. My eyes jumped from place to place trying to catch all the movement around me. I pulled out the goggles and adjusted the lens filters for daylight, then activated the battery pack.

When I placed the goggles over my eyes, the world disappeared into blackness. I came to a quick stop, yanking them from my face. I once again tried to attune the filters then replaced them on my head. Slowly, the world came into sharper focus as the tint of the lenses matched the amount of light outside.

The world looked like I thought it would through a welder's helmet as sparks showered about. White images showed the heat signals around me. I could make out all the inert items without bumping around like a blind person.

Turning to face the camp, I could not see the sign of any fire. I took my time trying not to miss the two people I knew were out there. Slowly, I progressed to the end of my imagined arc. I started back toward the point I had started from, forming the letter D search pattern. Moving through the brush, I stopped often, looking for the two people we had seen from the air.

In just minutes, I found what I was looking for. Lying behind some brush, I saw the heat signature of a person. I pulled the goggles down around my neck. I now saw the outline of somebody not that far away. Looking past them, I could see the small campfire with the other individual lying near the fire. I pulled the sheath off the Winchester while moving forward.

Counting my steps, I crept toward the closest one. To anybody who could really hear the forest, they would have known I was there.

Finally, I stood at the feet of the person behind the brush. I could tell now that it was a woman by the body shape. Reaching out with the Winchester, I placed the tip of the barrel on the base of her skull.

"Move and you're dead," I murmured. "I don't want to, but I do value my life over yours. Place your hands behind your head and interlock your fingers."

She laid the rifle down as she did what I had asked of her. "Now inch your way back away from the rifle. When I thought she had moved far enough I stepped over her, placing my foot on the weapon. It was an AR-7 .22LR survival rifle, a nice lightweight weapon for bush pilots.

"What's your name?" I demanded.

Through tears, she answered. "Lynn Carroll."

"That your husband Tony out there?"

"Yes, please don't kill us!" she pleaded. "Tony will give all the money back. I'll make him. I swear it."

I thought for a moment then I answered, "I don't have anything to do with Jose. In fact, I just spent the last few days getting your kids to safety."

Lynn jumped upon hearing news about her kids. "Are they alright?"

"We'll get to that later. Right now your husband has two weapons pointed at him. If he has a gun, he needs to toss it away from him." Though my knees protested, I squatted down to look her in the eyes. "Lady, I don't want to see anybody get hurt, but you'll be the first to feel pain. Now tell your husband to surrender."

She looked at me for a few seconds, making up her mind.

"Trust me, lady, it'll turn out well." I prayed that would help convince her to speak out to her husband.

"Tony!" she yelled out. "Tony, I have a rifle barrel pointed at me. Please, babe, throw the gun you have away!"

I reached out, grabbing her by the hair. I then pulled her to her feet. She cried in surprise and pain. I pushed her out in front of me. "If all goes right, you'll see your kids soon. Now step out where your husband can see you."

Staying behind her, I placed the rifle barrel to the base of her skull again then pushed. She took a quick step out of the brush with her hands still behind her head. "Greg! Bob! Stay where you are for now," I yelled out. "Mr. Carroll! I don't want to hurt you or your wife, nor do I want to chance getting hurt myself. Throw the weapon you have this way, so I can see it," I commanded.

Mr. Carroll looked in my direction, taking in the situation. "How can I trust you?" he asked of me.

"Sir, I don't know how to answer you. All I can say is if shooting does start, your wife here is the first one dead, then before you can fire again, you're dead. You'll never see your kids again. I can only ask you to trust me."

"Greg! Let him know you're out there. Bob, I need the same from you."

From somewhere I heard Bob speak first. "Here!" was all he yelled out.

Greg sounded off next. "Here."

"Sir, please listen. Just trust me. I know it's asking a lot, but I don't see that you have a choice."

Tony Carroll paused for a moment then threw the handgun he had away. I let go of Lynn, and when she realized I had released her, she ran to her husband. I stepped back to pick up the AR-7. With the Winchester aimed at the Carrolls, I walked toward them.

"My name is Wade Hampton," I said. "I pulled your kids out of the lake shortly after your plane crashed. Both are safe in Juneau, and hopefully you will be seeing them soon.

"Amanda, Charles, they are safe?" Tony stammered. "Where are they? Can we see them?"

I raised the radio then pushed the key. "Greg, Bob, come on in."

Not far away, Greg stood up. Off to my right Bob was making his way to the camp. I moved over to where Tony had thrown his handgun. It turned out to be a Ruger .22 revolver. I unloaded the revolver then the AR-7.

Making his way over to the fire, Greg watched the Carrolls carefully. "What's wrong with your leg?" he asked Tony.

"I got shrapnel in it after we crashed into the lake," answered Tony. "That looked like the black helicopter that had been chasing us that passed over about an hour ago. I suppose it belongs to you three?"

"No, it belongs to me," said Greg "But Jose's people aren't on board this time."

"Greg, Bob, meet Tony and Lynn Carroll," I announced.

Greg squatted down in front of Tony. "So you're the person that has Jose's life in turmoil? Let me be the first one to shake your hand." Greg extended his hand to Tony.

Nervously, Tony reached out and shook Greg's hand. Lynn started crying. "This is just the kind of cruel joke Jose would do. Now what? You take us to him, so he can kill us?"

Greg chuckled to himself without letting go of Tony's hand. "Lady, the last place I'm taking you is to Jose. No, you're going to Juneau to be with your kids. All we have to do is get you both to the Snooper." He paused. "That son of a bitch has had me smuggling drugs into the U.S. for way to long. Now he's at Wade's cabin with only five or six others protecting his slimy butt. There's never been a better time to free ourselves from him."

"Mr. Carroll," I said, "you won't really know about us until you talk to Amanda and Charles again. There will be some doubt in your mind. I can only ask you to trust us for a little longer."

Greg looked at me, shaking his head while smiling. "My new friend here is a little naïve on how Jose works."

"Your new friend knows a lot more about the world than you can guess," I quickly answered back. "I live out here to escape the madness

people like you call the civilized world. For the past five years, I haven't heard about someone getting killed, robbed, or other nasty things that the world can dream up on how to make life miserable. Now in just a short time I've seen people killed, and even killed some of them myself. Give me this life with wild animals all around me where I feel safe. Not the self-absorbed corporate types or the politicians who don't care about the people or the country."

I stood up straight, looking down at Greg. "If this makes me naïve then I gladly accept the title. If it's anything for a buck, leave me out." I walked away before I said more.

"Hey, Wade!" It was Greg right behind me. "Look, I'm sorry! You do appear to be a big Boy Scout to me. Now if we could get more people to act that way, maybe we could save the world."

"Look, Greg, people like me have put up with being stepped on time and time again. From grade school to adulthood, what is it with people that they have to crush others to feel good? Oh, I know, they're just a bunch of..." I paused "No; I won't say it I won't be pulled back into that life." Taking a few deep breaths, I continued. "Just leave me alone for a minute or two, please." I once again walked away.

That's the problem, I thought, *too many assholes in the world.* To think I was one of them at times. When I came out here it seemed to be the way. If you stood for peace, you got stepped on hard. The only peace the Republicans wanted was for the world to bow down at their feet. The Democrats weren't all that great either. They wanted to give away everything they could. Now all we needed was some idiot third group to start causing trouble. Every one of them thinks they know what people want. Yet time and again they prove they don't have a clue.

The anger I felt inside was the voice trying to break out of the cage. I held it in. I slowly started my way back to the fire. Mr. Carroll was talking as I made my way back to camp.

"I had just moved into Seattle, Washington after getting my certified public accountant license. A little after a month of opening my own office, some guy walked in. He wanted to hire me for three months' work. His client would be my only concern for those months. It would be a great start for my new business. The only thing was I had to head for Juneau, Alaska."

"He was told he could bring the whole family along also," Lynn added. "A three-month fully paid Alaskan vacation—who could pass it up?"

"As it turned out, we couldn't have," said Tony. He gently took his wife's hand. "After years of struggling to make ends meet, then to have this drop in our laps, we were hooked.

"I got friends to watch the house for us," Tony continued. "We paid for the office space four months in advance. We jumped into the car then used the ferry that went to Juneau. The first couple of weeks of checking every penny that came and went through some unknown company were shaky. Slowly, I started finding small amounts of money missing. Change was all it was—a few cents here and there. It never added up to much, even after going back three years in the books given to me. It only added up to $453 in those three years. Lots of companies lose more than that in one year. Well, the man who was paying me showed up one day. He introduced himself as Jose Hernandez; he was grateful for the discovery of the missing money. I tried to tell him that this was common to all businesses, but he wasn't listening to me.

"Jose had noted that I had a pilot's license. So he suggested I take the family out for some weekend trips. See the country, enjoy the outdoors, and use his floatplane. So we made plans to fly out to a lake for the weekend. To our surprise, Jose met us at the plane, announcing that he would accompany us. He was dressed in loafers, slacks, and a sweater. He brought no other equipment with him."

"It really made us all uncomfortable having him with us," added Lynn. "He insisted on siting in the back with Charles and Amanda. Before we even got off the ground, he had his arm around Amanda. He didn't touch her inappropriately, but it just didn't seem right. Tony flew around the glaciers that were nearby Juneau. He gave us all the best views of the countryside. All the time I thought I could hear Amanda whispering for Jose to stop touching her. Tony finally landed the plane on the lake we had chosen for our trip. Shortly after we grounded the plane, Amanda was eager to exit the craft."

"No sooner had we landed when two more planes appeared overhead," continued Tony. "One plane started a landing approach to the lake. The other one continued out of sight. They seemed to have been flying together. As the plane taxied to our campsite, Jose informed us that it was just some of his people. As they unloaded the plane, Jose pulled me aside, talking about going for a short plane ride with him.

"I felt I didn't have any other choice. Jose sat in the back seat with me. Lynn and the kids stayed on the beach. One of his men sat in the front passenger seat. We must have only been in the air for three minutes before landing on another lake. As we taxied toward land, I could see the other plane that had passed overhead earlier.

"We got out of the plane then headed for the trees. Just feet into the forest I saw more of Jose's people. I saw one person kneeling on the ground with a hood over his head. Then, one of Jose's men pushed me from behind.

"Jose stopped next to the hooded man. 'This is the person who you are replacing,' he said. Jose looked me in the eyes, smiling. He said, 'Don't fail me like he has,' then pulled out a handgun, placed it to the man's head, and squeezed the trigger. Jose walked over to me, putting his arm around my shoulders. As he steered me back toward the plane, he said, 'Welcome to the family.'"

Tony stopped speaking for a moment as he gathered his thoughts. Mentally pushing away the images of the hooded man's death, he continued his story.

"Right there I knew I had to get away from this evil. When we got back to the campsite Jose's men had set up the tents. A small table filled with food was waiting for my return. Lynn ran up to me with the biggest smile I had seen on her for some time. Amanda and Charles were both excited about the feast that Jose had put before them.

"That's when Jose leaned in close to me speaking softly. He said, 'You have one fine looking daughter there, Tony. I wouldn't mind being the first to get a taste of that. Do as you're told and she just may make it untouched.' He put his hand on my back, then said, 'Yes, I would like to teach her about life between a man and woman.'"

Tony's face was the epitome of disgust. He continued, "Jose laughed then called to his men as he made his way to the plane. 'Don't worry about the equipment when you leave tomorrow. I'll have these guys fly in to pick it up. Yep, things are looking good, Tony, looking very good.'"

Tony placed his head into his hands. "What else could I do but look the other way as the months went by? I just had to figure a way to escape Jose."

Lynn Carroll had remained silent as Tony had told us a little part of the story. Now, she spoke up. "After Tony told me about what he had seen, we both knew we had to get away. We just had to figure out how to disappear and not worry about Jose. So we went on several camping trips using Jose's planes. On one trip, Jose got really upset that we had taken his DeHavilland Beaver. We went back to look over the plane, trying to discover why he got so mad. We found a secret door just below the waterline on the right-side pontoon. We figured it had to be a waterproof compartment for carrying drugs.

"But when we opened it, it was too small for hauling any large amount into the country. Tony thought that was how Jose was getting some of the money by the authorities. He also started to work on an idea to get away."

"Yeah, moving the drugs onto shore was what he had me doing," said Greg.

Bob spoke. "Us, Greg—remember us, not just you. Don't ever forget that again, friend."

At that, Greg placed his hand on Bob's shoulder. "Not to worry, Bob, I have you to always remind me, friend." Greg smiled widely, but Bob couldn't smile back at him. "I'm sorry to interrupt your story; please continue."

Lynn took a breath, looked at Tony. "Go ahead Tony—it was your idea, you tell them what you did."

Tony looked down at his hands, clutched them into a fist, and released them. He finally looked up, staring out past everyone. "Since I was taking care of his finances and I knew all the account numbers, I made my own copy of those numbers then slowly changed the ones on record. I told Jose I was moving them around to avoid detection by anyone who may have been watching.

"When I got the last one changed to a bogus account number, Lynn and I figured it was time to make our run. I was hoping that having the original set of numbers might buy us time in case Jose found us. It was a weak hold card, but it was all I had. I put the original numbers into a waterproof container, then put that into the pontoon. We loaded the kids with our camping gear and took off."

Tony reached out, touching his wife. "Are our kids really safe? How can I…" He trailed off, then looked at me before continuing. "How can we believe you?"

I stood not far from the others. I found myself staring out into space just listening to Tony and Lynn tell their story. "Mr. Carroll, I asked you a while back to trust us. I also said it would be hard to do. Sir, ma'am, your children are safe, and if I have to swear upon my life or the Bible, or my father and mother's grave, I would. I try my best to always speak the truth. If what Greg says about me being a big Boy Scout helps any, so be it. I'm not lying to you now. I hope never to find a reason to later in life."

I walked the few steps to stand in front of the Carrolls, then bending down, I took their hands in mine. "Look me in the eyes." They both seemed to hesitate. "Look me in the eyes!" I repeated. Tony's eyes met mine. We locked in a stare for a while. I turned to Lynn, who raised her head up to meet my gaze. Slowly, I saw a tear form in the corner of her eyes. I let go of Tony's hand then wrapped my arms around her, pulling her close. "They're safe, lady; both your kids are safe."

When I let go of Lynn, Tony moved in to take my place. He held her close to him. Then he looked back at the three of us.

"We didn't plan on landing here at this lake," Tony said, "But Jose came up on the radio telling us he had some helicopter closing in behind us. It seemed one of his men saw us putting the container into the pontoon. If we knew about that compartment and were using it to hide something, it couldn't be good. Plus I was the one doing his books for him.

"When we saw the lake, I thought we could land then hide the plane," Tony continued. "I'm not sure what happened, but the plane dipped hard to the right. The wing entered the water then it stood up on its nose. The prop turned madly under the lake water for mere moments. Water poured into the cockpit, soaking Lynn's and my feet. The water raised up the outside of the window.

"Lynn insisted we get the children out of the plane. She began pushing against the door, trying to open it. I told her that we had to let the pressure equalize before we could open the door.

"As the plane sank we started hearing thud like noises. I yelled to the kids that we were being shot at. I wanted them to stay behind all the gear. That's about the time I felt a sharp pain in my left leg, and the plane had sunk enough so Lynn was finally able to open her door."

Lynn picked up the story again. "The water rose faster as I grabbed Amanda. I told her to get ahold of her brother and then take a deep breath. Amanda stopped me, saying that something was wrong with Charles. I was hoping he was only unconscious when I instructed her to hold his nose and mouth shut while swimming to the surface. That was the last time I saw them.

"Tony told me that he thought he had been shot. I really didn't know what to do after that. The water was so cold I wasn't sure if we could get out. With Tony's help, we got into the backseat while keeping our heads in the air pocket there.

"Looking through the windows, I could tell we were still sinking. We started pushing our gear in front of us. I could still see out the front window and watched the plane come to a stop. It rocked on the ledge it had come to rest on.

"We both heard the sound of a prop cutting through the water. Time really didn't have any meaning at this point. But the motor we were hearing stayed for a long time. When it faded, we were left with only the sound of our own breathing.

"I tied a waterproof survival bag we had to my ankle. Tony pulled out Charles' one-person raft. He told me to inflate it when we got out of the plane. He also told me to hold on really tight to the raft when I did."

Unable to stay quiet, Tony started talking. "Almost at the same time Lynn exited the plane, it started to slide over the ledge. I grabbed the doorframe with both hands, pulling as hard as I could. I came out of the plane, hitting a wing strut. I flayed around with my hand until I found the bag tied to Lynn. With a death grip on the bag, I hung there waiting.

"She must have pulled the cord on the raft because we started moving away from the sinking plane. I looked down and saw the plane tumble over the ledge then disappear. I felt the water rush past faster and faster, and I could see the surface light growing bigger.

"When my head broke the surface, I saw Lynn with her arms over the edge of the raft. We both managed to pull ourselves in, but the raft was overloaded with the two of us in it. I hoped it would support us until we got to shore. The water was freezing, but we hand-paddled to shore.

"As you can see, we got to the shore where Lynn started a small fire behind some rocks. She heated the rocks for us to get close to for warmth. We both stripped down while the rocks kept us fairly well warm. That was maybe three weeks ago.

"The bag held the handgun and the .22 rifle in it with all you see here. We've been trapping small animals to eat. The most amazing thing of all was two wolves—they would bring fresh kills close to the camp then leave them. Like they knew we needed help."

I looked at the Carrolls. "They were paying a debt they owned. I saved those two wolves years ago by sharing my food with them. They in turn kept other wolves away. So I guess they've returned the favor of sharing with you. I'll have to thank them properly someday soon."

"Right now we have to get you two out of here," I continued. "Mr. Carroll, do you think you can make two miles with your leg wound?" I asked.

"I've been hobbling about the camp some, but two miles...I'm not sure."

"How about to the lake, can you make it that far?"

"The lake I can do, with help," replied Tony.

"Greg, there's a small beach. I think you can fit your helicopter on not too far from here. It'll be the only one that looks slightly big enough."

"If Bob stays here to help, can you find your way?"

179

Bob set the GPS to lead Greg back to the Snooper. "Here, Greg, this will lead you to within two feet of the Snooper. See you in about an hour or so."

With GPS in hand, Greg entered into the forest, disappearing from sight.

I opened my backpack then stuffed the AR-7 and Ruger into it. Walking back to where I had first meet Lynn Carroll, I picked up the Winchester's leather sheath. My plan to get Greg out of here safely was taking shape now. I still needed to get Tony Carroll to the lake.

With my backpack on and Tony's arms around Bob's and my neck, I gave the Winchester to Lynn to carry. "I trust you with this. It saved Amanda's life, plus it's one of the only things I really have to remember my own family with, so be careful please."

We headed out to the lake shore.

CHAPTER 19

"**G**reg can't land the Snooper here!" exclaimed Bob. "I know that, it's why I chose the place," I answered him.

"I promised his wife that he would come home alive. This seems to be the way to keep my word. He can get low enough and close enough to load you three on the helicopter. It'll only take him seconds to get to the nearest landing site. But it's up to you to get him home. You understand, Bob? I don't care if you have to stick a gun in his face. Oh, by the way, I made the same promise to your wife. Don't make a liar out of me. You'll hurt my Boy Scout image."

"It's going to be dark soon. I don't need him wandering around. If he comes back tomorrow I can't stop him, but today with your help, I can."

About twenty minutes later I heard the whoop, whoop of helicopter blades. Greg came out over the lake waters then moved over to our small beach. The pilot's side skid set down on the rocks. The other skid touched the water surface.

We both picked up Mr. Carroll then loaded him onboard the helicopter. I helped Mrs. Carroll into the cargo area of the copter. I leaned close to Mrs. Carroll, saying, "Give the rifle to Amanda; she can return it to me later." I also asked her to hand me the bow hooked to the wall. "Good luck with Greg!" I yelled as Bob climbed in.

Giving me a thumbs-up sign, Bob made his way to the copilot's seat. I stepped back with bow in hand looking at Greg. His eyes were locked forward, but he was talking hard to Bob. I really had no idea what he was saying. I backed up more to be clear of the blades.

Greg worked the controls, keeping the Snooper level. It took almost all his concentration not to let the Snooper slip while everyone got on board. Bob finally sat in the copilot's seat. He picked up the headset, then placed it over his ears. "Bob, take the controls, then get these two out of here. I'm going after Jose with Wade."

"No!" came back over the headset.

"What did you say?" Greg asked.

"NO! I won't take the controls. You have a wife and kids waiting for you to return, plus Wade promised Marlene that he would get you back alive. You could fly to any landing site you want, but it's going to take you a while to get to the cabin. It'll be dark when you get back here. Wade won't know it's you when he fires on you."

"Take the damn controls, Bob, or I'll set this thing down right here."

"Look at him, Greg! Wade is waiting to make sure you leave. Do you think he'll really let you get off? I bet he'll wound you just to keep his word. You know he's that way!"

Greg turned his head to look at Wade. He stood by the trees, bow in one hand, 9mm in the other. Feet spread apart, dressed in camo, ready to make war. Wade raised the bow over his head and yelled something at Greg. He came prepared to hunt killers. Greg, on the other hand, was dressed in street clothes. Yeah, Wade was ready for the night's work.

"We can come back at first light tomorrow, Greg," said Bob.

Greg looked at Wade then nodded his head. *You win this time, Boy Scout*, he thought. The Snooper lifted up above the trees heading across the lake leaving one person behind.

"We'll stop and pick up Snooper One on our way out," said Greg.

I watched the helicopter make its way out of the valley. The sun was just starting to sink behind the western mountain. Darkness would cover the valley before I could get to the cabin. Nobody was pushing me toward this night but me. A light rain started, drizzling from the sky.

"Look out, Jose, here I come," said the voice.

CHAPTER 20

A fourteen-year-old boy shuffled his feet in the dirt outside of his mother's house in Mexico. He could hear his mother yelling at his brother. Emmanuel was twenty-one years old. The young boy respected his older brother. He had taken good care of him and Mother since Father had died. Emmanuel said he was going to move them into a big house. Emmanuel said he would get him a nice car to drive later.

The boy heard a thud of a fist, a scream of pain from his mother. He rushed inside the house, seeing his mother on the ground with her hand covering the side of her head. The boy could see blood between her fingers.

Emmanuel grabbed the boy's arm, pulling him toward the door. "Emmanuel! Don't do this to your brother, please, I beg you!" yelled his mother.

"Shut up, woman, we will be out of this mud pit soon!" Emmanuel shouted back at her.

"I will never forgive you, Emmanuel! Do you hear me? Never!"

"Then stay here and die; I won't. I'm getting out of this pit!"

Emmanuel dragged his brother out of the mud house. The young boy called out, "Mother, what's happening? Emmanuel, what are you doing? Mother!" he cried.

"You don't have a mother anymore, Brother. It's just us, but soon you'll have a new father. He will teach you about life."

The boy broke free of his brother then ran back toward his mother. "I won't leave, Mother. I want to stay."

Emmanuel caught the boy as he entered the house. "No! You're my way out of this place." He spun the boy around and brought his knee up into his groin. The boy collapsed on the dirt floor in pain.

Emmanuel grabbed a handful of hair then started back to the car. The boy's mother ran out of the house with a knife in hand. "Die, you pig!" she called out.

Emmanuel turned with a gun in his free hand, aiming it at his mother. "No, Mother you die," he said in a sad voice. "You could have lived in a better place."

The sound of the gun firing made the boy jump.

Jose sat up at the table in the cabin screaming, "Mother!"

A guard swung open the door with his rifle leveled ready for trouble. Jose stood up from the chair, pushing it with his legs.

"Go back outside!" he yelled to the guard. Looking at John, Jose told him, "Shut up. Not one word from you, you hear me!"

John raised his hands in a surrendering matter.

Jose stumbled into the bedroom, closing the door behind him. Leaning against the wall, he shut his eyes tightly. The memories came flooding back from where he had stored them.

Emmanuel's car pulled into the drive. The boy hurried to the kitchen, pulled open drawer after drawer. Finally finding what he wanted, the boy dashed for the door to greet his brother's return.

He ran into Emmanuel's arms like that other man had taught him to do. Emmanuel wrapped his arms around his brother. "I'm sorry, Brother, but it had to be done. I promise it'll never happen again."

Emmanuel felt the knife slide into his abdomen, and his eyes opened wide. The boy pushed away from his brother. "Doesn't that make you feel better now?" The boy pulled the knife across Emmanuel's belly. His guts spilled to the floor.

"I forgive you for what you did to me, Emmanuel. But I cannot forgive you for Mother."

Emmanuel fell to his knees with a death stare on his face. "Brother," was all he said. He toppled over, splashing blood everywhere.

The boy saw a handle of a gun in his brother's waistband. Pulling out the gun, he felt the weight of it in his hands. This he would keep, reminding him not to let anyone use him again.

Jose's eyes flashed open and sweat rolled down his face. He staggered to the corner of the room. His stomach tried to empty itself. Falling to his knees, he looked at the bed. With a lurch in that direction, he got halfway into it. There the memories took him again.

Emmanuel had put him in the trunk of his car before leaving their mother lying in the mud. It seemed Emmanuel drove for a long time when the car came to a stop. The trunk opened up. Emmanuel quickly took hold of his arm. The boy was jerked out into the dark of night.

"It's almost daylight, Brother. Today you will save both of us," said Emmanuel.

The boy hit his brother as hard as he could while trying to pull his arm free. "You killed Mother. You killed her!" Emmanuel's hand shot out to slap his brother.

"No, Emmanuel!" came a voice from behind the boy. "Don't damage him, please."

The boy didn't understand what the man had said. But he recognized the American accent. He turned his head to see a blond haired, fat old man. "Bring him here. Is this the boy you told me about?" asked the plump American.

"Yes, Mister Cruise," answered Emmanuel in a heavy Spanish accent. "I bring you this boy. You get me a house while I work for you, right?"

"That was the deal we made, and only if the boy pleases me you will get your house," said the American. "Come help me. It's almost sunrise. I find it exciting to start a relationship as a brand new day begins. So a new life for this fine-looking boy will begin today."

Emmanuel held onto his brother while leading him into the American's house. The man walked around the corner into a big living room. On the left of the foyer was a fireplace with two couches facing each other. Between them was a large table about two feet high.

The boy could see the whole wall facing him was glass. On the right of the entryway, he could see four metal bars coming out of the floor. Two of them were connected by another bar running between them. That bar, about three feet wide, was heavily padded and stood about three feet above the ground. Behind the padded bars were two other posts.

The American pointed to the padded bar. "Push him up to that with him facing the window."

Emmanuel forced his brother to the bar and held him there. The American bent to the floor, grabbing a chain with leather cuffs on the end. He wrapped one cuff around each of the boy's ankles.

"Emmanuel! What are you doing?" the boy begged. "Why? What did I do? Why did you bring me to this place?" Emmanuel remained silent.

The American walked to the other side of the padded bar. He stopped to look at the boy's face. He picked up another leather cuff attached to the pole on the boy's left. The man seized the boy's left hand then started to wrap the cuff around his wrist. Pulling as hard as he could, the boy jerked his hand from the man.

"No! Emmanuel, help me! Don't do this, please!" screamed the boy.

"I am helping you, Brother. You'll see," replied Emmanuel.

Emmanuel clutched his brother's arm and held it while the American attached the cuff on the boy's wrist. Emmanuel quickly snatched the boy's right hand, holding it for the American.

The American pulled the chains tight, forcing the boy's arms to raise up then spread out away from him. He pulled the right ankle chains so the boy's foot covered a mark in the floor. After locking the chain, he did the same with the left foot.

Tears streamed down the boy's face. "No, Brother! Don't do this." The boy was now held by the chains, bent over the padded bar.

Emmanuel turned away from his brother. "I'm sorry, Brother, truly I am. But this is the only way to get out of that mud house Mother had us in. You'll see, Brother. You'll see."

"Ah, the sun is almost over the horizon." The man reached around the boy's waist, undoing his pants. The man pulled the pants down along with the boy's underwear. He then produced a razor, cutting the boy's pants at the crotch area.

As Emmanuel walked away, he looked back to see the man unbutton his own pants. Emmanuel stood at the door listening to his brother crying for him to help. The boy kept calling Emmanuel's name again and again. Emmanuel had to get away now, or he would never see the house the American promised.

Emmanuel closed the front door then hurried toward his car. Just before he climbed in he heard his brother cry out in pain. The screaming went on as Emmanuel drove off, leaving his brother for the American to use.

Jose's eyes flew open to see the cabin again. His arms spread out before him on the bed. He crawled up into a standing position. It had been years since he had fallen into the nightmare he had escaped.

Breathing hard, the boy remembered the walk to the American's house now. When he entered at sunrise, he could hear the cries of another boy. He walked around the corner, facing the poles in the floor once again. The American was standing naked behind a different boy, his hips moving back and forth. The boy raised Emmanuel's gun, aiming it at the American.

"Mr. Cruise," he called out, just as he had been taught to address the man.

The man turned his head, seeing the boy with a gun pointed at him. The man just stood there staring at him. In Spanish, the boy commanded, "Get away from him, you monster, now!"

The man raised his hands while backing away from the boy strapped to the bar. The boy took a step closer to the American, still pointing the gun.

"Whoa, boy, there's no reason for this," said the man, looking past him.

The boy quickly looked behind him. The American rushed toward him as a loud boom sound filled the room, then another boom, and yet another. The man jerked at each boom, at last falling to the ground, twisting and rolling across the floor. The boy didn't even realize he had fired the gun.

He walked over to the man who was now trying to crawl away. Standing over him with the gun still aimed at the American, he could see fear in the old man's eyes. He could feel the power of the gun he now had. With his foot, he pushed the man over on his back.

The boy could see that he had only hit the American twice— once in the leg and the other in his fat side. Moving carefully, the boy lowered the gun.

The man cried out in English, "I showed you my love. I love all my boys. You know that."

He never understood a word the man said for the three months he had been chained to the posts. The man didn't speak the boy's language. However, he knew what this monster had done to him.

The gun stopped while pointing at the man's exposed genitals. The man was crying loudly now with fear in his eyes. None of his boys had ever come back, none had ever tried to harm him. He always treated them with love. The boy started pulling the trigger until the gun wouldn't buck against his hand anymore. The man was still alive afterward, but soon he would be with Emmanuel.

The boy put the gun in his back pocket, then turned his attention to releasing the boy now chained to the post. "How long have you been here?" he asked this new boy.

"I got here just today," cried the boy.

After the last chain hit the floor, the new boy ran out of the house with no pants to cover him.

There standing by the couches was another man. The boy pulled the gun out of his pocket then pulled the trigger again. Nothing happened.

"Hold on there, son," the man said in Spanish. He walked toward the boy. "The gun is empty, that's why it's not working. I'm not going to hurt you, son."

The boy stood his ground as he dropped the gun. He then pulled out the knife he had killed his brother with. He rushed the man, trying to stab him.

The man deftly moved to the side, tripping the boy as he charged by. The knife flew from the boy's hand as he reached out to stop himself from hitting the floor. As he worked to get to his feet, a foot came down on his back, pinning him to the floor.

The man reached down, enveloping the boy's neck with his hand. He leaned close to the boy's ear then spoke softly to him. "I'll let you go in just a moment; you can run or stay to talk to me. I have one question for you: How would you like to learn to stop men, ones like that one, from hurting you again?"

The boy struggled to get up but couldn't break the man's hold. "Well, how about it? You want to learn or let others keep on using you? You either learn to use people, or you get used. Which do you want?"

The boy relaxed and lay still. "I wish to learn," he said.

"Good," answered the man. "Come with me, then; do as I say. No one will hurt you again, you understand? What is your name, son?"

"Jose Hernandez."

Jose walked into the main room of the cabin. Mentally, he was finally in the present once again. He saw John asleep in the bunk. He opened the front door of the cabin to step into the cool night. He strode off the porch then passed the big tree stump. Jose continued up the trail thinking to himself, *Why would anybody live out in this miserable place?* It reminded him of the mud house he had lived in for so many years. His personal bodyguard followed him up to the trail, staying a few yards behind him.

Chapter 21

The sun had been down for about an hour when I could just make out my beach in the distance. I slowed my pace as I moved closer to the tree line. From talking to Greg, I knew there were seven men around my cabin. Five guards, John, and Jose living here off my hard work. No guts, no glory. To hell with glory.

I set my pack at the base of a tree well off the beach. I removed the night-vision goggles from my pack. After readjusting them for the night, I tested them to ensure that I was ready. I picked up the bow with the five arrows attached to it. I then notched the sixth arrow on the bowstring. It would be a long night if all went my way.

Time: 8:24 p.m. I moved more slowly into the forest, trying to picture myself as the hunter. I knew Jose had four guards posted out here. It was like playing hide and go seek, but the loser would be dead if I found him first.

Time: 8:37 p.m. I found myself within ten yards of the first guard. This would be just another man I'd killed in my lifetime. I was protecting my house the first time then and now. Once again, I had to remove the filth from my home. I was fourteen years old that very first time.

I had just got home from school. I entered the front door calling out, "MOM! I'm home." My call was answered with silence, so I tried again. Still nothing. I walked to the first step of the stairs.

Time: 8:39 p.m. I raised the bow, looked down the bowline to the arrow tip, and pulled back the string. I could hear the voice whispering to me: "Let me out, Let me out."

"Okay," I heard myself say softly. My mind went steady. My hands relaxed. My whole body went dead calm. Blood was going to flow tonight—some of it may even be mine.

I tried to move my hands. My head hurt, but I couldn't reach back to feel why. Something was holding my legs tight. It was like waking in the morning except for the piercing pain I was feeling in my skill. Somewhere I heard a voice: "Hey, you two, the kid's awake."

Then I heard my mother's voice: "Wade!"

"Shut up, bitch." Then I heard the sound of a hard slap. "You don't say anything, got it?"

Slowly, it came to me. I was tied to a chair with tape over my mouth. My eyes popped open. My parents' bedroom came into focus. I was tied to the chair my mother used at her small makeup table. I could see my mother trying to cover her naked body. I shook hard against the chair, hoping to break free.

Time: 8:41 p.m. All my senses running in high gear but still steady and calm on the outside. I finished pulling the string fully back. I took a breath, letting some it out, holding the rest. *I love you, Mom*, I said to myself, then let the arrow go. The arrow crossed the ten yards in seconds. The man's body jerked backward but didn't fall to the ground. As I had planned, the arrow passed through his neck into the tree behind him. I didn't know how long the arrow shaft would hold his weight, but to hell with him.

Well, Greg, how do you like my Boy Scout image now? I thought to myself. I pulled out another arrow and notched it on the string.

I had to sit there in the chair listening to three men rape my mother. That's when I first heard the voice inside my head. "Relax, save your energy; there's nothing we can do right now. Do you still have the pocketknife? Yes, we do, I can feel it in our back pocket." It wasn't a bad voice; it was my voice of reason. I was no good to anybody if I didn't remain in control.

I put my mother's cries out of my mind. I could still hear them, but I no longer acknowledged what they were doing. I reached into my left back pocket, barely touching the knife. I grabbed the outside of the opening of the pocket then pulled. The knife slipped out from under me, and I grasped it firmly in my palm.

Time: 9:53 p.m. I found my second target sitting on the ground. If I didn't have the goggles, I might have missed him. He sat in the dark with his back to some bushes. Branches and foliage above blocked whatever light penetrated down to the ground. He held his weapon pointed at the sky, the butt to the ground. His head moved slowly from side to side looking for any sign of movement. The man jumped onto his feet to look behind him. His rifle came up, the butt end held tight to his shoulder. Quickly scanning the area, as he turned to the right, I could see his finger wasn't on the trigger. I stood up, taking aim at the man's back. He started turning to his left again. His back came fully into my view.

I released my arrow and watched it fly through the space between us. I saw him drop his weapon, then slowly turn, looking my way. Both of his hands went down the shaft that was protruding from his chest. He sank to his knees wondering what had happened to him, then fell forward. His body jerked a few times then lay still.

I caught sight of two glowing eyes looking back at me. The male wolf walked out of the brush staring my way. He shook his head while walking over to the dead man. The wolf then lifted his leg to mark the body.

I whispered, "Thank you for distracting the man so I could get a clear shot." I wasn't sure, though, if the wolf wasn't trying to take the man himself—I may have just interfered with his hunt.

I used the pocketknife to saw at the rope entwining my wrist. It seemed to take a long time, but I finally felt the rope drop onto the floor. I froze, looking around to see if any of them had noticed. I worked the knife about to cut the rope securing my arms to the chair. I had only been trying to slice the rope a few minutes when one of the men got dressed and went downstairs.

I heard the refrigerator door open up. "Beer time!" he yelled.

Another man picked up his pants, almost tipping over as he tried to put them on. That only left one monster up here with me. Now was the time to act—if I could get the ropes cut before the other two returned.

I worked hard at the bounds around my arms. I couldn't see how much more I had to cut. I couldn't risk one of them seeing what I was doing. The third man got out of bed, gathering up his pants. I could hear my mother sobbing on her bed. When his back was turned she reached for a crystal angel Dad bought her years ago. She jumped out of the bed, swinging the statue at the man's head. He moved far enough away the blow only grazed his skull. He countered with a fist to my mother's chest, driving the air out of her lungs. She fell backward, gasping for air on the floor. I bounced in the chair, yelling as loud as I could as my mother scrambled to her feet, still holding the angel in her hand. The anger on her face hid the pain from the blow.

As she lunged for the man once again, he raised a handgun then fired. I saw Mom thrown back from the impact, hitting the wall. The noise of the discharged gun rang through my ears. My focus came to rest on the blood running between her breasts, the vacant look in her eyes as she tumbled across the floor.

Once again, I became calm, shifting my gaze to the man who had just shot my mother. Blood trickled down the side of his head. "Bitch!" he yelled at her. He stepped forward, kicking her with all the force he could. He fired one more time into my mother's dead body. "Bitch!" he repeated.

"What's going on up there?" came a voice from downstairs.

"The bitch hit me with something," the man called back. He held on to the doorframe for a moment then walked out of the bedroom headed downstairs.

I started working the knife again. Within seconds, the ropes around my chest loosened. I raised my arms, lifting the ropes up over my head. I then cut the ropes on my legs and stood, free at last. I walked over to where my mother lay. I looked down at her but didn't shed a tear. There would be time later for that.

Time: 10:30 p.m. I made it to the cabin path. From where I stood, I could see the cabin door. A man stepped out into the doorway, making his way out on to the porch. He quickly sidestepped to the right then leaned against the wall. I had to turn off the goggles because of the light inside the cabin. I could see him holding his head in his hands, and then he shook it like he was trying to drive something from his mind. I slowly brought up the bow with my third arrow notched and ready to fly.

Before I let loose the arrow, another man appeared from the shadows of my home. I watched as the two talked, but their words were lost in the distance. The first man pushed off the wall and stepped down on the dirt path. The two of them began walking up the trail. The second man stayed back, giving the first his own space. They both walked farther from the lake into the darkness.

One more man came to the doorway to look at the night. He stepped back, closing the door, barring the blackness from the inside of the cabin. I relaxed the pull of the bow, looking down the trail. There should be two more guards out there on the other side of the trail. At this moment, the count was two more guards out here, the one in the cabin, plus the two who walked up the trail. *I'm going to be one arrow short*, I realized.

This wasn't the time to cry for my mother. I exited left out of my parents' bedroom. I moved quickly and quietly down the hallway to my room. I passed between the window and the foot of my bed then went into the closet. I looked at all the trophies for marksmanship around the room. Killing targets was one thing, but killing people? Could I do it?

The voice grew a little louder. "Your mother is dead. They raped then killed her. Yes, we can kill them."

"Yes, I can," was my only whispered reply.

If one took the time, they would have seen all the trophies for rifles, handguns, and bows of all makes and models. I could hit whatever I fired at.

I reached into the closet, grabbing the rifle case. Inside was my Winchester model 1892 that my father had bought just the previous Christmas. I pulled a box of ammunition from the shelf. I swiftly loaded three rounds into the Winchester. I worked the lever action of the Winchester, putting a round in the chamber. I then took six more rounds out of the box to place in my shirt pocket.

I could hear the men downstairs talking angrily at each other. I sat down inside the closet to wait. The men suddenly stopped talking. One of them began making his way up the staircase.

When the stair climber entered my parents' bedroom, he called out. "Hey! The kid is gone."

"Then find him, you idiot. You shot the woman, now take care of the kid," came a voice from down below.

"Come on, kid, make this easy. I won't hurt you much. I'll make it quick, just like your mother."

"Like hell," I whispered to myself. "You made her suffer for a long time while you raped her."

I could hear footsteps working their way down the hallway. My brother was away at a high school wrestling match. He wouldn't be home until dark. Dad was at work, still hours before starting home. The door to my brother's room opened. The murderer was searching there for me.

I raised the rifle, aiming over my bed to the open door. Soon another life was going to end in this house. I saw the shadow against the hallway wall. Death was coming. I rooted myself were I was, waiting until he stood fully in the doorway. Then death reached out, tapping him in the chest.

The sound of the rifle going off in this closed place was deafening. Jumping to my feet, I worked the lever again, watching the empty cartridge fly out to my right. I rolled over the top of the bed, coming to my feet on the other side. The murderer was on the floor staring toward the ceiling. The hole through his chest spoke to all: He wasn't getting up again. I stepped over him, hurrying to the banister. Hugging the wall, I knelt to the floor, putting the barrel of the Winchester between the posts.

Another man showed up at the foot of the stairs. "Carl!" he yelled out. "Carl! What are you doing?" He climbed to the second step when death slammed him back against the wall. Blood smeared the wall as his body slid down it. He then tumbled over to stop at the bottom of the stairs. I levered the action, watching that shell fly out. I reached inside my shirt pocket, seizing two more rounds. I pushed them into the rifle.

Time: 11:59 p.m. I crossed the trail entering the dark shadows of trees. The hunt was on for the two guards on this side. It only took minutes to find number three walking along a route he made for himself. He passed in and out of the shadows as he moved among the trees. The goggles showed me clearly wherever he went.

I moved in behind him after he passed me up. After he was five yards past me, I took aim. While tracking him with the arrow, I called out softly, "Hey."

The man sidestepped while spinning around, raising his rifle to the firing position. I let fly the bowstring. The arrow cut through the air. As it found its target, the guard dropped his weapon. He stood there looking at me then to the arrow through his arm. I pulled my knife out of its sheath as he went for his handgun. I flipped the knife in my hand, so I now held it by the blade. He started to pull the gun from its holster. Taking a step forward, I let loose my Rambo-style knife. The gun was almost pointed my way when the knife struck him in the chest.

"You can keep it for now," I said to him, though he was already dead.

I pulled my fourth arrow and placed it on the string. One more guard, then I can clean the cabin.

I heard the back door slam shut. I raced down the stairs then out the front door. I started looking for the last rapist to come around the front of the house. With the rifle raised, I stepped off the porch. I moved to the corner of the house while looking down the sights. I moved around the corner of the house and toward the back.

The barn was to my left, and behind the house I could see part of the open garage doors. I pressed my back against the side of the house. Having not seen the man yet, I guessed he hadn't gone into the barn. *He could have returned to the house*, I thought.

The sound of a car starting came from the garage. I pushed away from the wall, ready to fire. The car charged out of the garage. Taking another step away from the house, I fired. The car changed course to head straight at me. I worked the lever once more, then fired again. I ran farther from the house, working the Winchester handle. The car was going too fast to change its path. I stopped moving and trained the rifle barrel to where the driver should be. The rifle kicked against my shoulder. I fished two more rounds from my pocket as the car flew past me.

I inserted two more shots into the Winchester, then sprinted to the garage and jumped on my brother's Kawasaki 175cc dirt bike. The dirt bike kicked over the first try. Holding the rifle across the handlebars, I headed out after the car. The car had already reached the paved road. I wouldn't know which way to go when I got there.

As I approached the road, I looked left. Going over a small rise, I saw a car of the same color. Without stopping, I turned left onto the road then gunned the small engine. The whine of the dirt bike settled down as I shifted into fourth gear. Coming to the rise, I saw the car fishtail as it tried to turn left on Franklinton Drive.

The driver punched the gas, making the tires spin. He headed toward town on Franklinton. I could see the car swerve back and forth as it sped along the road. I shifted down, getting ready to make the left turn the driver had missed. Once around the corner I opened the bike up again. My full attention was on the road ahead of me as I passed the "Welcome to Franklinton, Arizona" sign. The white road markers flashed past as I raced to catch the car.

I shifted down when I entered Franklinton town limits. I locked up the brakes as I skidded past the car, which had slammed into a parked car in front of the general store. With the Winchester in hand, I dropped the bike when it had come to a stop. The engine was still running as I walked away from it.

I was barely aware of the people coming out of the store. Some already gathered around the car. A car on the road came to halt because the dirt bike was in its way. People started taking notice of me as I walked toward the rapist's vehicle. I could hear people talking to me, but I couldn't hear anything they said.

"Get away from him!" I screamed out. I raised the Winchester up, preparing to fire. The few people around the car moved back. I walked up to the driver's window then poked the rifle barrel inside the car. Somewhere I could hear the sound of my name being yelled.

Time: 12:25 a.m. I found the fourth guard sleeping against a tree. I worked my way to the sleeping man for a better shot. I was only three steps from him as my arrow pinned him to the tree. I moved forward, placing my hand over his mouth. His eyes came up to meet mine. The look he gave was full of the fear of death. "Boo," I said.

Now there were only three more from my count. I placed another arrow on the bow.

I looked into the man's eyes, seeing his fear of what he knew was coming. The rage of what he had done to my mother took over, the new sound in my head yelled at me. "Pull the trigger now!"

So I did.

A hole appeared in his face. The back of his head exploded, spattering blood, brains, and bone all over the inside of the car.

I turned away then walked back to the bike. Somewhere in my mind I could see people staring at me as I picked up the bike. I kicked its engine over, got it into gear. I left the town, behind riding carefully home. Mom was waiting for me.

Time: 1 a.m. I stood by the door to my cabin, ready to push it open. Slowly, I moved the door until I could step inside. Bringing the bow up level, the arrow tip scanned the room, automatically looking for any target. Empty—the main room of my home was empty. I moved farther in, closing the door as I cleared it, then leaned back against the door.

My home was trashed. Things were thrown all around. Two of my chairs were broken into pieces lying next to the fireplace. The shelves were torn from the walls. All the things I had sitting on them laid piled across the floor. The bunks were ripped apart for firewood. The mattresses covered the floor. They had been sliced open for some reason.

I took two steps from the door, looking at five years of my life scattered everywhere. A footstep sounded from the porch, the door handle moved. I raised the bow, pulling the string back as the door opened. The arrow hit the man point blank in his chest.

I reached out to close the door while looking at the man's surprised face. I slammed the door, hearing him take a step backward, then fall heavily to the ground.

"Wade! It's Sheriff Taylor! I'm coming in," came from the front door. I had left the Winchester leaning against the outside doorframe knowing that they would come after me. I had also covered Mom with a blanket when I got home.

The voice spoke to me once again. "Don't worry, Wade, we'll be okay. Now just rest for a while."

The footsteps coming up the stairs filled my ears. Sheriff Taylor's voice cut through the near silence of the house. "You men search down here. If you see Wade, don't shoot unless he fires first. After that, move outside. If you find him, call out. Pete, you come upstairs with me."

The footsteps started up again, coming closer to me. I simply sat there with Mom's head on my lap. "Don't fret, Mom, it's almost over; they'll take care of you," I whispered into her ears.

Sheriff Taylor stepped inside the doorway of my parents' bedroom. "Oh, Christ! Pete, get the others outside, keep everybody out!"

"What about Mr. Hampton? Do we keep him out, Andy?" Pete asked.

"Especially him, Pete," Sheriff Taylor called back. "Pete, keep the brother out of here too if he happens to show up. Call 911, get an ambulance out here along with the coroner," answered Sheriff Taylor.

I just sat there with Mom, my eyes dry, my hands calm, my mind quiet.

Time: 1:10 a.m. I locked the door then dropped to the floorboards. I heard feet on the porch once again. A handgun appeared in the broken window. It pointed to the corner where I had stood. Six wild shots sounded off, striking the wall above me. I pulled my 9mm and pointed toward the window, firing off four shots of my own.

Jumping to my feet, I fired one more out the window. The back door was already open, so I ran straight through onto the path leading away from the cabin.

As I turned the small bend on the trail, I came face to face with a tall blond man who was rushing back to the cabin. I placed the 9mm to his chest. "One sound and you're dead," I told him.

Turning him around, I pressed the weapon to his back. I dug the barrel into his back to encourage him to move. We hurried away from the cabin. After a short while, I indicated for him to get off the trail. We made our way across the dark forest landscape for ten yards then stopped. I stood still, listening for pursuers.

"Kneel down," I ordered the blond-haired man.

As he was doing as I asked, I pushed hard against his back with my foot. He toppled forward onto the earth. "Now stay there." I searched him, but found no weapons and let him roll over on his back. "You stay flat on your back," I told him. "Or you will be just another dead man out here."

"Look, mister," he said, "I just want to get back to my wife then get out of here."

"What's your name?"

"John Bolger," he answered me. "I work for Greg Woods as one of his pilots."

Keeping the 9mm pointed at him, I stepped back. "Look, I don't want to be the one to tell, but Sandy's dead."

He started to sit up. "What!"

I raised the gun higher so John could see it up close. "Lay back down," I ordered him.

"Okay, okay," he said while lying back down. Tears swam in his eyes. "How do you know she's dead?" he asked.

"I was in Juneau when it happened. She tried to take Amanda at gunpoint. Greg and I chased her to a plane on the other side of the airport. When she saw that neither Greg nor I was going to let her take the girl, she turned the gun on herself. Before pulling the trigger, she asked Greg to tell you that she loved you."

"I don't understand—who's Amanda?"

"Amanda is one of the kids Jose is looking for."

"Okay, but you're telling me you and Greg killed Sandy."

"No! The person who gave the information about her killed her. That someone is also backing Jose. That's who killed her. They gave her nowhere else to run to. Not Greg or me—we tried to get her to surrender."

John sat there in silence for a few minutes. "I'll help you kill Jose," he said in a deadpan voice.

"No, Jose is mine, alone," I told him. "You need to get out of here before Greg comes back in the morning. You want to kill someone, go find Jose's informant. But if you get between Jose and me, you're dead.

"We can go back to the cabin, get you some supplies," I continued. "Canada's Highway 37 is eighty-four miles east of here. Make your way to the U.S. Border. That should keep you out of trouble for a while. You better hurry, though, winter is on its way. You don't want to be out here when that happens."

"I can really help you with Jose," he repeated.

"By my count, Jose is all by himself. I just took out his big bodyguard," I informed John.

"How did you do that? The man wears a bulletproof vest all the time. So I know you didn't shoot him with that thing," replied John, implying the gun.

"No, I shot him with an arrow, right in his bulletproof vest. Maybe he's not dead. But I must have scared him, though, when he opened the door." To stop him from pleading to help me again I asked, "How did you get involved with Jose, anyway?"

"I'm getting up. You can shoot me if you feel like it. Without Sandy, I have nothing to live for," he spat out.

"One of the reasons I am trying to send you away. You could get me killed by not caring for your own life. But go on, tell me how you got involved with Jose," I answered back.

Running his hand through his hair, he began. "Before I met Sandy, she got mixed up with some guy in Pennsylvania. Turned out he was a big-time drug dealer. Sandy testified against him in a court of law. The government put her into the witness protection program. They gave her a new life in Oregon. That's where I met her. Her name wasn't Sandy at the time. We got married, lived about a year in Portland. Then some Senator Blankenship from Pennsylvania showed up with two FBI agents.

"The senator said that he had been told that friends of this guy had been arrested. During the interrogation, one of them mentioned of finding Sandy's new name, where she lived also. So they needed to move her again. The senator found a place in Juneau, Alaska for us. The FBI gave us new names and pointed me to Greg's company. I worked there for three years, was happy. Greg and Bob were great people. Sandy and I were lucky to have found them.

"Then Jose showed up one day when I was at work. He told Sandy all about her past. He said if she called anyone he would kill me, and then ship her to South America. She knew what he meant by that: life as a prostitute for stinky, fat old men. So we did what he asked. First thing was to get Freddie hired. Then I had to get Greg to fly the Raptor out to his ship. I still can't believe I betrayed Greg like that.

"That's the short version. Jose owned us, plus Greg and Bob too. Now for the first time we had a real chance to get rid of Jose, to be free again. Greg would have never known that it was Sandy and I that set him up. Jose wanted that Raptor of Greg's bad, really bad.

"Now Sandy's gone, and it's Jose's fault." John's voice cracked. "If only he would have left us alone. No! I'm not running while he's still breathing."

"You're going to leave Jose to me," I countered. "You're going to walk back to the world. Let the authorities know that Jose found out about Sandy. Please try leaving out Greg's helicopter if you can."

"Why should I leave Jose to you?" John said coarsely.

"Because I have the gun, remember? If I shoot you now, you're dead. If you walk out, maybe you can find out who threw your wife to the wolves. But you're not staying here, understand?"

John stood a bit taller and put his hands on his hips. "Jose killed my wife. I need to help pay him back," he heatedly replied.

"One, Jose didn't kill your wife. She took her own life. That alone released the hold he had on you." John started to interrupt, but I continued, "Two, you need to find the informant to take care of him anyway you see fit. Three," I spat, then moved even closer, "you had your chance when he walked into your life. You failed to stop him then. Greg and Bob had their chance to stop Jose. They failed too.

"The only one that took a chance was the Carrolls. It almost killed them, no thanks to you, Greg, and Bob. Now it's my turn. I'm not going to let Jose touch those kids, ever. He's a dead man walking. He just doesn't know it yet." I took a deep breath then continued, "The Carrolls brought Jose to me. You, Greg, and Bob brought him to me. You pushed this fight on me. The animal is mine now, not yours, not Greg's—mine. Do you understand?

"Jose intruded into my life," I continued. "What he doesn't know is that I have a lifetime of hate built up inside. It's screaming to be out now. I can tell you right now, you don't want to be around when that happens."

John shot back. "I wouldn't know how to find the informant, but I know where Jose is."

Still shouting, I answered, "Then you have a long walk back to the border to think of a way." I moved up so our noses were about an inch apart. "Your friend Greg thinks I'm some kind of Boy Scout. I promise that's the last thing I'll ever be. That's the end of this talk. You walk or die right here, which is it?"

"That's no choice! Do it your way or die? What are you, the Taliban?"

"No!" I answered him sternly. "I protected my home when I was fourteen years old. I can protect my home now too. I lost someone dear to me back then. I killed the people who invaded my life. I didn't need you or anybody's help then, nor do I now! I stood by myself against the coward, and not one of them walked away. You had your chance." I pressed the barrel hard against his head. "Greg had his turn when he flew into the trap. Neither one of you stood up then, and now your turn has passed. I'm not letting Jose leave here alive. DO YOU UNDERSTAND ME?" I screamed, knowing that Jose could be close by.

"Okay, calm down," John said as his eyes questioned my rage. "I'll go. I'll find the senator to let him know that he has a leak somewhere."

I grabbed John by the arm and forced him to the cabin's backdoor. A rummage pack still hung on the wall. I started filling the pack with bags of dried meat, some canned food, salt, and a water filter. I found a water container for him to fill down the trail about two miles.

I picked up a compass then exited through the backdoor. It took only moments to set it up for the first leg of his journey. "There's a cabin about two days' travel on this course I've set here. All you have to do is follow this arrow. You can't miss it. I keep it well stocked with food. Take what you can carry, turn the dial to here, then follow the new course. It should take you two weeks to find the road. You'll have one more week of walking to reach a town. That is, if someone doesn't give you a ride. Now get out of here before I change my mind."

John started to open his mouth to speak again. I pulled back the hammer to the 9mm. "Shut up and go!" I snarled through clenched teeth. I stood there watching him walking away from the cabin.

Time: 3:45 a.m. I moved up the trail in the opposite direction that I sent John. I had to find Jose and the big guy before they found me.

Time: 3:55 a.m. The big guy's footprints turned out to be easy to track in the dark. He has absolutely no idea how to cover his prints. Maybe he did know how to set traps. That could be why he was being easy to follow. I moved off to the right side of the trail. After a short distance, I checked out the trail again to see if I could find his prints. Yes, there they were for anybody who knew how to see them. Right beside one of his prints was the sign of a loafer. The big guy was stepping on Jose's tracks as they worked their way up the mountain. At least Jose went this way too.

Time: 4:20 a.m. Hell came out of the bushes straight at me. Big arms attempted to encircle me. I dropped down to a three-point stance. The arms closed around the air where I had been. Planting my feet, I drove my shoulder into the big man's kneecaps. He stepped back, bracing himself with his other foot. A big hand grabbed the back of my shirt. I wrapped my hands around his ankle. With him being off balance, I lifted up his foot, straining hard. For a moment, I thought his foot would never move, but then I found myself in control of his balance.

I continued raising my arms over my head, then took a step backward, dragging him forward. The big man did something like the splits. He screamed loudly as the muscle and ligaments in his groin area stretched in new ways. He hit the ground hard while covering himself with both hands. I kicked his groin as hard as I could then repeated the move a couple more times. He still wiggled on the ground, refusing to give up the fight.

205

I worked my way around him to grab his shirt collar. I started to pull him along the ground to a small rock ledge. The drop off was only a few feet. I dragged him so his neck was on the ledge. A big hand reached out to swat my hands away. His neck fully exposed, I slammed the edge of my palm on top of his Adam's apple. His feet came off the ground in reaction, and he tried to yell out. His hands grasped his own throat as he rolled off the rock and fell several feet below, landing heavily on his head.

I watched as he thrashed about, attempting to breathe. He would have been much better off if I could have broken his neck like I had planned. His body stopped twitching about. He finally laid still. That only left one more monster to go now. The anger had built to a level I couldn't control any longer.

The uncontrolled rage formed on my lips. "FREEDOM! Free at last. Do you hear me, Jose? I'm coming for you!" I bellowed into the night. Now like an animal I roared out across the valley. Not far away, Bear roared back.

Like so many years ago, I felt I was riding the motorcycle up to the dirt driveway after the last coward, feeling this anger like it was the first time. I stepped into the night in search of my prey.

Every fiber of my body was alive; every nerve was feeling, tasting the air around me. Every sound reached my ears, listening for the last one of the intruders of my home. Nothing mattered—just kill the intruder, this last one.

Freedom! Freedom! Freedom was here once again. To be released of all restraints, to forget the law of men and heaven. There was no voice inside my head anymore. The two had become one; we were made whole again by death. All the people this Jose had killed with his drugs, the lives he had ruined. Today he would pay for his crimes.

I started up the trail as the rain fell down harder. It found its way past the tree limbs, past the leaves and needles. Large droplets of water rushed to the ground. They struck other leaves and needles, making bigger drops of water. Gravity pulled them to the earth, to my already soaked body. The hunt was on, the game was afoot, and dying time was here.

Chapter 22

E ven in the rain, Jose wasn't hard to track: a broken twig here, a crushed leaf there. The rain-soaked trail formed pockets of mud. Puddles of water filled the footprints where Jose had gone. I could almost smell him up ahead. The sky was starting to lighten up. This part of the earth had swung around for the sun to touch it again. The dark clouds overhead looked like shadows of cotton balls.

A big rock in the middle of the trail came into view. I had been here many times, standing on top, looking out over the lake I called home. I touched it like a mother does her child. My mind started to quiet, but the rage remained. I thought of Amanda and Charles, reminding me why I was hunting this man.

I stepped around the rock to find approaching me the person who had brought his pain to my world. Jose stood staring at me for a second, and then we both moved. Jose's hand shot to the 9mm he carried. I, in turn, raised mine to strike Jose's nose with the palm of my hand. I raised my foot, knocking the weapon from his hand. It flew out into the darkness.

He staggered backward while pulling his knife. He wiped the blood from his upper lip then thrust the knife my way. I jumped back out of reach, and there we stood face to face, killer facing killer. After tonight, I would have to agree with the townspeople. I would kill again, they had said. They just didn't know how many times I did. I was happy to remove this evil from the world.

"I killed my own brother with this knife. It hasn't tasted blood for many years. It will be the last thing you ever feel," spat Jose.

I started to move to my right. I could only think about all the Hollywood knife fights I had seen. Two men facing each other while going around in circles until one of them makes a move. My hand went to my revolver, only to find nothing to grab. The holster was empty. I must have lost it somewhere back with the big guy. My hand moved to my 9mm that rested in the shoulder holster. Wrapping my fingers around the handgrip, I pulled it out.

Jose lunged forward. I leaped backward, trying to clear the 9mm. Jose came at me again, swinging the knife and cutting the back of my hand. The handgun fell to the ground between Jose and me. His eyes shifted to the gun for a second. I kicked at the knife, connecting with his knife hand. It flew into the night, lost from sight. Now the only weapon was the 9mm. Jose launched himself my way, wrapping his arms around my waist, pushing me backward.

After three steps, I finally planted my feet, stopping his advance. I reached my own arms around his waist then lifted upward. Jose's feet left the ground, but he refused to loosen his grip. Leaning back, I swung Jose to my left. I turned circles, inching closer to the boulder. The plan right now was simple: smash his legs against the rock, then kill him. Jose grabbed the back of my belt, freeing up one of his hands. He then struck me in the groin with the other. When I released him, he flew only a few feet.

I spotted the 9mm lying near the trail. As I reached for it, Jose tackled me, gripping the gun. Now we both had our hands on the weapon. Jose managed to sit on my back, raining blows to my head. It was clear that he was going to win control over the weapon. He ripped it from my grasp, then rolled away.

We both stood, facing each other. This time Jose was pointing my gun at me. A smile formed across his face as blood still flowed from his nose. He took careful aim at my forehead and pulled on the trigger.

He was surprised when nothing happened. He drew back the hammer—it wouldn't lock in place. Trying to pull back the slide, Jose finally saw that I had set the safety. As he released the safety, I leaped forward, driving my toes into his kneecap. Jose cried out as he collapsed to the ground. I scooped up the 9mm while moving back from him.

I aimed the gun at him then ordered him, "Get up, I'm not done with you yet." I fired the gun into the sky to show the gun was live.

Jose slowly got to his feet, not putting much weight on his left leg. "I set the safety before you tore it away from me," I said. "You can feel lucky I'm not going to shoot you." The magazine dropped into my hands when I pressed the release button. I then threw it deep into the bushes. I drew back the slide and the round in the chamber jumped out, falling to the ground. I grasped the gun by the barrel and tossed it away.

"Come on; let's finish this, Jose! Just the two of us, hand to hand. I have a lot of issues to resolve about people like you."

Jose laughed. "You've injured my knee now. How is that fair?"

"I'm old, you're young; that evens it up in my eyes," I answered. "One way or the other, someone isn't going back down this mountain. I plan on it being you who stays here."

"I'm sorry, but it'll be you here when I walk back to your cabin. By the way, who the hell are you? Why do you care what happens to those kids? They are nothing to you."

"Who I am doesn't change a thing, but my name is Wade Hampton. Those kids didn't do anything to you. You, on the other hand, have terrorized them and their parents."

"One thing I learned early in life, Mr. Hampton: Take what you want out of life. Use people all you want, because they don't count for spit. They're only here for the strong to rule over."

I shook my head. "You're a sorry person to know. People like you fill this world with hatred. You start wars for your own profit. Let others die for your own glory. Your heart is cold and hard. You should have been a banker or a politician, but you're just a small-time drug dealer."

"You'd be surprised how many bankers and politicians are backing my enterprise, Mr. Hampton." Jose charged me as best he could. It was easy to sidestep him. He raced right on by me, stopping on the edge of the clearing. He bent over to pick up his knife.

"Now, once again, you'll feel the sharpness of my blade."

I was right back where I started. Jose had his knife in hand. I had nothing but air. Jose stepped forward, swinging his knife in short figure eight movements. I dodged each swipe. I was trying to scan the ground for anything to use for a weapon.

Because of his knee, Jose was unable to move that fast, but he wasn't giving me much time to look around. I saw the bullet I had dropped just moments ago. Slowly, I worked my way over to it. When I picked it up, Jose laughed.

"What are going to do with that, shoot me? I think I can kill you before you find the gun," Jose said with humor in his voice.

Jose approached, swinging his knife, stepping closer. I pretended to throw the bullet at him, which he ducked by reflex. Jose stepped closer to me.

He now stood within five feet of me. He kept moving his knife. I faked throwing the bullet once more. Jose only laughed, then took another short step my way. A desperate plan formed in my head—I would have one chance to get it right. I would have to move fast if I failed.

Take two more short steps, Jose, just two more, I thought. Jose edged himself forward one step. *Come on, one more, get closer*, I screamed in my mind. Jose launched himself at me. I fell to the ground as the knife flashed above me. I stuck my foot between his legs and grabbed his ankles. I lifted him up off the ground, then forced my heel to the earth. Jose had no choice but to go over backward. He tried to soften the impact with his arms. He landed hard on his back, splashing water into the air. I quickly got to my feet to only watch Jose rise sluggishly. He still held on to the knife.

Jose let loose with another of his laughs then raised his hand to show that he still had the knife. We were standing only four feet away from each other. He pushed the knife out at arms length then smiled. Jose looked at his outstretched arm with the knife still in his hand. This was the moment I'd been waiting for.

It was almost like slow motion. My fingertips tightened on the bullet, my arm dropped to my side as I twisted my body. Around on one foot I went, watching the landscape turn into a blur. My head completed its turn, my eyes locked on Jose's forehead, my arm stretched out fully behind me. There was no doubt that at this distance I would find my target.

The bullet left my hand, sailing across the few inches that separated us. Jose's knife moved to defend himself, cutting the right side of my torso. I found myself looking into Jose's eyes as he halfway comprehended what just happened. The bullet connected with his forehead, dazing him. Taking no chances this time, I dropped back a step then kicked out at Jose's right elbow, rendering it useless. The knife dropped to the ground where I stepped on it. I brought up my knee up as fast as I could. I only stopped when I couldn't lift him by his groin area anymore. This seemed to take all the fight out of him. I, however, wasn't close to finishing with Jose.

I tackled him to the ground and straddled his chest. With the palm of my hand, I hit his forehead were the bullet had impacted. I landed another blow to his forehead, then two more times just to make me feel good.

Getting to my feet, I hollered at him. "Get up! Get up now, you piece of shit. I have more anger to transfer to you. In fact I have a lifetime of it for you. So get up."

I reached down, grabbing him by his shirt, pulling him halfway up. I knew he couldn't comply with my demands. I started dragging him to the cliff that was close by. Through the brush into trees I hauled him.

The sun had come up enough for me to see the drop off. Jose started to twist a little as I got closer to it. I released my hold and stepped back, then kicked the bottom of his feet and yelled at him again. "Get up, Jose, or I swear I'll throw you off this cliff."

I noticed that the rain had stopped, that the sun was breaking through the clouds, lighting up the mountain peak across the lake. Shifts of sunshine ripped through the clouds on other mountaintops. Sunshine reflected off the lake waters, birds started to fly through the columns of light falling from the sky. This was my home, my refuge from the world, my place of peace in this world.

With blood running down his face, Jose had managed to get to his feet. He turned away clumsily to run. He ran four steps then stopped abruptly, trying to come to a stop, one good arm waving around in an attempt to regain his balance. Then he disappeared. Jose had found the cliff on his own.

I didn't hear a scream like I had expected. I didn't hear the sound of a body striking the rocks or the trees below. I looked over the cliff to find Jose hanging there with his one good arm. Now it was my turn to laugh. "I guess I was wrong; you are going to beat me off the mountain. How long do you think you can hold on, Jose?"

The look on his face will always be with me. It reminded me of the rapist before I shot him. He had spoken to me, so softly that I was the only one who had heard them: "Mercy, don't let me die."

My answer now was still the same as before. I placed my foot on his hand. I applied my weight on it. I could see the pain on his face. "Die, you monster." When I removed my foot I closed my eyes. Yes, there was the scream, the sound of him hitting the rocks on the way down. Lastly was his body crashing into the tree limbs far below.

I turned to start back to the trail.

CHAPTER 23

I stopped where Jose and I had fought. The 9mm that I had thrown in to the brush could wait another day. I felt something under my foot. It was the bullet I had hit Jose with. Picking up my trophy, I put it in my pocket. I stretched my body—every muscle cried out in pain. Mindlessly, I made my way down the trail the kids and I had used just days ago.

By the time I reached the lake, the sun was coming over the mountaintop. The birds had been up for some time now. The fish were just starting the hunt for insects close to the water surface. The clouds had parted even more, allowing sunshine to pour into my world.

I finally made my way to the inlet where I had sunk the pontoon. I worked my way to the cabin side of it. After building a fire, I stripped for a plunge into the ice water. The cold water gripped me, trying to force the air out of my lungs as I made my way to the pontoon.

After searching, I found the small compartment in the pontoon. The door was missing so I reached inside. My fingers closed around a small box, which I pulled out, then headed to the surface. I approached the fire, shaking and thankful for its warmth, still holding the box I had gotten from the pontoon.

The door had not been closed properly, so when the plane settled into the lake it ripped off the pontoon. The force of the water entering the compartment broke the pontoon free from the plane. The missing pontoon sent the plane on its wild right turn.

I put my clothes on before I was completely warm or dry. I walked past the cabin path a short distance. Working along the beach, I found my pack. I fell to my knees as my eyes welled up with tears. "I saved them this time, Mom. I was able to do for them what I couldn't do for you. Please forgive me, Mother; I was working to save you, but that nightmare got you first." I could feel tears on my face. "I'm sorry, Mom."

The sound of a helicopter cut through the air. Once again the birds screeched out a warning: Man was coming, man was near. I put the pack on but didn't fasten the straps. The wound on my side let me know it wasn't going away. I headed back to the cabin, box in hand. I hoped it was Greg returning, as I knew he would.

I stood on the trail after hiding the box. Greg came up the trail with his .38 out, not knowing what to expect. The silence that I had come to love covered this small part of the world. I raised my palm toward Greg and he returned my gesture. "Looks like something the cat drug in."

"I feel like the mouse that cat played with but got away somehow," I said.

"What about the cat? Is it still around?" asked Greg.

"The cat took a big fall. It won't hurt anymore mice in this world," I replied.

"That's a pretty bad looking scratch on your hand there. I bet that's an even nastier one on your side."

"Yep, the cat had a big claw. Guess I better do something for it. But first I need help removing the whole litter."

We spent the rest of the morning loading up Jose's men then tying weights to the bodies. He flew over to a nearby lake, where I pushed them out. It took longer to get the big guy from the trail where I found my revolver. We searched for Jose's body but couldn't find it anywhere.

Greg sat on the porch listening to what happened after he had left. He hung his head while running his fingers through his hair. "Thanks, Wade," he said. "Thanks for putting your life on the line for us. I know Amanda and Charles will be happy to hear that you're okay.

"Bob and I will be back tomorrow with some supplies for you," he continued. "We'll bring the kids also, if you don't mind."

"Bring them all, if you can," I offered. "It'll be nice to have some friendly faces around for a day or two."

Greg finally got up. "You could come back with me tonight, sleep in a bed have a good meal."

"Thanks, Greg, but I think I would like to be alone."

With that, he started to walk back to his helicopter. "Hey," I called out, "I can walk with you; it's not that far."

We walked in silence to the lake. At the lake I told Greg where I had left the rest of the money I had pulled out of the bank. "Use it to buy the supplies," I told him. I stood at the trail watching Greg fly back around Nimbus Mountain.

Walking back to the cabin, I retrieved the box I had left along the trail.

CHAPTER 24

I was at the edge of the lake when two helicopters came around the mountain. The birds cried their usual warning as the helicopters made their way toward me. I no longer wore the camouflaged clothes I had yesterday. Today I donned an old pair of blue jeans, an olive drab cotton shirt, and a pair of well used hiking boots. These were the clothes I had worn when I first hiked into this valley.

The helicopter landed on the small beach, blowing the loose sand into the air. After the blades came to a stop two small figures jumped out of the closest helicopter. Amanda and Charles sprinted toward me. Amanda carried with her the Winchester I had asked her mother to give her for safekeeping. Not sure what to do, I spread my arms out for them. The two ran into me as I circled them, picking them off the ground.

We all stood around for a while saying our hellos. The kids stayed by me wherever I went. Tony Carroll's leg was in a cast. He was getting around pretty good with the help from crutches. Lynn stayed by her husband's side, watching her kids hug this stranger with all their might. She wondered what had happened that her kids hadn't told her about.

Bob and Caroline held on to each other as they wandered up the trail. "Amanda, go make sure Bear doesn't find them first please," I asked her. "Can you go with your sister too, Charles?" Both of them took off following Bob and Caroline.

"Tony, Lynn," I called out, "would you two please walk with me to the cabin?" Greg, Marline, and their kids also started up the trail.

Greg called back over his shoulder. "I've got some supplies for you in the Snooper. Four windowpanes, some real chairs too. Those wooden things you had were really uncomfortable to sit on. I also have a few other small things for you. Bob and I will be back for the next couple days to get my stuff at the depot. I'll be bringing more to you on those trips."

Amanda and Charles stood in shock at the inside of the cabin. I had tried to clean some of it that morning but there had been too much damage. It was going to take a day or two for things to look orderly once more.

"Okay, kids, I need you to find something to do outside while I talk to the adults. Amanda, you're in charge; Charles, you listen to your sister this time. Oh yes, Charles, protect all the others for me. I'll try making this as short as I can," I called out.

After the kids had gone outside, I got everyone's attention. I walked over to a pile of clothes by my bedroom door and picked up the small box.

Lynn recognized it first. "That's the container with Jose's account numbers in it."

"Yes it is," I answered back. "I spent most of last night prying it open. After going through the contents there was some four hundred million dollars here."

"$400,560,000 to be exact," added Tony.

"Wow," escaped the others' lips.

"Yes, you're right, Tony," I said, acknowledging the figure.

"As you can see, I have divided the accounts up into five different groups. Four groups have a hundred million in them. I'm sure Tony will help get us further access to the money. Now, I don't care what you do with your share; you can flush it down the toilet if you want. Give it to charity of your choosing. You can spend it on yourself, but you people with kids should at least put some aside for a college fund. You will take it home then decide what to do.

"That leaves $560,000 left for a drug rehabilitation center. Let Jose pay for the cleanup of some people's lives he's ruined. Does anybody have a problem with my proposal?" I waited for a few seconds. There was a calm quiet. "I'll take the silence as no one disagrees with it. So put your account forms away so we all can get back to the kids."

Caroline spoke up. "Tony, Lynn, if you watch the kids, the rest of us will get the first round of supplies up to the cabin."

As everyone started on their assignments, Greg stopped. He looked my way then took a step or two closer. "Thank you, Wade. You put your life on the line for all of us. If I had some champagne, I would offer it up right now with a toast."

"How about some beer tomorrow?" I suggested.

"Done," said Bob. "I'll help you drink it too. We may have to stay the night if we bring enough."

Laughing, we all went to work. Before any of us knew it, we had the cabin on its way to being ready for the winter. The windows had been replaced, the shelves back on the walls. We filled them with cans that had survived Jose's invasion. It would still take a few more days to get it where I liked it.

I said my goodbyes to Tony and Lynn then did the same for Bob and Caroline. Greg and Marlene stood arm in arm as I wished them well.

That only left Amanda and Charles to bid goodbye. My old knees popped as I knelt in front of Charles. "You take care of your parents. Remember you promised to protect your sister, though I think she can take care of herself, okay?

Charles put his arms around my neck. "I'll protect them all, Wade, like you did us."

"What more can I ask of you? Now go find your parents. Get started on the protecting them part."

I eyed Amanda as I stood. Yes, she was going to be a knockout—breaking boy's hearts, then later some men's, too.

"Wade," she said, "do you still feel pushed?"

"Funny thing, Amanda—I found out that I wasn't being pushed at all."

"What was it then, Wade?"

"I was hiding a part of me that was crying for release. I was scared for a long time to acknowledge it. It was all the anger with what life had put me through. It finally came clear to me the other night." I reached up, wiping a tear from her cheek. "What's this for?" I asked her.

"I wish you were my dad so I could live here with you."

"No, don't say that; your father is a fine man. He took the beginning steps to topple a bad guy. He helped rid the world of a monster. Don't ever think small about him; in a lot of ways he's braver then me. He got married, had two great kids, and protected you the best he could. You got that, and no matter what happens in the future, you have wonderful parents. I believe they would give their lives for you."

I reached out, taking Amanda in my arms. "Go now, you'll be safe." Without looking back, Amanda ran to the helicopter to her family.

I stayed to watch them lift off. I stood watching the helicopters as they rounded the mountain then disappeared.

As I closed the door of the cabin I reached into my pocket, pulling out the bullet I had thrown at Jose. I put it up on the small mantel over the fireplace next to the only photo I had of my mother. Then I went outside to cut some wood.